ZELLE AND THE TOWER

FAIRELLE BOOK FOUR

REBEKAH R. GANIERE

FALLEN ANGEL PRESS

ISBN: 978-1-63300-007-0
ISBN: 978-1-63300-008-7

Cover art by Rebekah R. Ganiere
www.vwzdesigns.com

DEDICATION

For the Dreamers, The Survivors and The Bitten.

NEWSLETTER

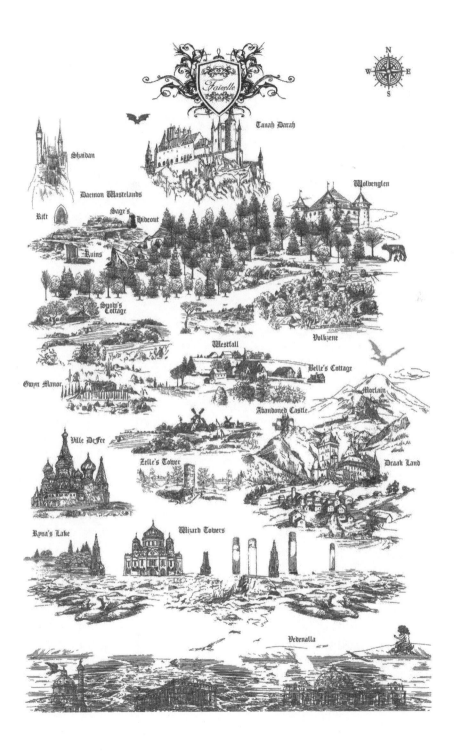

PROLOGUE

PEREUM, FAIRELLE YEAR 200

In the year 200, in the city of Pereum, the heart of Fairelle, King Isodor lay on his deathbed. With all of Fairelle united under his banner, his four sons vied for the crown. One by one the brothers called forth a djinn named Xereus from Shaidan, the daemon realm, to grant a single wish. But Xereus tricked the brothers, twisting their wishes.

The eldest wished to forever be bloodthirsty in battle, and was thus transformed into a Vampire. The second wished for the unending loyalty of his men, and was turned into a Were-wolf. The third asked for the ability to manipulate the elements of Fairelle; he became physically weak but mighty in magick, a Fae. And the last asked to rule the sea. A Nereid.

When the king died, each brother took a piece of Fairelle for himself and waged war for control of the rest. Xereus, having been called forth so many times, tore a rift between his daemonic plane and Fairelle, allowing thousands of daemons to pour into Pereum.

Years upon years of bloody warring went by with all races

fighting for control and eventually the daemons gained dominion of the heart of Fairelle. Realizing that all lands would soon fall into the daemons' control, the High Elders of the Fae and the Mages from the south, combined their magicks to seal the rift. The daemons were banished back to their own plane, but Pereum was wiped off the map in the process, leaving only charred waste behind forever known as The Daemon Wastelands.

Upon the day of the rift closing, a Mage soothsayer prophesied of the healing of Fairelle. Over the next thousand years the races continued to war against each other, waiting for the day when the ancient prophesies would begin.

Eight prophesies, a thousand years old, to unite the lands and heal Fairelle. Now has come the prophesy of the Banished.

CHAPTER ONE

VILLE DEFEE, FAIRELLE - AUTUMN, 1211 A.D.
(AFTER DAEMONS)

With precision and speed, Flint pushed through the crowded street. He shivered and scowled at the silky touch of magick in the air. Pulling his cloak tighter about him, he kept his head down.

The footsteps of the king's guard pounded the cobblestone street a block behind.

"Find them!" the captain shouted.

It'd been a mistake to stop and ask for directions, but Flint had only been to Ville DeFee once, and with all the blasted brightly colored structures and sweet fruity smells he'd gotten turned around. Standing out amongst the slender, graceful fae, he lumbered through the streets.

His stomach growled as he passed a pastry store.

"Check every shop," a guard called.

A shrill call from a bright pink bird pierced Flint's ears, making him wince. He thanked the gods he hadn't been born in Ville DeFee. Such brightness and merriment were overwhelming.

3

Dax shoved Flint sideways into a darkened alcove, away from an oncoming merchant carrying a basket full of blue fruit. Dax squeezed in next to Flint as the fragrances from the basket made his stomach growl once more. How long had it been since he'd eaten?

The merchant passed without a glance in their direction. Flint stuck his head out and scanned the area. The guards were still several shops away.

"We have to keep moving. We're close now." He darted onto the street.

"Do you really think this is a good idea?"

"No." He kept walking.

He was on a mission, and only the king himself would be able to stop him. He rounded a pale blue building and headed toward the end of the row. A fae youngling stopped skipping to stare at Flint.

He dropped his head again. His boots looked even filthier against the immaculate stone road. When was the last time he had washed them? Or taken a shower?

All of the days since leaving Tanah Darah and then Wolvenglen seemed to blend together into a horrible nightmare that he continually lived and relived. Only his hours spent in a drunken stupor and a couple of hazy memories with several tavern wenches broke up his personal hell. His gut clenched at the thought of seeing Snow as a vampire. Her skin, her eyes, her hair; it was all different. She was different. Gone was the sweet younger sister that he'd tried to teach to dance. What she was now… was a creature he was bound to kill.

A screech and a crash yanked him from his dark thoughts. Flint stopped and turned.

"Excuse me. I'm so sorry."

Dax threw apples into an overturned barrel as the shop-keeper looked on wide–eyed, mouth slack.

"Leave it." Flint scanned the street for the guard. People stopped to stare at Dax. Hood off, his shaggy blond head and tan skin screamed human.

Flint's skin itched and he clenched and unclenched his fists to keep from scratching his arms. The magick of the fae permeated everything. From the large, juicy, unnaturally colored and tasting foods to the highly polished, never dirty streets. It wasn't natural, it wasn't right.

Dax righted the barrel and stood.

Flint glanced skyward past the twinkling lanterns floating above. The moon had barely made an appearance but already the streets were crowding. They needed to get out of sight before night fell. Then the streets would be packed with fae, singing, dancing, and making merry on this Beginning of Spring Celebration.

"End of the street," Flint pointed. "Move it."

Dax nodded.

He hadn't wanted Dax to come along, but somehow the giant werebear had gotten the notion that he was responsible for Flint. After one fight together in which Dax saved his neck from being chewed on, and suddenly they were best buddies.

In the past months though, Flint had come to appreciate Dax's company. Having lived with his six brothers and Snow for so long, the loneliness of being parted from them was not something he had thought about when storming out of the castle at Tanah Darah. And despite what he said, he liked Dax. Dax didn't talk too much and didn't pry. He kept his head straight and Flint's neck out of a noose.

They moved at a quickened pace until they reached the end of the street. Rounding a corner they found a smaller, darker area where the shops had already begun to close down for the night.

A bright peach building with purple awnings sported clusters of people coming and going. Shouting, laughing, and glasses clinking floated out the open windows of the pub. Flint's eye twitched and he licked his lips at the thought of getting a drink. The sounds of a flute lured him closer.

"Not here." Dax's large palm fell on Flint's shoulder.

He shook it off and continued on.

Drinking was not something he'd done regularly before. Now, it seemed more like a daily routine. What would father think? Flint pushed the pain aside and stomped towards to a mint green building. The worn red apothecary sign swayed in the breeze. A giant bluish tree wrapped the building in a hug. Vines in every color and variety snaked up the sides in a cocoon of protection.

Flint looked through the front window, but could see nothing except shelf upon shelf of bottles and herbs. He pushed open the door and two birds chimed a tune in unison. The scent of nature filled his nostrils. Roots and plants, herbs and flowers. It reminded him of Snow's cabinet where she kept her healing supplies. Again he was hit with a pang of guilt. But it didn't matter; all that separated them would be gone soon.

A beautiful woman of about forty with light brown hair arranged bottles on shelves in the corner. She turned at the sound of the birds. Every surface of the shop was covered in jars, bags, and containers of various sundries. Flint removed his hood, as did Dax, and the woman started, dropping a bottle. The contents splashed on the floor, the glass shattering. A silent scream played on her red lips.

Flint threw up his hands. "I'm sorry to frighten you. I just need to speak to Lord Rondell and then we'll go."

The woman's green gaze lit on Dax. Horror remained solidly planted on her features. She stared at him without blinking.

Flint turned and gave Dax a questioning look. He shook his head and shrugged. Voices floated in from the street. If the woman screamed the guards would be alerted.

He turned to the woman. "Madame, I know we should not be here but—"

A beautiful young woman with bright blue eyes and rosy cheeks appeared from the rear of the store. "Stepmother, is there a prob—"

She scanned from Flint to Dax and then swiftly stepped around the counter and approached the woman, taking her by the arm.

"I'll take care of this. Why don't you go home while I clean up and close the shop."

The woman finally tore her gaze from Dax. She stared at the girl for a moment before yanking her arm away and composing herself. With another a sideways glance in Dax's direction, the woman nodded.

"Yes, of course you will. That's your job." She straightened her dress and hefted the hem so as not to step in the mess she'd made. "And if these two get caught in here, I'll not take the blame."

Tension thick as dragon-scale cracked in the air.

The girl nodded. "I understand."

The woman looked at Dax once more and then strode out.

When the door slammed shut, everyone sighed.

Quick as light the girl rushed to the entrance, magicked down the shades and dimmed the lights with a flick of her fingers. "Flint Gwyn. You sure do know how to make an entrance, don't you? Do you know what will happen if you're caught here?"

"I'll be thrown in prison."

"*I'll* be thrown in prison." The girl waved her hand and mumbled a word he couldn't hear. The smashed bottle reformed, and the liquid on the floor disappeared. She strode to it and put it on the shelf, then faced him again, a smile on her lips.

Flint relaxed. Coy girl. "Cinder. You're looking well. Last time I saw you, you appeared no more than a teen and I was no more than eight or nine."

"I was already in my late thirties back then. Good to know that I have aged well," she laughed. "I'm old enough to be your mother."

Taking several strides forward she reached out and embraced him with more strength than he thought her capable of. Pushing him to arms' length she looked up at him. "You used to pull my braid and hide my favorite book when we would come visit."

"And you would magick my pants so they wouldn't allow me to wear them."

"That was only after you tried to kiss me."

"Trust me, a disaster I would never dare to repeat. Besides, if I remember correctly you had a prince whose affection you were vying for. Did nothing ever come of that?"

She blushed. "Rome and I are just good friends."

He nodded and smiled. "Yes, I can see that."

Her fingers twitched. "Don't make me turn you into a mouse."

They laughed in unison and hugged again.

"Don't misunderstand me. I am happy to see you, but what in Fairelle are you doing here? You could've been seen."

"I'm looking for your father."

Cinder's eyes misted. "He is no longer with us, I'm afraid."

Flint's heart sunk. Lord Rondell had been his last hope.

"I'm sorry. I had not heard of his passing."

"It was quite sudden. We aren't exactly sure what happened. But he is in the Fade, with Mamette. And I know they are happy together."

"Of course." Flint blew out a heavy sigh. He'd come all this way. "Well then, it seems I've traveled for nothing. It was good to see you, Cinder. We should go before the soldiers come."

"Wait." She grabbed his cloak. "You came such a long way, what is it you need?"

"I doubt you can help, but thank you." He patted her hand and nodded to Dax. They replaced their hoods and turned.

Cinder harrumphed behind him. Arms crossed over her chest, she slid between Flint and the exit.

"You listen to me, Flint Gwyn. I am my father's daughter. And anything he could do, I can do. You look as though you haven't eaten in weeks, and your scent says you've bathed even less. You and your friend will sit at my counter, eat my food, use my washbasin and tell me why you came. For if you do not, I shall spell you and force you to. And I know you don't want that." With a wave of her hand, two chairs dragged themselves up to the shop counter.

She flashed him a brilliant smile and pointed to the chairs. Dax shrugged and headed for the counter. *Traitor.*

Flint wasn't sure if she was lying or not about the spell, but he was sure about one thing. She was definitely her father's daughter.

CHAPTER TWO

THE HIDDEN TOWER, FAIRELLE - AUTUMN, 1211 A.D. (AFTER DAEMONS)

Z elle meandered to her aviary. Loca, her snowy owl, perched delicately on her shoulder as she ascended the staircase to the uppermost floor of her home. Her hand slid up the wooden banister, knowing the texture by heart, and her bare feet made no sound on the cold slate.

Opening the large wooden door, the flutter of feathers and soft cooing of birds filled her ears and soothed her loneliness. All around her winged friends perched, or dozed, or primped. Loca hooted and flew off to a dark corner high in the cathedral ceiling.

Moving about the room Zelle threw aside the thick curtains from the barred window. She inhaled the fragrant air heavy with the scent of nature. Thin trees just beginning to show the blush of spring lined the area. They were so tall that even from the fourth floor window, she could not see over them. They stood as centennials surrounding her tower in a protective barrier against the rest of Fairelle.

Below her window, vibrant apple green grass grew plush as

her duvet, rolled out like a rug greeting the trees. Purple and yellow flowers dotted the meadow lending their fragrance to the warm breeze.

She let the scent of life fill her. For the millionth time her heart longed to go outside, but she could not. Staying locked away was for the good of all Fairelle.

"Good morning my lovelies," she sang, turning to her birds. "How is everyone?" She walked to the closest perch and inspected a speckled dove that lay on a bed of twigs, protecting her eggs.

Several of her birds had been gifts from her father. But others had found their way into the top of her tower searching for food, or warmth, or healing, and Zelle was more than happy to oblige them.

Moving to a wren that had come in with an arrow through its wing, Zelle inspected her patient. "You look better." She patted the bird's head and poured a mixture of berries and seeds into its feeder. The wren chirped and hopped to the bowl.

For more than an hour she talked to her birds while feeding them. Then she swept and mopped and finally took her dustpan and dumped it out the window. The sun fell across the back of her hand. She placed the dustpan on the floor and reached through the thick metal bars letting the light hit her skin once more. It warmed her whole body and made her smile.

"There she is," came a male voice.

Zelle yanked her arm inside and searched below for the familiar voice. Three men emerged into the meadow.

"Oh, beautiful lady, come down to see us today," one of them begged.

Zelle's face flushed with heat and she withdrew, hiding

herself behind the curtain, her heart racing. The men closed in on her tower. Part of her craved their visits because of her solitary life. But part of her sensed the danger and violence they carried; their reddish auras dotted with brown. Always armed with weapons, the men were often boisterous and crass. Yet despite the way they frightened her, there was another part of her, one she couldn't put her finger on, that awakened whenever the men drew near. It made her whole body tingle in anticipation. But in anticipation of what, she had no clue.

"Oh, lovely, lovely," one of the men sang. "Come to me tonight. Lay with me under the moonlight, and let me drink you in."

The tallest of the men shoved the singer, his aura flashing crimson. "Knock it off, Craigen."

"I was just playin', Klaus. Sheesh."

Klaus turned to the tower. "Lovely maiden, will you give us a song today? We've traveled far, and still have a ways to go. Just one song will ease our way." Klaus smiled up at her and her heartbeat quickened. He was handsome. Not that she had much to compare him to, except for his two friends.

"Or you could let us in," Craigen said.

Zelle couldn't hear the exchange below, but Klaus shoved Craigen and soon the men were nose to nose. Their auras flashed in a dazzling display of colors. Eventually Craigen turned away. Klaus glanced up once more to where Zelle stood, hidden by the curtain.

"Are you still there, maiden? I apologize for my friend's rudeness. Please, will you sing to us?"

Zelle bit her bottom lip. She didn't want them to go just yet, despite her fears. Besides her father, they were the only people she'd seen in years. They'd discovered her about six months prior and came every week or so to hear her sing.

"All right."

The men hooted and hollered. Zelle headed to her sleeping chamber, the floor below. She picked up her lute and dragged a chair to her bedroom window. The men stretched out on the grass, almost hidden by the tall blades. She strummed the lute several times before opening her mouth to play and sing.

The tune floated out, smooth and clear. Her voice was a sound to behold, even to herself. She sang of a forest far away. Where deer and lions and rabbits played. For several long minutes she sang and strummed, lost in her own story. When the song ended, her music held her in a cocoon of peace. A light violet mist surrounded her. She lifted her hands, mesmerized by her own power.

"That was enchanting, Daughter," came a voice from her bedroom doorway.

Zelle's head snapped up. Her father stood staring at her. She swung to look out the window. Her mystery men had vanished.

"Is something wrong?"

Zelle smiled. "No, sorry. I just get so light headed when I sing."

He gave her a knowing smile. "I understand."

"I didn't realize you were coming today." She set down her lute.

"I was in the area and thought I would come and check on you. I brought your elixir and a present."

Zelle stood. "Really? A present? What is it?"

"Come and see." Her father put his arm out. His deeper green aura of harmony flecked with blue shone around him in a halo of color. She'd never told her father that she could see auras and over the years, she'd guessed at the meanings of the colors by how her father's changed depending on his mood. Her father, and then herself, and the men who had come to hear her sing were all she'd been able to observe.

Zelle raced to him. He patted her hand as she set it on his arm. She rubbed her fingers on the soft dark fabric of his blue cloak as they glided down the stairs together. Her father's rough hand lay atop hers while they moved.

"So tell me, Daughter, what were you looking at out the window when I arrived?"

"Oh." Zelle swallowed. "I thought I heard one of my birds."

"And how are your birds?"

"Very well, thank you."

They'd reached the second floor and entered her library. In the middle of the floor stood a stack of new books, as tall as she.

"Oh, Father!" She took off at a run, almost knocking into them. She tilted her head and scanned the spines of all the titles. Half way down she spotted one that intrigued her, took all the other books off and removed it from the stack. It was an encyclopedia of the birds of Fairelle. Turning she grinned. "Thank you."

"You are most welcome, my dear."

Zelle flipped open to the first page as her father walked about the room closing books and putting them on shelves. "I do believe that you might have as many books here as I do in my mage tower."

Zelle's head snapped up. So rarely did her father mention where he lived when he wasn't with her. He was important to the mage community and because of that he had to keep her secret because of her powers. As dangerous as her magick was to the outside world, her father warned her that evil mages would come and take her to try and steal her magick if they ever found out about her.

"Such a mess. Such a mess," he muttered.

She shut the new bird book. "I'm so sorry, Father. If I'd known you were coming…"

"Books hold great power, even when they aren't being read. You must treat them with respect."

"Of course, Father."

He finished shelving books and then turned. "I can't stay long today, I'm afraid. I must get going. But I wanted to see how you are. It's been what? Four days, since I was last here?"

"Five days."

"Five? How time does fly." His brown eyes softened and he took her into his embrace. "I am sorry, my dear. I have been so preoccupied as of late. I apologize for neglecting you."

"I understand." She clung to him. For all his frail appearance, she was always surprised at how solid his body was when she hugged him. "You have many duties to attend to. You cannot spend your life trying to keep me from killing people."

Her father took her face in his palms. "My darling daughter. It's not the world I worry about."

Zelle warmed at the though of her father's devotion. He had ever been her constant guide in life. Taking care of her, keeping her safe.

"Have you had any problems?" He let her go.

"No. No episodes." She swallowed, remembering the feel of the dead sparrow in her hands the month before.

"Well, I brought my things so I can drain you. If you think you might need me to."

"No, I think I am good." She smiled.

"Are you sure?" His heavy eyebrows furrowed.

Zelle knew he only wanted what was best for her. To try and save her from the pain of her powers.

"I may not return for several more days."

The longest she'd been able to go without being drained was two weeks, and that had been by sheer force of will. She remembered her violet mist from earlier.

"Maybe we should."

"Of course, dearest."

Zelle set down her book and pulled a chair close to the fireplace. She clutched her hands in her lap, trying to relax the panic that scratched up her throat, threatening to make her scream.

Her father moved in close and pulled a large red amulet from beneath his robes.

"Oh, before we start." He handed her a vial. "Wouldn't want to forget to give you this."

The small blue glass bottle of liquid pressed into her palm. Her father's own elixir to help her sleep.

"I should take it, before the nausea hits." She opened the bottle and gulped down the bitter liquid. Though she took it every few days, the taste was something she had never become accustomed to. She handed the empty vial to her father and took a deep breath.

"Do you still have the emergency vial?"

She nodded.

He chanted familiar words that she didn't know the meaning of. The stone at his neck glowed bright red and then it swung open like a locket. Her father took his palm and laid it on Zelle's chest.

The warmth from his palm grew white hot. A searing pain that shot through her limbs and caused her to quake. Her breath caught and pressure squeezed her body. Purple mist floated from her and channeled itself into her father's amulet. She grabbed the arms of the chair in an effort to hold in the scream building inside. Her lungs faltered and her gaze locked on her father's face. Her vision darkened around the edges and her heartbeat pounded in her ears. Pressure built behind her eyes and every inch of her chest felt as if it was ready to bust outward. Just when her thought began to become fuzzy, the amulet snapped shut and its grip on her loosened.

Zelle sucked in a deep breath. She concentrated on breathing as her vision blurred and then returned. She loosened her hold on the arms of the chair and hugged herself.

"It was good that you chose for me to do this today, that one filled the amulet to capacity," her father said.

Zelle nodded, her head still spinning. Her stomach lurched.

"Do you wish me to stay?"

Zelle shook her head. "I think I might nap." She got to her feet and almost fell back into the chair. Her father offered her his arm, but she declined. He kissed her on the forehead.

"I'm going to see if I can find a book I think I left here, and then I'll be on my way."

"Of course, Father."

"I'll see you in a few days."

"As you wish, Father." She slid one foot in front of the other in an effort to make it to her room.

"Rest well."

Zelle made it to the stairs before her knees buckled. She hoped she made it to her wastebasket in time. She didn't want to mop again today.

RASMUSS WATCHED ZELLE MAKE HER WAY TO THE STAIRS AND disappear up them. His fatherly smile dropped the moment she was out of sight. The weight of the bloodstone amulet reminded him why he put on the charade. He'd drained her a bit more than was necessary, but he had some things to attend to, and he was going to need the extra essence to get it done. His sister Terona had gone missing, and from what he'd heard, the vampire prince Sage was on the throne.

Rasmuss turned and resumed his search of the library for his prophesy tome. He'd brought it here months ago in an effort to give Zelle something fun to read. She was such a complacent girl. No man could have asked for more in a daughter. Too bad he was no regular man.

Rasmuss scanned the book cluttered shelves. Parchments, tomes and more lined every wall. The scent of wood hung heavily in the air. It was a smell he loved. The scent of knowledge.

He had to get the book, but where had he put it?

HE RAVAGED THE LIBRARY AND THE FIRST FLOOR FOR SEVERAL hours before making his way into Zelle's room to search. She slept on top of her bed, breathing heavily. He looked everywhere possible before deciding to check the library one last time.

An hour later a roar from a nearby glen pulled Rasmuss from his search. He froze. The squawks of terror at the sound from Zelle's birds floated down to him. Someone was near. He needed to go. His ride wouldn't stay silent forever. And if there was someone near the tower, he needed to find them, and silence them before they discovered Zelle.

Giving the room one last glance, Rasmuss cursed under his

breath. The book would have to wait. Morgana wouldn't be happy about it, but he could handle her.

He moved swiftly from the library, his deep robes swishing down the stairs as he headed for the sitting room and entrance. Setting his hand on the door he called for his magick to force open the portal. The doorway dissolved and Rasmuss stepped outside. The beast roared again and Rasmuss rushed for the trees.

CHAPTER THREE

"Dax, what the hell are you doing?" Flint yelled, running from the beast they'd come across moments before. Dax stood motionless, staring at the monster. Cursing, Flint ran and grabbed Dax by the arm "Dax! Move!"

Dax looked over at Flint, his eyes glazed. The dragon hissed and lumbered forward. Sweat trickled down Flint's brow and for the first time in a long time, fear rippled through him.

"Dax, let's go!" He yanked the large man by the arm, producing another roar from the dragon. Rearing its head back, the dragon spit in Flint's direction. Searing pain flew over his hand and up his arm. He cried out and cradled his arm into himself. The skin bubbled and blistered immediately and his shirt turned to ash and dissolved. He sucked in a breath and stumbled backward.

"Dax!" He moved toward the edge of the trees, his gaze never leaving the dragon.

Why the hell wasn't it attacking Dax?

Dax turned and blinked several times. He looked at the dragon and then at Flint. As if waking up, Dax's eyes widened and then he turned and ran for Flint. They tore through the trees the smell of burning hair wrinkled Flint's nose and churned his stomach.

When they reached a safe distance Dax slowed, and shook his head.

"A dragon!"

"Yeah, I could see that." Flint bit against the pain.

Dax looked down at Flint's cradled arm.

"Dragon spit." He grabbed his waterskin and opened it, pouring the water over Flint's wound.

Flint cried out. The water hit his skin like a storm of glass shards pelting his bones. The raw and blistered flesh had already begun to open.

"We need to get you to a healer," Dax said.

"I'll be fine."

"No," Dax insisted. "Not this time. We need to get to Adrian's. Hanna or Redlynn can help."

"I said no," Flint grunted. He glanced at the dragon. Even from the substantial distance the beast's gaze tracked them with precision but it didn't move toward them to attack again.

Flint hit his head against the tree at his back. Why was he out here? Why couldn't he just swallow his pride and go home?

"We need to get out of here. Someone is obviously with this dragon and they'll be on their way from all that roaring."

Flint got shakily to his feet. With quick strides he passed mossy gluman trees and jagged jebestine rocks, trying to keep his bearings. He'd been burned once by tumbling into the fireplace as a child, yet, that felt nothing like pain that threatened to devour him.

Sungold flowers sprouted from the ground, but all he saw was gleaming, green scales and the rows of two-foot long, razor sharp teeth. Flint swallowed hard and slowed when a cramp hit his side. He doubled over.

He hadn't been training daily. That, combined with the lack of food and over indulgence of spirits, had caused his deterioration.

"Man, I can't believe I just stood there in front of that thing," Dax mused.

"It's called dragon fear." Flint sucked in a long breath and tried to expand his abdomen to ease the cramp, but he couldn't. His arm burned and throbbed in pain.

"No," said Dax. "I wasn't afraid. I was…"

Dax's face held a concentration he'd never seen before. And Dax was right. Flint hadn't seen fear in him.

"Come on," said Dax suddenly. "Let's get out of here. We need to deal with that arm."

"Just give me—"

"Shhh!"

Suddenly Flint found himself thrown to the ground behind a downed tree. He cried out in pain, but Dax covered his mouth. When Flint stopped yelling, Dax rolled off him and Flint pushed himself into the trunk.

"What the hell?"

Dax held his finger to his lips and sniffed the air. It was a strange sight. But given Dax was a werebear, Flint assumed he'd picked up on a scent. Dax's head swiveled to the right and he pointed. A man in a blue robe rushed past about ten yards away.

They waited until the man was out of sight before getting

to their feet and heading in the opposite direction. Soon the beat of flapping wings came from above them. They made a run for it and reached the edge of wood, waiting as the dragon and blue-robed rider circled overhead and then turned south. Flint tried to focus through the pain. They had to get to safety.

He spotted a building in the distance. A large square tower with barred windows, covered in vines and flowers loomed in the grassy glen.

They made for the tower at top speed but the dragon circled back and they dropped to the ground, letting the tall grass and flowers camouflage them. His arm burned as it connected with the soil. He bit the inside of his cheek until he tasted blood.

The dragon headed to the forest and they hopped up once more. Racing for the tower they came to the front and found the door open wide. They stepped inside just as the dragon passed their direction and then disappeared again.

The entry to the tower shimmered like water flowing over a glass surface behind them. Flint swallowed. *Magick.*

"Whoa," said Dax.

Flint jumped back outside and stared at the shimmery surface.

"Flint, what are you doing? That thing could come back."

He stepped inside again just before the shimmering surface swirled and then darkened- turning into what resembled a door.

Getting stuck inside a mage tower was worse than begin caught outside one. Flint stepped forward and touched the door The wood felt solid. He tried the handle and the door disappeared again and after a minute reappeared. He stared at the door for several moments. They'd grab supplies and then be on their way.

Flint turned to find a comfortable sitting room. A fire shone from the corner fireplace. A rough hewn heartwood table and chairs, a deep brown loveseat with a matching settee filled out the room. It'd been almost six months since he'd been in a real home. A place that smelled like a home. Felt like a home. The cold damp scent of rock surrounded him and set his teeth on edge, weighing him down as if the stones were piling on top of him. Images flashed in his mind. Memories with his mother, his siblings, his father.

"We should go." Flint walked to a window and glanced outside.

"The dragon and rider could return."

"Exactly. This could be their place."

"If this is their place, from the looks of that robe and the way the door closed, I would say this is a mage tower. We need to find something to put on that arm. And we could at least eat first. We haven't eaten since Cinder's yesterday."

A lump lodged in Flint's throat at the thought of his visit to Cinder.

"Vamperism isn't an ailment Flint. I'm sorry. There is naught but death that can reverse it."

Her words haunted him. If he couldn't help Snow, what good was he? Once again he was reminded that he was second eldest, and second best. If it was Erik, his elder brother, trying to find a cure, surely she'd be cured already.

Flint shook his head. Word of his actions over the past months had to have reached his brothers. The drinking and whoring. He'd failed his family name once more.

Flint cursed and his gut cramped with need for sustenance. He looked down at his arm. The entire sleeve to his tunic was gone. Blisters and burned skin showed from his shoulder to his fingers. If he had to fight, he didn't know how well he'd be able to grasp his sword.

"All right, look for food and ointment, but nothing else. Then we go. They could return any minute and I don't want to be here when they do."

Dax nodded and headed to the rear of the sitting room. Flint sighed and dropped on the soft, plush couch, making it creak. Once more he was flooded with the longing to go home.

He shook his head and rubbed his face. He couldn't return now. Not without Snow, Kellan and his parents. Maybe in time…

Slinging his bag off his shoulder he rummaged inside for his flask. He located his large hunting knife and put it between his teeth while continuing to search.

A soft gasp to his right caught his attention.

His head whipped up.

A willowy, petite woman with pearlescent hair down to her thighs stared at him. The terror in her wide amethyst eyes brought him to his feet. Her beauty was unparalleled. Her fine features so delicate. A surge of longing coursed through him at the sight of her. Finally he found his voice.

"I'm sorry." He pulled the knife from his mouth.

She scrambled away, ready to scream.

Shite. Flint was on her in a flash. "Shhhhh….We mean you no harm." He grabbed her around the waist pulling her soft frame against his and covering her mouth with his palm. Flames of agony licked up his arm. "We didn't mean to intrude. There was a dragon, and the door was open. We just needed a place to hide—"

She screamed against his hand.

Damn. He was doing this all wrong. "It's all right. I'm not going to hurt you, I just need you to stop screaming."

She struggled against him, scratching his arms and stomping on his feet. He tried to convince her that they meant no harm when her knee connected with his groin and he let go. Pain burst through his body as starbursts lit behind his eyelids.

She slapped his face as he doubled over. "Stay away from me!"

"What the hell is going on?" Dax ran into the room.

The woman yipped with fright, caught between Dax and himself. Flint tried to suck air into his lungs but he felt like his stones were in his throat.

"I was trying to calm her," he croaked.

"Well done," said Dax. "You probably scared her half to death with that knife in your hand and the way you look."

The woman looked between them, her hands clasped over her breast. He wanted to apologize again. To tell her once more he wouldn't hurt her. To reassure her that he was a decent person.

"How... how did you get in?" she finally asked.

"The door was open," said Dax.

"Open?" She looked at the door.

Flint sucked in a huge gulp of air and straightened once more. She eyed him and he showed her the knife, then set it on the floor and kicked it toward her.

"It closed itself," Flint said. "We won't hurt you. We just needed a place..." His mouth dried and for some reason he found himself unable to take his gaze from hers. She pulled him in and he was suddenly unable to look away.

"Are you going to rape and kill me?" she asked.

Dax's brows furrowed. "Wait, what? No."

"You... you can take what you want. I... I don't want you

to… just take whatever you need and please go." She inched into the corner behind the couch.

"We aren't going to hurt you," Flint said again. He tried to give her a reassuring smile but it'd been so long since he'd smiled that he was sure he looked like a dolt.

Dax set down the food he'd gathered and help up his hands. He was better at this than Flint had ever been. Dax's calming nature set everyone at ease. A pang of jealousy ran through him. Erik would have had her sitting on the couch and smiling by now as well.

She took a deep breath. "Are you sure you don't want to hurt me? If you do, you can tell me." She reminded him of a cornered doe. So soft and feminine and hesitant.

"No," Flint said. "We have no desire to hurt you."

She stared at them for a long minute. Flint relaxed his posture and held his hand out to her trying to remember what his mother had taught him about being a gentleman. "What is your name?"

She swallowed hard. "My name is Zelle." Her accent was slight but lilting. Flint had never heard anything like it.

He pushed at his hair and tried to straighten his ragged tunic in a vain attempt at looking somewhat presentable. "I'm Flint Gwyn, and this is Dax. Like I said, we were trying to hide from the dragon."

Her gaze traveled up and down Flint's body, taking in every inch of him, finally locking on his arm.

"What happened?"

"I was burned."

Flint cleared his throat as Zelle moved to his side; her movements graceful, like she floated. She shook her slender limbs out from underneath her cream colored gown. Her light fingers lifted his arm and she inspected it with fingernails longer than he'd ever seen on a woman.

Her touch warmed him in unexpected places. Her long white hair slid down, hiding her face. She barely reached his shoulder, she was so petite. He swallowed hard. Something about her soothed him. Her calming nature reminded him so much of his mother.

She looked up, and her almond shaped amethyst eyes connected with his. Again he felt a pull to her that he couldn't betray. As if she was looking directly into his soul.

She couldn't be though, if she had she would run from him in terror.

"Your face carries many burdens," she said.

"More than you can imagine."

Zelle trembled. There were men in her home. Real men. And not the men that had been there earlier. Two large, ferocious looking cloaked men appeared to be raiding her kitchen of all food. She tried to make her brain work, but she was terrified and excited all jumbled into one jittery bundle. No one besides her father had ever been inside her tower. She wasn't even sure how they had gotten in.

Her father's portals were active for a few minutes, sometimes only seconds after he left. She wondered if something had gone wrong. Part of her said she should force the men out. It was dangerous for them to be near her. But another part longed so deeply for companionship that she couldn't possibly send them away so soon. Especially the dark haired one, Flint, with the sad eyes and the aura that radiated a gray shroud flecked with black and red. It depressed her just to look at it.

But nothing about it said he was dangerous or meant her harm. The red was merely small flecks, like dust settling in sunlight. Not like the bright brash halos that covered the men from that morning.

He appeared to not have slept in weeks. The way his body had sagged into her couch made her want to comfort him.

"We'll go." He pulled his arm from her grasp and nodded to Dax.

"Wait." It was reckless, and if her father found out... "You said you haven't eaten today. And your arm. You need that tended to."

Zelle inspected the large broken blisters and recognized them. "Dragon spit."

"What?" he asked.

"You said you were being chased by a dragon. Probably father's dragon, Fader. That's a dragon spit burn. You need it cleansed or infection could set in. And you already have food out. It won't take but a minute for me to plate it."

The two men exchanged a look. *Why did they keep doing that?*

"Thank you." Flint inclined his head. "That would be most kind of you. And more than we deserve."

Zelle scooted toward the table, gathered up the fruits, cheese and bread that Dax had dropped and ducked into the kitchen.

Dax bowed and smiled as she passed. His aura glowed a bright yellow, brandishing his power. Yet the muddy brown that surrounded it left her wondering if something was missing. As if his yellow aura of power had been blocked by something, or hidden from him.

Zelle smiled tightly and continued through the dining area. Pressing herself into the wall of the kitchen she blew out a large breath.

"Feel free to sit at the table and make yourselves comfortable," she called. What was she doing?

She may not get the chance to speak to anyone again for years. So no matter the outcome, she was going to do this. Besides, they said they meant her no harm, and they'd done nothing so far. Nor did they leer at her the way the men who came to listen to her sing did.

Glancing around she grabbed two plates and a platter and piled them with food. Then she grabbed a pitcher of water and took it to the table.

"Let me help you with that." Flint rose from his chair.

"No, no. I can get it." She smiled. He was so handsome. In a scruffy, muscular, terrifying kind of way. His eyes sad and his expression pained. She wanted to touch his face but she didn't.

She set the plates on the table and took a seat next to Flint. The men wolfed down the food and water. She'd never seen anyone eat with such fervor before.

She picked up a grape and popped it into her mouth, chewing slowly. When it hit her stomach she realized how hungry she was herself. Having been drained earlier and then the nausea that followed, she was famished.

Her gaze lit on Flint. His chestnut eyes scanned her face, then he stood and moved past her. He returned with a plate full of food for her. She opened her mouth to speak at his kindness, but she had no words. Retaking his seat, he poured water into a cup and passed it to her.

Zelle dropped her gaze to her plate. She reached for a piece of bread and noticed purple mist wafted off her hands. She shoved them under the table hitting it with her elbow and causing the plates to rattle.

What was happening? Her father had just drained her.

"Is something wrong?" Dax asked.

"No." She cleared her throat. "I'm fine, thank you."

"You're pretty far from a town out here. And I saw no stables, how do you get around? Your husband?" asked Dax.

She slid her hands out of her lap. No mist. Relieved, she tore off a piece of the bread. "I'm here alone."

"Alone?" Flint's gaze held concern. Once again confirming his noble nature.

"My father comes by to see me frequently, but I am usually by myself. Except for my birds."

"Do you ever go out?"

Zelle shook her head.

"Never?" asked Dax.

"Father says... well, he just wants to keep me..." How could she tell them the truth? That she was a born killer and she possessed powers that were uncontrollable at best, and deadly at worst. "It isn't safe."

A sudden self-conscious overtook her. It might be strange that she had never been out, but surely other women in Fairelle didn't go out whenever they wanted.

Flint reached for a piece of cheese and Zelle glanced at his arm. "I need to tend to your burn."

"How did you know it was dragon spit?" asked Dax.

Zelle stood. "Fader usually does as he's told but every once in a while father has arrived with a small burn. They are beasts after all."

Zelle pushed from the table. "Come. I know what to do. It will hurt, but it must be done. Otherwise you could lose your arm."

CHAPTER FOUR

F lint followed Zelle up the stairs. What was wrong with him? Why was he acting like a blushing maiden in front of her?

He watched her gracefully take the stairs one at a time until she stepped onto a landing and opened the only door. A giant library made up the second floor. Stacked from floor to ceiling, there were bookcases filled with more volumes than even Snow could read. He choked at the thought of his sister again.

"Sit there." She pointed to a large chair.

Flint removed his cloak and set it on a table. He watched the sway of Zelle's hips as she drifted about the room and over to a cabinet. He glanced away, trying to find something else to concentrate on. He had no right to look at such a pure vessel of innocence. Not with where his body had been.

"So what do you use on dragon spit burns?" he asked, trying to clear his impure thoughts.

"Wasteland ash to pull out the poison and fernblend to

heal it, but first we must scrub the burn to make sure all of the spit is removed and to break the remaining blisters." She turned and locked eyes with him.

Flint nodded, and cracked his neck, trying to loosen his tense muscles. "How do you know about this stuff?"

She glanced around and the lilt of her laughter made his chest squeeze. "I read a lot."

She removed a brush, gauze and jars from the cabinet and then knelt beside him. Inspecting his arm, her fingers playing over his skin light as butterfly kisses. The feel of the contact both pained and soothed him.

"I'm sorry for having to do this," she said.

"What's on the upper floors of your tower?" Flint asked, trying not to stare at her.

"My bed chamber and aviary." Zelle arranged her items.

"You like birds? My sister likes birds."

Her eyes lit up like fine set jewels. "Some have been gifts from my father. Others have found their way here."

Flint nodded, wrapped up in the sight and sounds and smells that were Zelle. Her hair framed her in a shower of white pearls. His fingers itched to run through the length of it. Her soft touch left a trail of warmth on his skin awakening every muscle while her scent cocooned him in a blanket of safety. Desire threatened to drown him, forcing him to shift his position in his chair. Pain shot up his arm. He jumped, all desire fleeing from him like a vampire from sunlight.

"Sorry." Zelle lifted the brush and held it over his arm. Her hand shook and she gave him a tight smile. "I'll try to be quick but this is not going to feel good." She lifted the lid off a dark black paste and spread a thin layer over his hand and arm.

His leg bounced in anticipation of what was to come. "So your father is a mage?"

"He's a very important man, which is why he can't live here." She wiped her fingers on a towel and closed the lid.

"And mages aren't supposed to have children. Is that why you live here?"

Zelle's eyebrows furrowed. "Um… yes."

Nice way to make conversation. "I'm sorry. That was insensitive."

Zelle dropped her gaze to his arm.

He wasn't good at this. Never had been. Around women, he choked. And with this beautiful creature, nothing seemed to come out right. The way she affected him had him tied in knots. He didn't know what to say or how to thank her for her kindness.

The last time he'd tried to court a girl he'd been seventeen. It had gone pretty well until she'd met Erik. The moment she laid eyes on him, Flint had ceased to exist. He hadn't attempted any sort of relationship outside of straight sex since then. And now, in the presence of a genuinely kind and beautiful human being, he wished he's paid more attention to his mother's advice.

"Ready?" Zelle looked up at him, her eyes apologizing for what she was about to do.

"Don't worry about me," he said. "I'm used to pain." He gripped the sides of the chair and gritted his teeth. He took a long, deep breath and then nodded. The brush scoured his arm in a painful stroke.

His fingers clenched and he bit his tongue to keep from crying out as the blisters popped, releasing more acid and revealing the raw skin beneath. The wood creaked under his grip and a wave of nausea rumbled through him.

Like a thousand tiny steel blades scouring his muscles the brush ripped through his flesh. Over and over she scrubbed the area until blood smeared the surface of his arm. His breath came out ragged and weak, his knee bouncing so hard he thought he might crack the stone floor. Holding on to what little dignity he still possessed, he refused to let her see him cry.

Setting the brush in a wash basin, she took a cloth and tenderly wiped away the mess, then she opened a green container of fernblend ointment and liberally applied it to the wounded area. The aroma of moss and mint drowned out the pungent smell of open wound.

Flint kept his eyes focused on the side of her face as she worked. The tip of her ear peeked out from under her hair and he noticed the pointed apex at the top. Longer than human ears, but much more pointed than fae ears, he thought it the most amazing thing he'd ever seen.

"Almost done." She smiled, set the ointment aside, wrapped his arm with gauze and tied off the ends. Flint released the chair arm and stopped his leg, which wobbled more than bounced. He relaxed into the soft overstuffed chair and closed his eyes.

He breathed deep while listening to her move about the room. A strange sensation over took him. She reminded him of his mother.

Memories of the times his mother had stitched him up, floated to him.

"It's not your job to save all of Fairelle, Flint." She'd smiled at him with sad eyes, knowing too well the burdens he cared within.

"Father says we can't just stand around and watch injustice. We have to do something."

His mother nodded. "And your father is right. But maybe learning to use your words instead of your fists might get your point across a bit better."

"*True. But there are also times with a punch to the jaw is quicker.*"

His mother sighed and shook her head. "*So much like you're your uncles.*"

Memories of growing up and being loved by his family left him lonely and on edge. Being alone with Dax these past months made him miss his old life even more. And now, as he sat in the cushiony chair in Zelle's tower, feeling for the first time something he hadn't felt in many years. Peace.

ZELLE TUGGED A BLANKET FROM THE SOFA AND DRAPED IT across Flint's long form. His gaunt face held a peaceful quality. His dirty clothes were rumpled like he'd slept in them for days, but they were well made. She wondered if he had a home.

She'd never touched a man before. She'd never touched anyone beside her father before. Reaching out, she ran a finger down his cheek, feeling the stubble of his beard prickle her fingertips. Purple mist swirled where their skin touched and a stirring sensation built within her. She stumbled away and shoved her hands into her sleeves. The response of her mist to Flint was a terrifying and thrilling prospect. Her mind slammed into action. *No. You know what could happen. You could hurt him.*

Memories of dead birds flooded her. *The tickle of the soft downy feathers in her palms. The choking, gasping sound as the birds were surrounded by purple mist that burned white hot in her hand.*

Zelle pressed on her temple, trying to force the images away. It wasn't her fault. She hadn't meant to kill them. It was the mist. Her eyelids flew open and she shuffled to the stairs and down to the first floor. Confusion flooded her at feelings she never knew were possible. Loneliness had plagued her, her entire life. But the stirrings inside when she touched Flint... Stirrings that made her want to touch him more, and see him smile; something had awoken. She couldn't put her finger on what it was, but her life would never be the same.

Dax cleared the dishes from the table.

"Here, let me do that." Where was her hospitality?

"You fed us. The least I can do is help with dishes. Where's Flint?"

"He fell asleep upstairs in my library."

Dax stopped and blew out a heavy breath. "Finally." His heavy broad shoulders sagged with relief. His concern for Flint palpable.

"He does not look well." She folded the napkins they'd used for eating.

Dax glanced at her before putting the plates near the washbasin. "He hasn't been. Not for quite some time."

"Do you two have no home?"

Dax shook his head. "He and I have many places we could lay our heads, but he has no wish to be there right now."

"You are good to care for him so much. Are you kin?"

"Not in the blood sense. But he is family to me, even if he doesn't see it."

Zelle picked up the cups. "He holds great sorrow."

"Yes. Yes he does."

Dax tracked Zelle's movements with a wary expression. Heat warmed her cheeks and she dropped her gaze. She finally had someone other than her father to talk to. Her insides clenched like they might burst. She had so many questions she wanted to ask.

Dax finished the dishes and they moved into the sitting room. "What's it like out there?"

Dax's heavy boots clunked on the stone floor as he followed and sat in a chair opposite her. "You've never been out there? Not even once?"

"For as long as I can remember, I've been in this tower."

"Have you never tried to leave?"

"No. I... I feel safe here." Zelle refused to meet his eye. The truth was she had tried to leave once and it had almost killed her.

Dax relaxed into his seat and rubbed his face. "I've seen a lot of Fairelle these past months. From the vampires to the werewolves, to the fae. We even met a beautiful young blue haired woman named Jak who could make flowers and plants grow just by thinking about it. But I can honestly say, a maiden in a tower is a new one."

Zelle swallowed hard. *Vampire? Werewolves? Fae? Blue haired magic user?* She had no idea they still existed outside her books. "You've... you've seen them?"

"I stayed with the wolves for a while. King Adrian and Queen Redlynn are good people. King Sage and Queen Snow of the vampires are also good people. Queen Snow is Flint's sister."

"Flint is a vampire?" Zelle heartbeat raced. Questions swirled and zoomed into her mind so fast she couldn't even catch them all.

"No, he's a vampire hunter actually."

"So he's normal... like us, then."

Dax looked at her quizzically. "You mean is he human? Yes, he's human."

"So then, how is his sister Queen of the vampires?"

Dax looked down at his hands and cleared his throat

before looking up again. "You'll need to talk to Flint about that. It's his story to tell."

"But if he's a vampire hunter, then does he hunt his sister?"

Dax stared at her but didn't speak.

She hadn't meant to pry. Her gaze traveled to the ceiling. To be a vampire hunter when your sister is Queen of the vampires had to be a pain beyond what she could imagine. To hate and hunt that which you loved.

He was like one of her birds. He had come in injured, and needed her help. But Zelle was at a loss as to what kind of help he needed.

"So tell me." She smiled again. "Tell me about all the things you've seen in Fairelle."

FLINT AWOKE TO THE SCENT OF ROASTING VEGETABLES AND warm bread. At the soft feel of the blanket covering him and the smell of food, he smiled. *Home.* He moved to sit up and his arm twinged in pain. His eyes shot open. *Not home.*

"You've been asleep all night and day."

Flint looked to his left. Dax lay covered with a blanket reading a large book.

"Why didn't you wake me?"

Dax shrugged and turned the page. "You needed the rest. You haven't slept well since... Let's just say you don't sleep well."

The recurring nightmares of rushing into the room to find Snow pale and almost lifeless on Remus' bed had plagued him. Her weightless cold body in his arms. The crushing load of her coffin as they'd hefted it to take her home.

He ran his hands over his face. Surprisingly, he hadn't dreamt about it last night though.

"What are you reading?"

Dax turned the book over to look at the spine. "History and prophecies of Fairelle and the men who discovered them."

Flint hung his head. "Sounds boring."

"It is."

"Then why are you reading it?" Flint scrubbed his hands over his face.

"Because I have nothing else to do, and because it's the first time I have been able to sit and read in months. No offense, but hanging out in the woods and sleeping in taverns hasn't been as stimulating as I had hoped."

"I didn't ask you to come with me."

"But you needed me just the same. Besides," Dax flipped a page. "I found the other prophecies in here."

Flint's gaze shot to Dax's impassive face.

"The other ones?"

"It lists all of them. The first pertaining to the wolves. The second having to do with the vampires–"

"What's next?" Flint's heart galloped.

"I'm not sure, but here's what it says."

Invited through a door, the privileged let in the evil
The greedy he did betray
And yet through them, humans will find a friend
And love will make her stay

Flint stared at Dax. "What the hell does that mean?"

"I am as clueless with this one as I was with all the rest."

Flint replayed the words in his head trying to make sense of them. After several minutes he gave up and looked down at his clothes. He'd been sleeping in them for weeks. Though Cinder had forced him to bathe, and had washed their clothes, they were beginning to look quite worn. And his current tunic was missing a sleeve, thanks to the dragon spit.

"Do we have anything clean to wear in the bags?"

"We have the clothes Cinder gave us, as well as one or two tunics left." Dax placed the book in his lap.

Flint stood and stretched. His arm burned and he pulled it to him.

"How's the arm?"

"It hasn't fallen off, but it feels like a dragon set it on fire."

Dax snorted. "You should have Zelle look at it again."

Flint studied Dax. "You like her."

"She's sweet, gentle and kind." He laughed. "That's not the kind of woman who stirs me."

The only kind of women who'd stirred Flint in the past were the kind that knew when to raise their skirts. But Zelle was the complete opposite and somehow, she struck him in a way that no one had before. Not, that anything was happening with her. He wasn't going to let anything happen with her. She was in a tower in the middle of nowhere. Obviously she wanted her solitude.

His stomach clenched and hunger raced through him, leaving him dizzy.

"What time is it? I'm starving."

"You should be, it's about four in the afternoon. Zelle saved some soup for you from earlier."

As he descended the stairs the smells of food made his stomach cramp. He looked around the room for his bag but it was nowhere in sight. He made his way to the kitchen and found Zelle stirring a large pot.

"Hello." He ran his fingers through his hair.

She jumped and turned.

"You're awake. How does your arm feel?"

He looked down at the bandages. "Better," he lied. "I was looking for my bag. I thought maybe I might clean up before we leave."

"Leave? That wound is still fragile, you should let me check it."

The depth of her sincerity pricked at Flint's heart. "We'll eat, and wash, and then we should probably go."

"Go where? Dax said you don't want to go home."

Flint stiffened. "What else did Dax say?"

She bit her lip. "Was he not supposed to tell me about you being a vampire slayer?"

Flint opened and closed his mouth several times. "Go on."

"He said your sister was a vampire and you are a vampire slayer, but he wouldn't tell me how because that's your story to tell. He lived with the werewolves and you went to see the fae and that you've been traveling for months and this is the first house you've slept in since you left Tanah Darah. Is that because you like sleeping in taverns?"

Her eyes were wide with genuine interest. Again Flint open and closed his mouth several times.

"Is that too much? Did I say too much? Dax said I talk a lot and that I ask hordes of questions."

"Um… You talk just fine." What did that even mean?

She stared at him as if weighing what he'd said, and then turned to her pot.

She looked so natural in her environment. Her white hair hung down to the backs of her legs in a cascade of opalescent loveliness. Her plain dress stopped just above her ankles revealing her small bare feet. He rubbed his fingers together, wondering what her skin felt like.

A vision of her in the kitchen of his manor house, cooking, with small children running around her, made him smile.

Flint shook his head. *No.*

For a fleeting moment hope lit inside him. Why not go home? The vampires weren't much of a threat. The evil behind the throne had been killed. Sure there were more prophesies, but they had nothing to do with him. Why couldn't they all just go back to the way things were before the mantle of being a Slayer had been thrust upon them?

He let out a heavy breath. They were the same thoughts he'd had for weeks. But how could he go home as if nothing had ever happened? The running, the lies, the gambling and drinking and–

Licking his lips, he craved a bottle to drown himself in.

Zelle turned toward him. "The soup will be warm again in a few minutes. If you'd like to sit, we can eat, and then I'll look at your wound."

"Thank you." Flint's voice came out rough and gravely. He sat at the table and blew out a heavy breath. How had he become this person?

CHAPTER FIVE

During dinner Zelle and Dax talked about books and the nearby flora and fauna. Then she recounted how her father had brought her to the tower to keep her safe. Flint listened, adding little. He knew nothing about flowers and plants. Weapons and killing? That was his world, but what he'd say would've only upset Zelle. How did you tell a lovely, sheltered creature what killing vampires was like?

After helping clear the table he lumbered up to her bedchamber on the third floor. Furnished to rival his own parents' bedroom, Zelle's father had spared no expense in making her comfortable. The large and soft bed invited him to lie down but a buttercup yellow shawl lying atop an ornate ivory vanity caught his attention. Flint crossed to the vanity and looked at the various feminine items. He touched the hairbrush, the comb, and then picked up the shawl. He caught the scent of her hair on it.

"I should look at your arm." Zelle walked in with more ointment and several other items, making him jump and bump into the table. The mirror shook and he dropped the shawl and grabbed onto the mirror to keep it from falling.

"I'm sorry. I wasn't trying to pry."

"I have no secrets. Look at whatever you like." She set down the items on her nightstand and patted the bed. "Sit."

He swallowed as his gaze lit on her immaculate bed.

"Come on, don't tell me you're worried about me hurting you."

"No."

"Well then come over. I promise not to bite you 'til after you've cleaned up." She sat on the edge of the bed and waited.

Flint walked over and eased down on the bright white comforter trying not to transfer any dirt onto it.

"Take off your tunic."

His gut clenched at the thought of her seeing his body. The scars he bore were a stark reminder of what he had become. No one outside his family and Dax had seen him with his tunic off. He rolled up his sleeve instead.

She didn't question his decision. Instead, she unwrapped his wound. He winced when she reached the last layer.

She groaned and turned his arm over. "The covering is stuck in the injury. I let it sit too long. I'm so sorry."

Flint tried to hold it together as she picked at edges of the bandages. The pain made his dinner turn sour in his stomach.

"I think maybe we should go into my bathing room. This is going to make a mess."

"Of course."

She gathered her things and headed to the bathing room.

Flint hung his head. He'd had wounds before, even bad wounds, but this might be the worst. Perhaps Dax should help him. He didn't want Zelle to witness his weakness if he cried out. Heavens knew Dax has seen him at his worst more times than he cared to remember.

"I'm ready," she called.

Flint lifted his head and sighed. Dax wouldn't know what he was doing. The bed creaked as he stood and headed for the bathing room.

"Sit here." She pointed to a wooden chair.

His legs trembled slightly as he eased into the hardback chair.

She turned, a pair of scissors in her hand. "I'm going to do my best not to hurt you."

"I've had worse."

She pursed her lips. "You don't have to be strong with me. I can already tell what a mighty man you are."

He wasn't trying to let her in, yet somehow she knew as much about him as if he'd opened up and told her everything. How did she do that? He'd never gotten close enough to a woman to let one see inside.

"How do you see me like that?"

"It's a gift I have, I suppose."

"Reading people is one thing but you know more than that. What are you?" He searched her face, watching as a flash of fear coursed over it. Her eyes bore the strike of sadness before softening again.

"I'm just a woman. I suppose being alone for so long, I'm more accustomed to seeing what people don't say as much as what they do."

He wanted to tell her that made no sense, but she smiled and broke his train of thought.

"Now. Let me take a look at this arm."

ZELLE TRIED TO KEEP THE FEAR OFF HER FACE AND OUT OF HER voice. She wasn't an ordinary woman. She'd never once read about a woman having to have her essence drained by her father and kept in an amulet around his neck. Or being able to kill a bird with uncontrollable magick. Especially when she didn't want to.

She took the small scissors she kept in her needlepoint kit and cut down the outside of the cloth on Flint's arm.

"Tell me about your home, your family. What are your parents like?" If she could get him talking about something else, maybe he wouldn't focus on the pain.

"My parents are dead."

She stopped cutting and looked up. "I'm sorry."

"Me too. They were the best people Fairelle ever had the opportunity to be graced with."

He stared past her to the wall and after a moment, she resumed cutting.

"My mother was beautiful, with long dark hair and eyes like sapphires. She was gentle and kind, but fierce as a dragon if anyone dared to harm her family."

"Sounds like how Dax described you."

He snorted. "I wish. My father was strong and just. Hair like corn and shoulders as broad as an ox. Together they were a magnificent couple."

"What about your siblings?"

"I have– had– six brothers." He looked down.

Zelle's throat dried. The sadness emanating off him was painful to witness.

"There are only five of my brothers left. One was killed by vampires."

"So you lost two siblings to vampires. No wonder you hate them so much."

She finished cutting the outside of the bandage and turned his arm over so she could cut the inside. Out of the corner of her eye she noticed him staring at her. It made her cheeks heat.

"What about your home?" she asked.

"Much of it's farmland whereas the area down here is woods."

"Dax said Fairelle is different all over."

"That it is."

She placed her scissors on the washbasin and ran her finger under the edge of the bandage. Yellow salve mixed with the blood that had dried into it.

"I'm going to wet down the bandages with warm cloths to see if I can get them to loosen."

He nodded.

Zelle grabbed several towels that had been soaking in the water basin and applied them to his arm.

"So you've never spoken to people before us?" he asked.

"I met an old woman once. She was traveling south. She stayed in the meadow for two nights and spoke to me. I made her food and gave her a few items of clothing before she left. I couldn't give her too much or father would be suspicious."

"Does your father visit often?"

"About twice a week. Sometimes he gets busy and forgets to come, but for the most part he's been very faithful about visiting me."

She placed the last washcloth on his arm and then wiped her hands on her dress.

"Have you always lived here?"

"As long as I can remember." She sat on the edge of the tub.

"Did he live here with you when you were a child or did your mother live with you then?"

48

Zelle opened her mouth to speak but then shut it again. Had her father lived here when she was young? She tried to remember her childhood years, but when she thought about them, her mind was a complete blank. Like a cloudless sky on a spring day.

"I... I don't remember," she said. "I seem to have forgotten my childhood for the moment." Her gaze met his and his brows furrowed.

"You don't remember anything?"

She tried again and a wave of nausea overcame her. She took several deep breaths and swallowed down the bile that clawed up her throat and coated her mouth. Her vision pulsed with dark dots and she blinked rapidly to clear it.

"Are you all right? You look as if you might be ill."

She took in several more breaths and set her hand on her stomach, willing it to be still. "Must have been something I ate," she said. "It happens sometimes. I'm fine."

She stood and grabbed on to the wash stand for support until her vision cleared.

"I should check on your bandages. I have to be honest. This is probably going to hurt worse than yesterday."

Flint chuckled. "The one time I wish you would have lied to me."

She caught his eye and a hint of a smile crossed his face. For a moment she imagined him as a young boy playing with his brothers. The image tugged at her heart.

"I did unfortunately, I told you in the other room I wasn't going to hurt you."

She removed the washcloths and lifted the edge of one of the bandages. It came off of easily at first, but toward the middle it stuck. She tried to pry it up little by little but his

49

discomfort was apparent. She took a step away and assessed the situation.

"They're stuck tight aren't they?" he asked.

She tried to lift another bandage and the same thing happened. She chewed her thumb. There had to be a way to get them off.

"Just do it," he said.

Her gut coiled tight as a snake. "I'd rather not," she whispered.

He took her hand in his large calloused one and ran his thumb over her knuckles. Sparks of desire traced over her like a feather.

"I need you to do this for me. I can't do it myself," he said.

Her chin quivered but she nodded. The warmth of his hand on hers sent a chill up her neck. If he was being strong about this, she could be strong for him as well. She'd gotten him into the mess, she needed to help him out. She wished that she could do something for the pain. Offer him something that would take off the edge. She thought about her extra vial of tincture her father had given her to help her rest. But she couldn't give him that. What if she lost control of her magick? It was the only thing she could use to knock herself out and calm her mist.

She stepped forward and gripped the first bandage.

He clutched the edge of the basin stand with his good hand and nodded. "Do it."

Zelle hesitated only a second before ripping the fabric from his arm. Flint grunted and his hand shook.

"Keep going," he panted.

Zelle flung the bandage to the floor and gripped the next section. Over and over she ripped the fabric from his wounds causing them to weep blood. When she reached the second to last bandage, he cried out.

"One more, only one." A tear leaked from the corner of her eye. She ripped the last bandage from him and he let out a horrible wail. She sniffed and stepped away. "That's it. That's the last of them." She grabbed the salve. Opening the tin she gouged her fingers inside and tenderly spread it over his wounds.

He sat silent, body shaking, head hung low.

She worked as swiftly as she was able over his arm. Then she applied the salve to the bandages to insure they didn't dry out again. Finally she rewrapped him and cleaned up the bloodied dressings.

"I think I should lie down," he said.

"I can help you," she offered.

He lifted his head, his eyes red from fatigue and strain. "I'll be all right." He rolled his sleeve down and cradled his arm. Rising he swayed slightly.

She ducked under his good arm and put it over her shoulder.

"Come on. I'll help you downstairs."

The weight of his body seemed to crush her with its power as she walked through her room with him and out into the hall. Getting him down the stairs proved to be almost fatal for both of them. But after several minutes she finally ushered him into the library.

Dax looked up from his book and rushed to help. "What happened?"

"I had to yank his bandages off."

Dax dropped Flint onto the small couch. He barely made a sound. She looked around and located the hand knitted green blanket she'd given him the night before and draped it over his body.

His deep brown eyes fluttered open with a glassy sheen. On impulse she brushed the dark curls from his face and then stepped away. He caught her fingers in his.

"Stay for a minute?"

She glanced over at Dax who looked at their joined hands and went back to his book.

She smiled. "All right."

Flint dropped her hand and she sank to the floor beside him. She lifted his palm once more as he closed his eyes. She ran her fingertips over each of his in turn and hummed. Before long she began to sing a soft melody. The words were in a language she did not know, but the sweet tune of it was all too familiar.

When she finished she looked up. Flint was fast asleep and Dax stared at her, mesmerized.

CHAPTER SIX

The following morning Zelle awoke on the floor next to Flint on the couch. She pushed into a sitting position and her neck twinged. She went to reach for it and found her fingers entwined with Flint's. When had that happened? His large hand wrapped around hers like a giant, warm glove. She slipped her fingers from his and rubbed her neck.

Despite the pain, she found Flint and Dax's presences comforted her deep in her soul. She couldn't remember the last time her father had spent the night in the tower. As far as she could remember he'd always come for a few hours and then left again.

She'd never really thought of the past before Flint had mentioned it.

She struggled to recall her childhood- trying to locate her first memory, but things grew fuzzy when she reached back further than a year's time. As if a blanket obscured her past.

She swallowed hard and a wave of panic mixed with

nausea washed over her. How old was she? How long had she been in the tower? Years? Decades? Why had she never questioned it before? Another wave of nausea slammed into her and Zelle scrambled to her feet. Trying not to wake Dax or Flint she made her way to the door and out onto the stairs. She headed to the kitchen where she poured herself a cup of water and gulped it down.

Questions swarmed her mind like bees in a hive. She stared out the small window over her washbasin. The scenery collided in a blur of colors.

Why couldn't she remember anything? Why had she never questioned her existence in the tower? A fresh wave of nausea made her belly churn. She bent over and breathed deeply.

"Stop, stop, stop," she whispered.

"Zelle?"

Flint's voice made her snap her head up. He stood in the kitchen doorway, sleep still obscuring his features.

"Is something wrong?"

Was something wrong? Yes, something was very wrong. She just couldn't pinpoint what.

"My stomach's a little queasy this morning." She gave him a weak smile.

"Probably from sleeping in the same room as Dax and I. I'm afraid our stench is a bit uncivilized at the moment. Why don't you sit down and I'll make you some tea."

She stared at him, her stomach calmed at the small handsome smile that painted his face.

He chuckled. "Believe it or not, I do remember how to make tea."

His eyes crinkled in the corners and a small dimple appeared on his left cheek. She etched the sight into her memory to carry her through lonely moments after he departed.

Remembering herself, she nodded and headed for the table. When she reached the narrow doorway, the two of them squeezed past each other. Every sensitive inch of her body tingled at the press of his hard chest against hers. She lingered allowing the moment to stretch out.

He stared down at her and she tried to remember to breathe. For that moment as their bodies passed, time seemed to stand still and her heart thundered. His purely masculine scent filled her head and made her swallow.

"I'm sure it wasn't the smell that upset my stomach," she said.

His head cocked slightly to the side.

She made her way to the table and dropped into a chair. Setting her hands on the table she stared at them. Purple mist swirled over her palms. Rubbing her fingers together she watched it disappear and reappear.

"Zelle?"

She shoved her hands into her lap. "Yes?"

Flint peered at her and then looked down at her hands. She hid them deeper in the folds of her dress.

"Uh… where's the tea?"

She started to lift her hand to point, but stopped herself. Instead she motioned with her head. "The last cupboard on the left."

He nodded and headed for the kitchen again. She checked her hands. The mist was gone. She blew out a low breath. She needed to be careful. For some reason Flint seemed to make her mist more prevalent than normal.

FLINT CARRIED THE DELICATE TEACUP AND SAUCER AND PLACED it in front of Zelle. She lifted it and sipped.

"That's nice, thank you."

He sat opposite her and cradled his still painful arm. "Are you going to tell me why you were feeling ill?"

She blinked several times. "I don't know."

"You can tell me to mind my own business."

"No, that's not it." She shook her head, her long hair shimmering as she did. "I honestly don't know."

"Has this happened before? Do you have a health condition?"

"Not that I'm aware of. It started when I was thinking about my past."

"Your past?"

"Last night you asked about my childhood. When I try to think about it, I feel ill."

Flint's chest constricted and his throat dried. "Perhaps something bad happened and that is your mind's way of trying to keep you from remembering."

She looked down at her cup and swiveled it around. "Mayhaps. The strange thing is, it isn't just my childhood. It's everything."

"Everything?"

"When I try to even think past a year ago, I can't. Somehow I can't hold on to my memories."

A sinking feeling punched Flint in the gut. "Dax remembers nothing before he was found by the werewolves five years ago. When you try to remember, what do you feel?"

She studied her tea, her light fingers tracing the rim of the cup. "Like a dark cloud forming a wall in my mind. I know there is something behind it, I just can't quite see through it.

Sometimes I catch glimpses of people and places, but I can't understand what I see."

She caught his eye. "The funny thing is, I don't really care. I mean, I suppose I care, somewhere, otherwise I wouldn't keep poking the cloud. But on a whole, I feel so happy and contented with my life that it doesn't matter. Does that sound right to you?"

"Sounds like magick."

"Do you think whatever happened to Dax to make him forget who he is, could have happened to me as well?"

"It's possible. But who could have gotten close enough to you to do it?"

"My father would never let anything happen to me. Maybe it was something my mother did."

She hadn't mentioned her mother before. "Do you remember her?"

"No. But I don't know anyone else except my father."

"Are you sure he couldn't have done this?" He tried to tread gently, but the more he learned about Zelle's father, the more leery he became.

"Why would he?" Her brows furrowed in the most child-like way.

"Maybe you should ask him the next time he pays a visit."

"I probably should. But it might make him angry. I don't care for him when he's angry."

Flint's knuckles cracked as he ground his fists together. Strange that he was so protective of her, though he barely knew her.

"Don't get me wrong," she said. "He's never hurt me. It's just... When he gets angry, his whole countenance changes. Even his face seems to morph into someone else. And his aura—"

"His aura?"

Zelle stopped short. "Yes, well, I…"

"What kind of aura?"

She looked down at her hands and studied them for several seconds. "I… I can see people's auras," she said. "I've not even told my father I can do it."

"Can you see mine?" His tone was hushed.

Her gaze locked with his again and then they traveled his face. He wanted to know what she saw, but was terrified all the same.

"What do you see?" he asked.

"You're sad and lonely, but brave and strong. Your aura is conflicted between wanting to be happy and wanting revenge."

His heart felt like she'd gripped it in her fist and squeezed. This lovely innocent creature saw to the very depths of him. Terror set off warning bells in his mind. He stood so fast that the chair behind him tipped to the ground.

"I'm sorry." She jumped to her feet. "I wasn't trying to—"

"I know you weren't." He floundered for something else to say. "I should go wash up. We need to leave soon." Heat flushed his cheeks and he strode past her.

"What did I say?" she called behind him. "Tell me. What did I say that was wrong?"

"Nothing," he said, as she reached the stairs. "You did nothing. You were absolutely right."

LOCATING THE BATHING ROOM IN ZELLE'S CHAMBER, FLINT walked to it, placed his bag on the counter and surveyed the contents. It had been weeks since he'd looked at his supplies.

He pulled out a clean tunic, rummaged around for a comb, and touched the smooth silver surface of his father's flask.

His fingers lingered over the polished surface, running over the engraved lettering, knowing the initials by heart. His body burned for the taste of the fiery liquid.

The one thing his father had given him after his first real fight. It had belonged to his grandfather before him.

"I'm proud of you Flint. You stuck up for your younger brother. Protected him." His father squeezed his shoulder. "One day Erik will be Lord of Westfall. His hands will be tied by the law. You will not be so tethered. I will be counting on you to do what is necessary to protect your brothers and sister. Do you understand?"

Flint wiped the blood from his nose, staring at his father through his one eye not swollen shut. "Yes, Father."

"I want you to have this." His father pulled his flask from his pocket and unscrewed the cap. He took a swig and then handed it to Flint. "Remember Flint, gentlemen and Lords drank from their own flasks and only out of a goblet at a feast. Never straight from a bottle and never in a tavern."

Flint nodded and took a burning swallow from the flask. His father clapped him on the shoulder and then pulled him into a hug.

"That's my boy."

Flint stared at the flask. Just one more way that Flint would have been a disappointment to his father. Drinking at taverns too many times to count. More bottles than he could remember.

He was a disappointment to everyone. His father, his brothers, his sister, and most of all, to himself. The fact that even a sheltered lady like Zelle could see the misery upon him, spoke volumes.

Go home, everyone said. Make amends. But how did he make

amends for his anger? His hatred and his failures? How did he let go of everything he'd been dealing with for these past several years and live? How did he forget the swiving and drinking and killing? What kind of woman would want a man like him?

Taking out the stopper he lifted the flask to his lips. The liquid burned his mouth, nose, and throat. He gulped down the alcohol along with the loneliness that threatened to overwhelm him.

The familiar sensation warmed and numbed his body. He set the empty flask down and resumed searching his bag. He found two empty bottles of ale. Getting to his feet he moved to the small barred window and tossed them out so Dax and Zelle wouldn't see.

He needed to wash, and leave Zelle in peace, no longer diminishing her light with his presence.

"What the hell is wrong with you? The lady in this tower is obviously in trouble." Erik's voice echoed through his mind, making him shake his head.

"It's for the best," Flint replied.

"For who? You? Or her?"

He swore several times and then grunted. It *was* for the best that he leave her be. Then, when he found someone trustworthy, maybe he'd ask them to help her. She wasn't his burden and he wasn't her savior.

The washbasin sat next to a tall white pitcher of water. A large ornate metal-framed mirror hung over it. Flint made his way to the mirror and gave himself a good looking over. His face was thinner and both his hair and facial hair were longer than usual. Bloodshot tendril woven through his sunken in eyes like threads in a tapestry. This was what he had always imagined looking like on the inside. The part he let no one see. But now it showed on the outside as well. He wondered how a woman as sweet as Zelle could have dared to let him stay in her tower. No wonder she'd been terrified when they'd shown up.

He shook his head and ran his hands over his face before pouring water into the basin and scrubbing his skin. The cool water hit him like knives, pulling him from the dullness that had begun to settle into his bones. He looked in the mirror again. A sudden urge to be clean hit him. A need to not let her see him like this again. To not have anyone see him this way. How many bar patrons had seen him? How many snickered about the downfall of the second eldest Gwyn brother? The one who never measured up. The one who couldn't even save his own family. The one thing his father had asked him to do.

He located the razor in his bag. A cup with soap sat next to the basin. He dipped his fingers in the water and then smooshed the sudsy cream onto his palm, rubbing it on his face and over his thick beard. He was about to reach for the razor when there was a knock on the door. He glanced over and saw double for a split second. The fuzz of the alcohol crashed through his head.

"Yes?"

"I… I brought you a towel and a bucket of water for bathing."

"You can leave them outside the d-d-door." *Crap!* Was he slurring his words?

"Are you all right?"

"I'm fine." Flint tried to place the razor on the counter, but hit the pitcher, causing it to crash to the floor. *Dammit!* Maybe a shave wasn't the best idea while semi intoxicated.

"I'm coming in."

"No! Don't—" The door swung open. Zelle held a large creamy towel in her arms. She looked Flint up and down. He gripped the counter so as to not sway. Her eyes narrowed. She spotted the broken pitcher on the floor, took a breath and marched in. He backed away and bumped into a chair. Zelle grabbed him by his good arm, pushing him down into the chair. Then she knelt and picked up the piece of pitcher from the floor, mumbling words in a language he didn't recognize.

"I'm… I'm sorry for breaking the pitcher."

"Yes, well. If you hadn't been consuming spirits in here, I am sure it wouldn't have happened." She didn't look up.

He knew that tone. Snow frequently used it with him when he was drunk.

She cleaned up the pitcher pieces and took them out to her bedroom. When she returned, she placed her hands on her hips and twitched her pursed lips. In his fuzzy state he found her skin gave off a beautiful purple glow. It flowed around her in a fine mist, tinting her hair and making her eyes even brighter.

"So you were going to shave in your condition?"

"I'm fine."

"Really?" Her eyebrow cocked. "So you intended to shave with one arm bandaged and unusable and the other supporting you so you don't fall down?"

"I…" He hadn't really thought that bit through. Maybe draining the flask hadn't been a wise decision.

Zelle shook her head and picked up the towel. He tried to move away, but she fanned it out and wrapped it around him like a babe. Her delicate smooth fingers moved over his throat and neck as she tucked it into his shirt, trailing sparks of delight across his skin. His desire rose as her hair fell over him and he breathed in her wonderful scent.

He yanked the towel down a couple inches to cover his lap. The last thing he wanted was to scare her with the way his body responded to her touch. She stepped away and again he saw the purple mist.

Lifting the razor from the counter, she flicked it open and stepped forward.

"Do you know how to do this?" he asked, suddenly aware that she would be holding a blade to his throat.

"I've read about it in books."

"In books?"

"I'm a good learner." She stepped into his space and tilted his head to the side.

"I really could—"

She pulled his head back by his hair so their eyes met. "No, you really couldn't."

She was right. And the only alternative was to embarrass himself further by asking Dax for help. He sighed and nodded. Her fingers trembled slightly as she put the blade to his cheek. She took a deep breath and began. Her strokes were light and swift.

After a moment the tension in his body left and he relaxed, allowing her to work. The warmth of her body flowed over him giving him a feeling of peace once more.

Zelle didn't know what had come over her, but finding Flint intoxicated and about to shave in the bathroom set her ablaze with anger. He was like her father's dragon, Fader. Peaceful and fine one moment and spitting acid the next.

She'd observed drunken men through her window. They'd come at night sometimes and call to her, telling her all the things they wanted to do with her, like she was a common whore. It made her skin itch like she was covered in scuttling bugs.

Seeing Flint partake of the same libations filled her with the same horrible sensation. She moved the blade up his cheek revealing tanned skin underneath, wiped the blade on his towel, and continued on. Purple mist swirled off her skin at the nearness of him, but he didn't notice. She tried to keep her hand steady as her hips leaned into his arm. The hard musculature of his arm pressed through the towel and her dress. She'd never been so close to a man, and against her better judgment, she liked it.

She wiped the blade on the towel again, surprised he hadn't mentioned how loud her heart beat. She tilted his face toward her. His looked up at her with a glassy stare, lips slightly parted as if inviting her to kiss him.

She'd read love stories where the hero took his maiden into his arms and pressed his lips to hers. She had always wanted to experience that.

"Thank you," he whispered.

She leaned close and her breast brushed his chest. The contact sent a jolt through her and she backed away.

"Are you sure?" he asked. "I can manage if—"

"I just need to move to the other side."

Flint nodded.

She scooted around the chair to his left side. He closed his eyes again and she worked the blade over his skin, playing and replaying the sensation from the jolt. If he'd felt it he gave no signs. Maybe there was something wrong with her. Like the purple mist and her father having to drain her. Zelle tried to think of other things to soothe her thoughts, but revealing more of his handsome face just made her warmer.

By the time she finished, she thought she might burst from

having him so close. Something inside of her needed to be with him. She lifted the towel and wiped his cheeks. His eyelids opened slowly.

Picking up the bucket of water she poured a bit into the washbasin and dipped the towel in. She wiped his face again and he moaned at her touch. Her breath caught at the sound. It was so manly, yet so needing.

Was she so lonely that she wanted any man? No. She hadn't felt anything for Dax, or the men who came to her window. Only Flint.

"Take off your shirt," she said.

His neck muscle twitched. "What?"

"Take off your shirt. I'm going to wash your hair."

"That's not necessary."

"I insist."

His gaze sharpened and he sat immobile for several minutes.

Zelle waited. She wasn't ready to be done with him. He would leave soon and she wanted to savor every memory after he was gone. The feel of washing him was a memory she would cherish.

His aura swirled with mixed emotions, like a rainbow in a windstorm. She caught every expression that shadowed his features. The ones that showed, and the ones that didn't.

"I don't want to make you uncomfortable," she said.

Finally, sitting up, he tugged his tunic out of the waistband of his pants. His eyes only left hers for the fraction of a moment as he pulled it over his head.

She took in every inch of his powerful torso, his tanned skin and sinewy arms. Curly dark chest hair trailed down between his abdominal muscles and dipped below his waistband. There was a beautifully cut v shape of his hips. But most of all, his scars. Some white, some pink, a few deep purple. They crisscrossed his arms, shoulders, chest and abdomen. Each one a testament to his ferocity.

"Battle scars," she whispered. The pain he must have endured. The battles he must have seen. Dozens. Hundreds maybe. Her fingers itched to touch them. "From being a hunter?"

Flint nodded.

She reached out, but stopped. "May I?"

He said nothing but his aura shifted to an anxious shade of azure.

Her fingertips fluttered over his skin and traced a long pink scar that travelled from his sternum, cutting through his dark curls to his left shoulder. At his shoulder she traced a scar down his arm. When she reached his forearm, he grasped her wrist in his strong grip. She swallowed hard.

"They're ugly," he said in a throaty voice.

"They're beautiful," she countered. "A testament to the kind of man you are."

"A murderer."

"A hero. Why do you see yourself that way? Do you hold other people to the same standard? Your brothers, are they murders?"

"Never. My brothers are good decent men—"

"Then why not you? Why are you not a decent man?"

"It's not just the vampire slaying. It's the other things I've done as well."

"The drinking."

"Among other things."

"What other things?"

"Things I shouldn't talk about with a lady."

His eyebrows knit together and he breathed in short, hard

bursts. Zelle trailed her hand over his stomach making his belly quake, and then over his chest.

"Like women?" Her voice was husky and low. "You've been with many, I assume. Do you have any children?"

"No." His eyes flashed. "I have no children. I'm sure of that."

"So, because you've had sex with lots of women that makes you bad?"

He stared at her. "Doesn't that bother you?"

For some reason, it didn't. "Sex is natural. Organic. People need a connection with other people and sometimes they just need release. I understand that."

"But you've never been with a man?"

The memory flashed in her mind, but a pain pounded her temple and she shoved it away. "I don't know. Like I said, I cannot remember anything from before a year ago. Maybe I have." His aura changed and she smiled. "Would it bother you if I had been with men before?"

"I'd be a hypocrite to say yes."

"You'd be lying though if you said no." She cupped his cheek with her palm.

He breathed deeply. Turning his head he kissed the palm of her hand. The contact made heat pool between her thighs. Something surged inside Zelle and at that moment she was sure she'd been with a man before.

Without thinking she reached down and pressed her lips to his. Stiffening, he didn't move. A wash of panic filtered through her and just as she made to pull away, he threaded a hand into her hair and guided her down onto his lap. He plunged his tongue deep into her mouth, making her heat further. A pulsing between her thighs pounded with the rhythm of her heart.

His sweet breath poured into her and she sucked it in. The sensation made her fingers tingle and her senses awaken. She wanted more.

Again he breathed and again she pulled his breath into her. The feeling rushed over her skin making her head light. She kissed him deeper, breathing in the euphoria that overtook her. Alarm bells rang in her mind and then a sharp pain pierced her skull. She broke from his lips and cried out.

"I'm sorry," Flint said. "I didn't mean to do that."

She rose from his lap as fast as she was able. Trying to hold back tears from the sharp pain shooting through her skull, she staggered to the bathing room door.

"No, no, it's fine," she said with a small wave. "I just– It's my head. A small headache. I think I should go lie down."

An image flashed into her mind. *Breathing in the breath of the dark skinned man with white eyes.* Another shot of pain wracked her head. Zelle stumbled toward her bed.

"I'm sorry," he said again, following her.

Zelle tried to steady herself. Falling onto her bed she cradled herself, pulling her chin into her chest. The sharp pain turned to pounding until minutes passed and the pounding turned to a dull throb.

"Can I get you anything?"

"Mayhaps a drink?"

"Of course." He raced down to the lower level.

Her head rang out with another thunderbolt and she cried into her pillow.

She shouldn't have kissed him, but she wanted something to hang on to. After all these years of isolation, she wanted a memory, that was all, because he wasn't going to stay. And she couldn't leave.

FLINT TOOK THE STEPS TWO AT A TIME, ALMOST FALLING MORE than once. He'd caused her pain. It wasn't surprising. Someone as gentle and innocent as her deserved so much more than to be kissed by a swine like him.

He swallowed hard, remembering the feel of her lips on his. Her soft body pressed into his. Her tender touch on his skin. She hadn't called him a monster after seeing his scars. She had called him a hero.

Dax looked up from the pile of books at the dining table. "Where's your shirt?"

"Zelle needs water." Flint stalked forward, grabbed a clay cup, and poured water into it from a pitcher.

"Flint." Dax's voice was a warning.

Flint caught his scrutinizing gaze. "I didn't do anything."

Dax's face was passive. "I didn't say you did."

"You were thinking it."

"I can smell that you finished off your last bottle from over here. Remember we are guests in her home. She isn't one of the bar wenches."

Flint moved so suddenly toward Dax that it surprised even him. "No, she isn't," he spat. "I know my place. I know what I am, and I would never do anything to disgrace the only woman who has been kind to me in months without being paid."

Dax stood his ground. Flint's snorted, anger branding him like a fire poker and whisking away all sense of reason. He worked his jaw muscles for a minute trying not to crush the glass in his hand. Without a word he strode back to Zelle's room.

She lay on her bed, no longer curled in a tight ball. At least she was somewhat relaxed. Flint moved to her side. She rolled over and took the glass from him. She drained the whole thing in several large gulps and handed it back. Flint sat it on her nightstand, unsure what to do next.

"Can I get you anything else?"

Her face was pale with a waxy sheen. "No, thank you. I think I just need to rest. It's been a long day."

He looked out the window. The sun was setting. He should be going. "I'll let you rest. We should be on our way soon anyway."

"Could you not stay just a bit longer?"

Yes. "We've imposed on you enough."

"But where will you sleep tonight?"

Flint shrugged. "We always find somewhere."

"But there is nothing for miles, I'm sure of it. And I should look at your wound once more at least."

Her eyes filled with emotions he couldn't read. "You need to rest."

"Don't go," she whispered. "Stay. Just for the night. You can go in the morning. You and Dax can stay down in the library again. There's a fireplace and blankets."

Flint's heart wanted to give in. To stay with her as long as she needed. But his head reminded him of what had happened when he'd kissed her, and of the fact that her father was a mage. With a dragon.

"And you're a coward who will just leave her here," said Erik's voice.

"Just tonight. In the morning we must go," he said.

Zelle nodded.

He wanted to go to her, to sit with her and stroke her hair.

"I'll wash."

"Maybe later I can show you my aviary," she suggested.

"You should probably stay in bed."

"No, I need to go up and check on them anyway, and let Loca out."

"Loca?"

"My owl."

Flint nodded. Of course she had an owl. Her father was a mage. Didn't mages do that kind of stuff? Have owls as pets and such. The thought pricked Flint's mind. "Are you a mage?"

"Me? No. I've never trained."

"Because your father doesn't want anyone to know of you?"

"Something like that." Zelle glanced away.

The hairs on Flint's arms prickled. He headed to the bathing room.

ZELLE TRACKED FLINT AS HE WENT INTO THE BATHING ROOM. She wanted to tell him. To tell someone the truth about why she had to be kept from people. But to do so would put him in danger. And possibly make him run from her. She wanted him to stay as long as he would, and telling him the truth would shorten that length of time. So she kept silent.

Her headache had diminished, leaving her wrung out. Between the nausea and headache, she needed to rest. She wished she could get him to rest near her. Again she was struck with images of lying with a dark skinned man. The feel of his lush lips on her body. She shivered and shook her head.

Fifteen minutes later Flint emerged from her bathing room dressed in a clean tunic and breeches, his long wet hair had been slicked back. He looked like a new man. His eyes still sunken in and his cheeks were more hollow than they should have been, but he was strong and tall and handsome.

"I'll let you rest," he said. "Thank you for the use of your bathing room."

"Dax may use it if he wishes."

Flint nodded but stayed silent.

She studied his aura. "You don't fancy the idea of him in here alone with me, do you?"

"No."

"Do you fear he will harm me?"

"Not at all."

"Do you think I will kiss him?"

Flint's body tensed. "You may do as you wish. This is your home, and you belong to no one."

"That's true. However I would hope you would not think me the kind of woman who simply invites men into her home so that she may seduce them."

Again his face looked conflicted. "No," he finally said. "I do not."

"Then do you want to tell me why it upsets you that he would wash in my bathing room while I rest?"

"It doesn't." He turned and walked out the door.

Zelle wasn't sure what had just transpired. She hadn't been around people with much frequency, but she could swear that Flint seemed angry. Jealous possibly? She didn't know. But one thing was perfectly clear. Flint had a temper, and a stubborn streak. Probably the very things that kept him alive, despite all of his scars. But it also kept him from going home.

Zelle sighed. Flint wasn't homeless; he was prideful.

CHAPTER SEVEN

Zelle awoke to a roar. She leapt from her bed at the same time footsteps rushed up the stairs. Dax and Flint burst into her room.

"My father," she said.

"Where do we go?" asked Dax.

Zelle ran to the window. Her father had left Fader right outside. "He'll be in here any second." She spun in a circle. "Under my bed."

Dax moved to the bed but Flint stayed put. "Are you serious?"

"You can take a chance in my bathing room."

"Is there no other way out?"

"Zelle, are you awake, daughter?" came the call from below.

"No," she whispered. Her limbs shook and her palms grew slick.

Flint stared at the door for a moment.

"Zelle?" The voice was closer.

"Dammit." Flint squeezed under Zelle's bed and she rounded the end just as her father knocked on the door and entered.

Her father smiled at the sight of her. "I'm sorry, my dear, did I wake you?"

"No, no, Father. I was just using the bathing room." She crossed to her father and hugged him. "Why are you here so early? I wasn't expecting you."

"Oh, I had some business today and thought I might stop by and see if you needed for me to drain you. I hate to see you so burdened."

A chill ran down Zelle's arms and she released her father. "No. I'm fine, thank you."

"Are you sure? Maybe we should try just to be safe."

"No." She spoke too quickly, causing her father to raise an eyebrow. "I mean, I think waiting a few more days wouldn't be too terrible. You took so much just a couple of days ago."

"Better safe than sorry."

"Please, Father. I… I really don't want to."

His eyes flashed and his aura swirled with crimson. His features changed, but in a half a second he smiled and stepped forward to pat her hand. "If you think you'll be all right."

"I do," she said, relieved.

His gaze swept the room as if searching for something, making her throat squeeze closed.

"Come, let's go down and I can fix you some tea before you have to go," she said.

He continued to scan the room for a moment. "How is your tub working? Any more problems with the drainage?"

"None at all."

"Let me make sure." He headed for the bathing room.

Zelle bit the inside of her cheek to keep from screaming.

Her gaze darted to the bed but she couldn't see either Flint or Dax.

"What's this?"

Zelle held her breath as her father walked out holding the waste bin.

He pulled out a piece of the bloodied gauze. "Did you have an accident?"

She blew out a breath. "Yes. The pitcher was slippery and I didn't grasp it tight enough, I'm afraid. I cut my hand but it healed quickly as always."

"Too bad. I liked that pitcher. I'll get you another and bring it when I return."

She took the bin from him and set it on the ground. "Thank you, Father, that is very kind of you."

She linked her arm in his and guided him to the door. "Can I make you tea now?"

They headed down the stairs and he slowed as they came to the library. "I actually need to look for something first."

"Um…"

He cocked an eyebrow.

"I made a huge mess in there yesterday. There are books everywhere. How about you have some tea and while I straighten up and then you can look?"

His gaze turned suspicious.

"You can go in, it's just I know how you feel about me taking care of your books and how you like things orderly and I'd hate for you not to find what you're looking for because of my mess."

She kept her face passive, trying not to give anything away.

"Of course."

They continued into the front room. Zelle let go of his arm

and he headed toward the kitchen. She glanced up the stairs to see Flint and Dax heading for the library.

"Clean up," she mouthed.

Dax nodded a reply.

An hour after they'd had tea, Zelle held her breath as her father climbed the stairs to search the library. Luckily, when they'd gotten in there, all signs of Dax and Flint were gone. She'd straightened shelves and fought the mounting anxiety until he'd finally given up what he was searching for and kissed her goodbye.

She watched from her bedroom window as he mounted Fader and took off into the sky. A moment later, her bathing room door opened and Flint peeked out.

"He's gone," she said.

"Is he coming back?"

"A few days, a week maybe, probably not longer."

"What was he looking for?"

"A book, I think."

Flint pulled the door open wider and stepped out with Dax behind him. "What did he mean when he said he wanted to drain you?"

Zelle coughed. "Nothing."

"It didn't sound like nothing. You sounded pretty firmly against it."

"Well it is." She crossed her arms over her chest.

"Drop it, Flint," said Dax. "Lady Zelle's business is her own."

Flint looked between them and then inclined his head. "I apologize."

"Come on," she said. "I'll fix you breakfast and then after I feed my birds, I'll look at your arm."

For as much as she wanted them to stay, they were getting too close to finding out the truth about her. And when that happened, who knew how they would react.

CHAPTER EIGHT

Flint's body hummed, still on edge from the close call with Zelle's father. Even from the little Flint had seen and heard of him, it was apparent there was something strange about the man. His speech was that of an old man, yet he walked with a step that only a younger man possessed.

For all his suspicions however, he had no desire to upset Zelle by asking too many questions, so he remained silent.

She left the lower floor as soon as she'd finished cooking to bathe and then feed her birds. Flint and Dax finished eating and then cleaned the dishes. Together they headed back upstairs with Dax stopping on the second floor.

"Did you want to leave soon?" he asked.

Flint's gut told him no. Something was not as it should be with Zelle and her father. He felt the need to protect her, but he wasn't sure what from, or if he was even able to.

"In a bit," he finally replied, heading up to the top floor.

He waited in the hallway and peered through the open

door. The smells of dried grass and feathers reminded him of home. He sighed and looked out the barred window. His bones ached with the need to feel the comfort of his own bed. And his soul yearned for the company of his brothers.

Zelle's humming floated out the aviary door. She'd changed into a pale lavender dress, and a large snowy bird gripped the fabric in its talons on her left shoulder. Her silky hair clung to her, leaving darkened spots where the fabric soaked in the moisture. Her slender hips swished as she moved from area to area, tenderly stroking and feeding her birds. They chirped their joyous responses to her kindness.

The owl swiveled its head and screeched before flying toward him. Flint backed up and the powerful animal flapped its wings in his face, forcing him down a step.

"Loca, no." Zelle appeared in the doorway and stepped between them. She raised her arm and the animal screeched as it settled on her forearm.

"Loca. This is Flint. He's a friend." She turned to Flint. "He's not used to strangers, I'm afraid. He doesn't even like my father."

Flint stared at the round yellow-eyed animal and nodded. He suspected Loca had a good reason for not liking Zelle's father.

"Here." She smiled at Flint and lifted his good arm.

He crossed his arms over his chest. "That's all right. If he doesn't like me, it means he's smart."

She chuckled. "He won't hurt you."

The bird eyed Flint.

"Yeah, maybe you should tell him that because I think he has other ideas."

She shook her head. "Silly males."

Zelle retreated to the aviary. She set Loca on a perch and

continued to feed the other birds. Flint followed her, the tune she hummed wandered into his mind, captivating him.

He leaned against the wall, observing her work. Her movements were fluid, like the dancers his mother used to employ to entertain at parties. The calmness that surrounded her not only set the birds at ease, but him as well.

He'd never seen or met a woman like her before. Soft and fine, with the heart of an angel. Yet a fierceness lay beneath to rival even that of himself. Like a predatory cat lying in wait.

He wondered for a moment what it would be like to have Zelle at his side. Someone to keep his bed soft and warm at night, and to fill his days with mystery and joy.

Loca screeched, pulling Flint from his thoughts. The bird watched him as if it knew Flint's thoughts. The bird was right. He didn't deserve Zelle.

"What would you do if you weren't burdened by your past?" Zelle looked over her shoulder at him, her face beautifully framed by her silver hair.

"I don't know." There were a hundred things he'd do if he weren't who he was.

"Liar. You can't hide from me, Flint Gwyn. I know you must have dreamed of it a thousand times over." She pet a dove and filled its bowl with seeds before moving on to the next.

He scooped a handful of seed from a nearby bin and weighed it.

"What does it matter? I am who I am." The words stuck in his throat like a hunk of dry meat. The same words he'd spoken to himself a million times over, whenever he thought of moving on.

"You act as if this is your lot in life. To get drunk, be angry and sleep with women who want you for nothing more than the coin in your purse. But in your heart you know you could change if you wanted."

"Maybe I don't want to." He tossed the seed into the bin.

"Then you lie to yourself more than I. There are three men who come to my window to hear me sing every once in a while. They dress like you and act like you, but they are not you. They enjoy who they are, what they are. You're different. You hate what you've become."

He crossed his arms over his chest. "Why do you think that?"

"Because they laugh, and joke, and make merry." She turned and gazed at him. "I have not once heard you laugh. Really laugh. As if no one is watching and even if they were, you wouldn't care what they thought."

"So if I laughed, would I prove to you that I'm happy?"

She stared at him for a moment. "Would it prove it to you? I'm not the one you have to convince."

"For some reason I feel like you are." He hadn't meant to say that out loud. He shifted his stance. "All right. If I wasn't who I am, I suppose I would be married. Have children. I'd spend my days helping Erik run Westfall and I'd spend my nights surrounded by my family. On occasion I'd hunt, ride, play cards, maybe learn to make things with my hands."

"Sculpture?"

"No. Tables and chairs. Baby bassinets and beds." After the words left his lips embarrassment plagued him. He'd never told a soul he wanted to do that. Not even his brothers. "What about you? What would you do if you weren't in this tower?"

She stopped moving. "I don't know. I've never been out in the world."

"Now who's lying?" He stepped away from the wall and walked toward her. "You said you've read books. Hundreds of them. You must know some things about the world and what you'd like to do."

She brushed the seeds from her palm and faced him. Her gentle features held a mix of emotion.

"What's wrong? You can put me on the spot but don't care for it yourself?" he chided.

"It's not that I don't care for it," she said. "It's that… for me, there is no chance. I'm stuck here and no matter what I want, or who I want to do it with. The difference between us, Flint, is that you have the opportunity to change your future."

He continued walking toward her until they were less than a foot apart. "I see no difference between us. We are both trapped in our own towers, unable to leave."

She opened her mouth to speak and he touched his fingertip to her lips. She sucked in a small breath. She was so beautiful, so hopeful. Everything he was not. He brushed her lip with his thumb, wishing he could kiss her.

"Hey," said Dax from the doorway.

Flint dropped his hand and backed away.

"Is it all right if I clean up in your bathing room?"

Zelle coughed and then smiled as she stepped around Flint. "Of course. Let me get you some hot water."

"No need," said Dax. "I already heated some."

"Why don't I walk down with you? I'm finished anyway and can't stay up here dreaming of another life."

Flint caught Dax's gaze as Zelle glided out of the room without a backwards glance.

"We should help her," said Dax.

"We'll help her clean up the tower today and leave in the morning."

"That's not what I meant and you know it."

"She doesn't want help."

"Don't you find this whole situation just a little strange?"

"I find it more than strange, but honestly, after what I've seen in the past several years, maybe she's better off here, safe in her tower." At least that was the truth.

Dax stared at Flint for a moment and then left.

The thought of leaving Zelle opened a darkening hole in Flint's heart, but he couldn't hang around in the tower for the rest of his life. He needed to move on. She obviously wasn't going to choose to leave, so it was best if he did before he got sucked in to her dream any further.

ZELLE AND THE MEN SPENT THE REST OF THE AFTERNOON cleaning the tower and their things. They washed their tunics and breeches in her tub and hung them to dry. Zelle helped scrub their boots and prepared food for them to take with them. For as much as she hated to see them go, it was obvious they couldn't stay. Flint needed to bury his demons and Dax had exhausted her history books searching for the truth about himself.

Dax sat next to her on the floor as she scrubbed the bland gray stone with a rough brush. He grabbed a second brush and worked along side her.

"Flint said you have no memories past a year ago."

She stopped and glanced at him. Then she began scrubbing again. "I know there are memories there somewhere, but I just can't find them."

They scrubbed giant white circles in silence for a moment. Only the sound of the brush and slopping water filling her ears.

"That's how I feel as well," said Dax.

"Do you think it's similar?"

"How could it be? You've been here in this tower with no one but your father to visit and I'm from… who knows where."

"Do you ever remember anything?" she asked. "Have you ever had anything break through?"

"Once in a while I see the face of a girl."

"Your sweetheart?"

He shook his head. "It doesn't feel like that when I see her."

"A friend perhaps? Or a sister."

"Maybe." He scrubbed a large circle.

"In all your reading did you hear anything about our conditions?"

"Nothing."

"So there's no cure." She should ask her father about it, but what would he say?

"We can only pray there is."

"Why do you stay with Flint? Why don't you search for your past?"

"Because he needs me."

They scrubbed again in silence.

"I have to tell you," said Dax. "I've never seen him this peaceful before. I'm not saying he should stay here. I'm simply saying that you soothe him. He needs that."

Stay? She wished he could stay. In the past three days she'd become very fond of both of them.

"If you left," said Dax. "Your father would look for you, wouldn't he?"

Zelle threw her brush in the water bucket and pushed the hair from her face. "I can't leave. It's not possible."

"It's not right for you to be locked up in here. No matter

who you are."

"What if I was to tell you I was dangerous? That I was cursed and my curse was so deadly that if I was ever to leave this tower, I could kill everyone in Fairelle."

"Then I would tell you that no matter the curse upon you, I don't believe you to be capable of something like that."

She blew out a heavy breath. "Yes, well… You don't know me very well."

Dax peered at her over his shoulder. "I think you're wrong about that."

AFTER EVERYTHING HAD BEEN CLEANED, ZELLE MADE A SIMPLE supper and they ate in silence. The impending departure left them all with the depressed feeling of wet wool clothing clinging too tightly to their forms.

She'd cleaned the dishes with Flint, neither speaking. Every time their fingers touched she experienced the same spark as before.

She went to her room to brush her hair and then she took the stairs up to her aviary to let Loca out for the night. After ascending the steps, she found the door ajar. Flint strolled around inside with Loca perched on his shoulder. He looked at the sleeping birds, touching them every once and while. Loca's head swiveled and he hooted before flying to her shoulder. His heavy body and clawed feet landed with ease.

Flint turned and their eyes met. A flutter ran through Zelle at his appearance in the moonlight.

"Did I wake you?" he asked.

"No. I wasn't asleep yet." Loca nipped her on the ear and she laughed. "All right, all right." She pet the bird, walked to the window and pulled on one of the bars. It came loose and

Loca gripped her shoulder before taking flight out into the air beyond the tower.

"I thought the bars were solid," Flint mused, moving to her side.

"They are. Father made this one special. It can be removed only at night, so Loca can come and go. He's the only bird I can't feed."

"Your father seems to have thought of everything to keep you here."

Zelle frowned. "My father is a great man. He only wants me safe."

"I meant no disrespect."

"I'm not a prisoner here. It's for my own safety." Even to her own ears the words were now a thin excuse.

"I'm sure it is."

What was going on with her? Just yesterday she had been content to be in her tower. Keeping the world safe from what she could do. But now… Now having listened to Dax tell her of the wolves, and vampires, and fae. The forests and animals and trees. Now…she wondered if it would be so bad if she left every once and while. Not permanently, but just to see things, experience things, be around people.

She scanned the meadow and woods, her hope recklessly budding.

"What are you thinking?"

"About what it would be like living out of this tower. To wander as you do."

"And I wonder what it would be like to stay and no longer have to wander."

Flint's eyes softened and he raised his hand to touch her. Heat flushed her skin like a thousand tiny candles. She wanted nothing more than to feel his touch. His hand hung in the air, inches from her cheek. Tilting her head she closed the gap between them. His palm dragged rough against her skin. A warrior's hand.

Goosebumps rose on her neck. "Kiss me," she whispered.

He searched her face. "I can't."

"You did before."

"And that was wrong." He dropped his hand. "You're a lady, and should be treated as such. Like you said before, you don't invite strange men into your house to seduce them."

"No. I don't. But I've never had any man in my house before you and Dax."

"Even more reason I shouldn't. You don't know the ways of the world."

"I know the ways of my body. And right now my body is telling me that what I want more than anything in this world is the feel of your body."

Flint blinked several times. "Do you always say what you think?"

"Should I not?"

"Most women don't."

The idea confused her. "What else would I say?"

"Women are taught to be what their husbands expect them to be, I suppose."

"But I have no husband."

Flint rubbed his neck and shoulder.

"I've made you uncomfortable," she said.

"You see people. Really see them. You see the things they are hiding."

"I do."

He took a step closer and she pressed into the wall, setting the metal bar on the window ledge. She sucked in a shuddered breath, her skin tightened at the nearness of him. His deep intense gaze searched her face.

"What do you see in me?" Emotions played all over his features.

"You're scared."

"I've never been scared in my life," he retorted.

"You are now. You're scared of what I see. Of what I think. Of what I might say to you." His eyes betrayed him and she pressed on. "You feel sadness and are burdened by the things you've done. You're too prideful to go home, though you surely have people there who love you. And most of all you want to find someone. Someone who will see you for you and love you despite what you've done."

"And do you? Do you see me for who I am? Do you see the people I've murdered? The vampires I've killed with my bare hands?"

"I see that you have done what was required of you," she said in a soft voice.

His body stiffened. "Then you don't see me. Because I did more than was required. I liked it. The rush of anger that comes right before a fight. The feel of a blade as it takes a life. I know those feelings, and I like them. I live for them. They are what I am."

Zelle shook her head. "I don't believe you. How many months have you gone without killing? Was it when your sister turned? Is that when you stopped?"

He stepped away from her.

"You want to believe you are a killer, Flint. You want to believe you enjoy those things because it makes it easier to deal with. Easier to push people away. Easier than dealing with the truth."

"And what's the truth?"

"That inwardly, you want to be loved despite what you've had to do. You want to be told that it's forgiven. It's not who you are. You want to forget and be what everyone else is."

"A coward?"

"No." Zelle shook her head. "Normal."

HE'D NEVER TOLD ANYONE HIS DEEPEST DESIRES, YET SOMEHOW when she looked at him, she read him perfectly. He swallowed. Normal was not in the cards for him. As long as his family lay divided, and the mantle he wore made him an enemy of his sister, he would never find true happiness.

"You know that normal is only a fairy tale, right?" he asked.

Zelle inched closer to him. Her willowy form barely reached his shoulder. Her hands were delicate, shoulders slim, her neck long and slender. Every part of her looked like a fragile doll. Except the presence that wafted off of her. The confidence she exuded combated that appearance. Every inch of her oozed sensuality.

Her hand snaked out and splayed against his chest. "You won't hurt me."

"No, I won't." In the moonlight she appeared completely different. Sensual and beautiful but with a strength she held in reserve.

Flint swallowed hard. From the glow of her purple eyes, he knew there was a reason she stayed in her tower. Power was the only word he could think of. Power and magick.

He ran a shaky hand through her long soft tresses and pushed the hair over her shoulder revealing more of her throat. Her perfectly full, peachy lips waited for him, just inches away. His body stirred at the thought of kissing her again.

She stepped into him, pressing against him. Her supple breasts smashed into his torso and her hips found purchase between his own. The contact was like a lantern switching on inside him. Every part of him woke up and paid attention.

"Kiss me again."

He should be chivalrous and do the right thing. Leave the sweet creature be, and not poison her with his anger and pain. But the pounding in his ribcage, and the feelings she aroused in him, were like no other. Never before had he wanted to be with a woman so badly. And never before had one held so much sway over his person.

He wondered for a moment if she had bewitched him, before pressing his lips to hers and tasting her sweet fragrance. He lifted her from the ground, pinning her against the wall with his knees between her thighs. Her soft frame molded into his as she tangled her fingers in his hair. Their tongues swirled together in a dance of desire.

His body responded of its own accord, his need growing with each passing moment. She reached down to the hem of his tunic and lifted it, running her fingers underneath. He'd never let someone touch his scars before. Never even let people see them besides his family. The women he'd been with, he'd forced to face the wall until he was done.

The desire to take Zelle down to her plush bed and make love to her flooded him. He slowed his kisses, his brain screaming that this was wrong. He didn't deserve this. She pushed her hands higher, raising his tunic to his shoulder. She traced a scar with her mouth, kissing his skin.

Flint swallowed a lump in his throat and moaned. Her fingers twined in the dark curls of his chest hair. Moving over to his nipple, she flicked out her tongue and licked around it. He slammed his hands into the wall on either side of her, and pulled away, trying to control himself. She slid down a couple of inches and worked her way across his chest with her mouth and fingers, bringing him torturous pleasure.

He had no doubt she knew what she was doing, but the thought that she had done this before wasn't something he could comprehend. She'd said he was the first who had ever gotten into her tower. Had that been a lie? Pulling away from her was the hardest thing he'd ever done.

"What is it?" She looked up at him.

"Nothing."

"Did I do something to upset you?"

"No. You're wonderful. I just…" He swallowed hard. This wasn't good. He'd known her less than a week and already he had feelings for her. Feelings he hadn't planned on. Feelings he didn't know what to do about. Feelings he wasn't prepared to deal with.

Flint stepped away, leaving Zelle as frigid as the stone at her back. His tunic fell into place, covering his beautiful body. He was shutting down. She replayed in her head what had happened that might have upset him.

"I should go." He glanced at the door.

"So you don't want me?"

He snorted and then coughed. He ran his hands through his hair and over his face. "I don't know how you expect me to answer that."

"Sex. You don't want to have sex with me? I assumed from the way your body responded that you did."

The look on Flint's face was one of utter shock.

"I'm sorry, was I not supposed to say that, either?"

"No, Zelle, it isn't something you are supposed to say. And the answer is yes, I do want to lay with you. But I can't."

"Is there something wrong with me? Is that why you don't want me?"

"No, there's something wrong with me, and if I lie with you, I'll ruin you."

Loca screeched outside. Zelle turned as her bird flew in and landed on her shoulder.

When she turned back, Flint had vanished.

CHAPTER NINE

Flint woke with a cramp in his side. The couch in Zelle's library was the most comfortable thing he had slept on in months, but far too small. Dax's large form lay on the couch opposite, books surrounding him. Flint had never realized Dax was such a reader. The books looked like large history tomes about Fairelle. He scanned the titles and swallowed, understanding. Dax searched for something familiar.

Dax didn't speak about it, but a few months back, Flint had spoken at length with King Adrian about him. No one knew where he came from, why vampires had been chasing him, or how he had become a werebear. It was as if someone had reached inside Dax and scooped his memories out.

Flint remembered the way Dax had stared at the dragon days before and wondered if he may find the answers he was looking for with them. But one did not simply go into the Draak Lands and look for anything except a painful death.

"Morning." Dax yawned and sat up.

"Morning."

Dax grabbed the book off his chest and looked at it. "You slept well again."

"Find anything interesting in the books?" Flint got to his feet.

Dax shrugged. "Bits and pieces. Every now and again I'll read something and it seems familiar."

"Like what?"

"The dragons. The southern lands. Some of the pictures in the books are of places I've seen but I can't tell if they are memories from before or from our travels now."

"But nothing in particular?"

"No, unfortunately. As soon as something strikes me as familiar, it leaves again."

Flint nodded. "I'm sorry for that. We should get moving this morning. Maybe we should head south to see if we can find your people."

Dax's brows furrowed. "Did something happen last night? You didn't seem very happy when you came down from the aviary."

"I just think we've imposed on Zelle enough." Flint looked at Dax and then at the book. "If you wish to stay—"

"I go where you go," Dax said, his voice flat.

"You don't have to, you know. You aren't bound to me."

"I am well aware that I'm neither your squire nor your man servant. But I made a promise to Sage and Erik. I won't renege on that."

At the sound of Sage's name Flint's anger flared. He was the reason Snow was no longer safe at home in the Manor house.

"You're going to have to forgive her at some point, you know," Dax said.

Flint folded the blanket he'd used. "Forgive who?"

"Snow. For wanting to be with Sage."

"Snow did nothing. It was Sage who did that to her."

Dax shook his head and set down the book. "It wasn't Sage. Snow wanted to be like him. To be with him."

"But he made her—"

"I was there, Flint. I saw it. I saw the way she wanted to be with him. Hell, she asked Remus to take her and make her a vampire so she could be with Sage. I was standing there when she said it."

Flint shook his head and draped the blanket over the side of the couch. "You're lying."

Dax got to his feet in a flash. "I've never lied to you. And I wouldn't lie about this. I heard Sage refuse to turn her. She stormed out and Sage told me to get her safely home. Remus showed up, he was going to kill me, but she stopped him. She told him to let me go and take her instead. So if you want to blame anyone, blame me."

Until now, they'd never spoken about what had happened with Snow. Several times Dax had tried to explain, but Flint had always stopped him. Could it be true? It didn't matter. It was still Sage's fault. If he had just left her alone, she never would have fallen under his spell.

"You should make things right between you and your family."

"It's not that easy."

"It is that easy. Tell Snow you're sorry. Love her despite what she has become. Sage is a good man. He saved my life more than once. And I know both Adrian and Redlynn feel the same. You need to let go of the past and move forward. Make a life for yourself. Before it's too late."

"Is that what you are doing?" Flint retorted. "Forgetting the past? Making a life for yourself?"

"My circumstances are different."

"How?"

"Because I'm not running from my mistakes."

Flint stared at Dax for a long time. Some days he envied Dax for not remembering who he was or where he'd been. How freeing it must be to have no bad memories. No nightmares.

A whistle from outside had both men turning to the window. Flint leaped over the couch where Dax had slept and headed to a window at the back of the tower. He threw the curtain aside. Three men on horses rode into the glen. Their packs were full and their clothes that of travelers. Flint scanned each man, his eyes lighting on one that he recognized but couldn't place.

"Oh lovely maiden with the silver hair," called a wiry man with a face like a rat. "Come down to us today and sing."

"Are you up there, Lady?" yelled the one Flint recognized. "Will you let us in today?"

A growl escaped Dax's chest.

"I know that one." Dax pointed. "He traded humans to the old vampire king, who turned them into slaves. He hit Sage with something called a gun."

A gun? It clicked. *Klaus.* Belle's boyfriend and the thug who'd grown up with his younger brother, Jamen. Flint had known Klaus was into some unsavory dealings, mostly gambling. But he had no idea the man had become a slaver.

The rat-faced man jumped from his horse and walked to the wall of the tower. He hoisted himself up two or three stones before jumping to the ground.

"I could climb it," he said. "Maybe see if I could get inside."

"Don't be a fool, Craigen," said Klaus. "This is a mage tower. If you got inside you'd be killed. You're lucky you didn't die just from touching it."

"Not with the way she looks at me. You've seen it. She wants me and I'm going to have her."

Anger shot through Flint like lightning. He sprinted from the room and down the stairs.

Zelle raced down after him. "Don't! Flint wait!"

But Flint's only thought was to keep the men away from her.

"Flint!"

He ran for the front door and threw it wide, the shimmery surface appeared and he stepped into the sun. He raced around the side of the tower, catching the three men off guard. The small man, Craigen, was climbing the tower again.

"Holy crap! Where did he come from?" the third guy shouted.

Craigen looked down from his climbing position and dropped to the ground. He ran for his horse and swung into the saddle in one fluid movement before the three men took off into the trees. Flint chased after them. Zelle screamed his name from one of the windows.

He ran into the woods, leaping over branches and rocks in his bare feet. He slipped on a spot of moss and pierced his foot on something sharp, but didn't stop. He kept going until he could no longer hear the beat of their horses' hooves. He scanned the ground for the tracks, but the soil was dry and leaves blanketed the ground.

The crass way the man Craigen had spoken about Zelle hit Flint like a physical blow. He refused to allow any man talking about her so commonly. Or thinking about her like that. She was better than them. Especially someone like Klaus or one of his men. They were even lower than Flint himself. Selling people for coin? It wasn't possible to get lower.

He continued to stare into the woods, winded and his injured arm throbbing, for several more minutes before his heartbeat slowed and he turned back to the tower.

When he reached the tower, crying floated out the window. His heart sank at the thought that she had been upset. Dax tried to calm her, but her response was mumbled and unclear. Flint walked to the front door of the tower. It was closed. He reached for the handle but the image disappeared and the door became solid stone. Flint's heart shuttered as he placed his hands on the brick, searching for the knob.

"Zelle," he called. "Open the door!"

There was no answer. He jogged around to the opposite side of the tower. She stood at the library room window staring down at him. The heat of her fiery gaze burned him where he stood.

"You *Tzarreth!*" she spat. "You *Pothoc Sthyr!*" She grabbed the bars of the window, pressing her face into them, screaming at him as tears streamed from her eyes.

"Zelle, open the door," he said calmly.

"I can't!"

"You can. Open it so I can come inside."

Zelle shook her head. "No, you dolt! I can open it but you can't get in. Not without the spell!"

Flint's heart raced and his head pounded. This couldn't be happening. Climbing the stone wall, he pulled himself up the two stories to the window where she stood. Her beautiful purple eyes were brimming with tears. His bad arm shook with strain. Flint reached out and grabbed one of the bars on the window but slipped.

"Flint!" She reached for him.

The air whooshed out of his lungs and his vision fuzzed as he impacted with the ground. He lay there for several moments trying to catch his breath. His head pounded and his arm ached. Getting to his feet, he looking up. Dax stood at the window, but Zelle was gone.

"Go to the door," Dax called.

Flint stomped to the tower, rubbing his shoulder and neck with his good hand. The wall had dissolved and the door stood open once more with Zelle on the inside. They stared at each other for a minute before Flint realized that he could not touch her.

"I'm sorry," he said.

She nodded with fresh tears welling.

Dax appeared behind her, holding both bags in his hands, as well as Flint's boots.

So this was it. He really was leaving.

"You don't have to come," Flint said to Dax. "Maybe it would be better if you stayed here and kept her safe."

Dax's expression hardened and he stepped out. "I'll meet you at the edge of the wood." Dax handed Flint his boots.

Flint nodded and watched his friend take off with both bags. He gave Zelle a sideways glance, unable to meet her eye. "I'm sorry."

"You said that already."

"Well, I am. When those men said about you—"

"They say it all the time. It's nothing. As you can see, they can't get in."

"Come with us."

Zelle shook her head. She pushed her sleeve up to her

shoulder revealing an arm cuff with a red jewel in the middle. "This cuff keeps me from being able to leave, even if I wanted to."

The sight of the red stone struck Flint with horror. He had seen those stones before. In the bottom of the pond, on Sage's ring, and on the necklace he'd taken from Terona.

"Where did you get that?"

"From my father."

"Take it off."

"I can't."

"Take it off!" Panic settled in his chest and wound its bristly fibers into his heart.

Her eyebrows furrowed. "What's wrong?"

"You need to take that off." Flint tried to make his voice even.

"I can't. I told you."

"Please," he pleaded. "For me. Please. Take it off."

"No." Zelle shook her head. "You don't understand. I can't." She reached up and yanked on the bracelet.

It didn't budge.

"It won't come off. I've tried."

The need to protect her roared to life inside him. "I need to get you out of there."

"My father would never let me go."

"I'll get you out."

She shook her head. "Where would I go? I have no money and know no one."

Flint stayed silent. He wanted her. At that moment, more than anything, he wanted to make her his. To take her home with him and make her his wife. "I'll figure out a way to get you out. It isn't safe for you in there."

She scanned his face. "Will you take me with you when you break the spell?"

The familiar twinge from being near her shot through him. The desire to protect her, to touch her. The feel of her lips on his skin the night before.

"Yes," he whispered. His soul rejoiced at the thought.

"I'd like that."

"I'll return for you. It might be a few days, but I'll be back."

"Do you know how to break the spell?"

"I know someone who might."

Zelle nodded. They stared at each other for another long minute. "You won't forget me, will you?"

"Never." He couldn't if he wanted to.

Zelle nodded, her expression somber. "Good bye, Flint."

"I'm coming back."

ZELLE'S HEART CONFLICTED WITH HER HEAD. IF HER FATHER knew what was going on, he'd be most angry. But she'd been in this tower, alone, for as long as she could remember, and she didn't want to be alone anymore. She wanted to be with Flint.

He turned and looked toward the wood. The sound of beating wings sounded in the distance.

"Go!" she said. "It may be my father. He can't find you here!"

"You said he wasn't coming back for days." Flint's face looked pained. He raised his palm and placed it on the barrier of the door. A blue current ran over the invisible surface. Zelle raised her palm to press against the same spot.

"Go."

Flint nodded, then turned and raced through the meadow.

She stood for a long time, watching the spot where he had been. How had she become so accustomed to him in such a short period of time? How long would it take for the pain of his absence to hit her? How long before it faded? So many questions flooded her.

She'd missed her father when he was gone, but only because she didn't want to be alone. This would be different…

Finally, she closed the door and headed up to her aviary. Loneliness pummeled her. Even her birds would be no comfort now he was gone.

CHAPTER TEN

K laus walked into his small cottage and threw his blunderbuss on the table.

"Hey!" Belle raced to pick it up. "It took me months to make that. Don't throw it."

Klaus glared at her. The last thing he needed was Belle telling him what to do. She picked up the gun and inspected it.

"Daddy!" Chloe ran straight to Klaus. He smiled and picked her up, swinging her in a circle, making her giggle.

"Hey, baby, how's my girl?"

"Mama took me to town today." Her eyes sparkled with wonder.

Klaus swallowed the words he wanted to say. "Did she really? And what did you do in town?"

"We saw the horses and the stores and mommy sold a few clocks."

"She did?" Klaus's gaze travelled to Belle.

She shot him with her icy glare and pursed her lips.

"Yes. And we saw Uncle Jamen and Auntie Scarlet and mommy bought me a lolli treat."

"I know how you love lolli treats. Oh wait, I think there's some left on your neck. I need to get that." Klaus dipped his face and nibbled Chloe's neck, making her squirm and shriek.

"Stop, stop." She giggled.

"Yes, stop." Belle took her from Klaus's arms and looked at Chloe. "Go wash up for dinner, Sweetums."

"Yes, Mama." Chloe smiled.

Belle placed her on the floor and Chloe ran off to the other room.

Klaus waited until she was gone, trying to hold his anger in check. "You went to town?"

Belle turned away. "Chloe just told you we did."

Klaus moved close and grabbed her by the arm. "And I told you not to."

Belle's gaze narrowed and she jerked away. "What did you expect me to do, Klaus? You haven't brought food home in weeks. Chloe was hungry."

"I make the money here."

She snorted. "Yeah, well, my clocks just put food on our table for the next month. So while you're out doing whatever you do to make money, I will be taking care of myself and my daughter."

Klaus raised his hand. The defiant look on her face angered him. "She's my daughter as well, Belle, don't forget that."

"It takes more than buying pretty gifts every few months to make a man a father. If that's all it took, you'd be father to half the whores in Fairelle."

Guilt rang through Klaus and he slowly took his knuckles and touched her cheek. "I'm sorry, Belle. It's been a bad day."

"More like a bad year," she shot back.

His temper flared, but he swallowed it. Her piercing blue eyes got him every time.

"I'm sorry." He pulled her into a hug, her body stiff in his arms. "I know this is my fault. Business hasn't been good these last six months. But I have something new on the horizon, a new buyer lined up and then everything will be good again. Just hang in there with me for a little longer. Everything will work out. I promise."

Leaning in, he kissed her on the mouth. She didn't respond, but she didn't pull away either. Klaus took it as a good sign. He kissed her again, his tongue tracing her bottom lip.

"I love you, Belle."

"I know," she whispered. "I just wish that fed Chloe." She pushed away from him and walked out of the room.

Klaus wondered for the millionth time why this was happening to him. A year ago he'd been almost as rich as the Gwyn family, and now he'd lost it all. The new vampire king wanted nothing to do with his human trade.

Klaus swallowed and his thoughts turned to Flint. Flint had been at the tower with the girl. Why had he been there? And how had he gotten in? A sudden hope burned in Klaus. The girl in the mage tower was obviously valuable. And if she was valuable, what else might be in there that was valuable? Jewels. Gold.

A smile played across Klaus's face. If he could get into the tower… If there were jewels, or treasure, it might be enough to set him up in a new business. And if not, well then, there had to be someone that he could ransom the girl to. Maybe even to the Gwyns.

His smile faded. If he did that, he'd have to run. Better to find what else was of value in the tower and take it. Leave the girl be. He would find a way in, grab what he could, and get out. She was just a woman, how dangerous could she be?

His gaze drifted toward the rear of the house. They needed this. If he did it, then Belle would forget about the bad times and he wouldn't worry about her leaving with Chloe. He didn't want her selling her clocks. If she did, she'd have her own money, and if she had her own money, it would enable her to leave, and that he couldn't have. He'd only barely been able to convince her to come home from Jamen's this last time. He wasn't sure he'd be able to the next time.

She and Chloe were his, no one else's. He'd kill them before he saw them with someone else. They were all he had.

CHAPTER ELEVEN

By the time Flint and Dax reached the walls of Ville DeFee the next day, the only thing left of the sun was the pinkish, purply hues that scattered the horizon. He would rather be doing just about anything than going back into the fae city, but he had no choice. Cinder was the only one who might be able to help him.

Leaving Zelle had been the most agonizing decision he'd ever made. The way her eyes had pleaded with him to return made him more desperate to free her from her father's magick.

"Look." Dax pointed to the golden gate.

The shift change was about to happen. They'd have exactly two minutes.

"Let's go." Covering himself with the cloak Cinder had given him, he headed for the gate.

Dax followed close behind. The cloaks were enchanted to keep people from looking too closely at them. But if someone had a strong enough will they'd see their true forms through the veil of disguise. A group of fae returning from the harvest walked up to the gate. Flint and Dax fell in behind them. Flint's heart thundered in his ears as they moved at a casual pace.

"Relax," whispered Dax.

There was no possible way he could relax. Moving slowly was as foreign to him as everything else in Ville DeFee.

He tried not to look at the guards who chatted with each other at the side of the gate. Dax grabbed his arm to calm him, and once inside they split from the group and headed to Cinder's shop. Weaving through the streets, anxiety pounded deep in his bones. More than once he felt eyes upon his back, but no one stopped them, or called for the guard.

The lights in Cinder's shop were bright, though the sign said it was closed. He glanced inside. Her stepmother was nowhere to be found, but two tall figures stood at the counter with her.

He rounded the building. Finding the rear entrance, he peered into the storeroom. Finding no one in sight, he pushed the door open and stepped inside. A small stove drove heat his direction. A kettle sat atop giving off the scent of mint. The tinkle of Cinder's laughter floated toward him, as did two male voices. He didn't know how long the men would stay, but he assumed it couldn't be too long as it was late already.

The tea kettle let out a shrill cry.

"I'll get it for you," one of the men said.

Flint scanned the storeroom for somewhere to hide, but there wasn't a place. He shoved Dax out the door and closed it as the curtain separating the front of the store from the back, moved aside and a tall, well built man with blond hair and richly made clothing stared at him.

"Hey, what are you doing in here?" He blinked several

times and then his brows furrowed. "You're not fae! Stil! There's a human in here!"

A second man ran into storeroom, but he wasn't fae, he was human in long red robes that flowed to the floor. A mage.

The fae male advanced on Flint as the mage retrieved something from his pocket.

"Stop!" Came Cinder's voice from behind the men. "Rome, stop!" She rushed to Flint, stepping in front of him. "This is my friend, Flint."

Emotions flew over Rome's face. When he looked at Flint again, his eyes were filled with suspicion. "What are you doing in Ville DeFee and where did you get that cloak?"

"I gave it to him," Cinder said. "Flint's father, Lord Gwyn, was an old friend of my father's. I've known Flint since he was a babe."

It was strange to hear Cinder talk about him as if she were so old.

"He shouldn't be here, Cinder. You know the law," Rome said.

"Yes." Cinder placed her hands on her hips. "I know the stupid law, but that doesn't keep you from bringing Stil in here does it?"

So this was Cinder's Prince.

"To say such things about my father's laws is punishable by death." Rome scowled.

"Then take me in." Cinder shrugged.

Cinder and Rome stared at each other. The tension thick as a fluffy down blanket.

Finally, it was Stil who broke the silence.

"Why don't you two marry already? You fight like lovers."

Rome's posture relaxed and he laughed loudly. "As if I could handle her."

"No, you couldn't." Cinder gave a radiant smile. Her gaze traveled to him. "Flint Gwyn, this is Prince Rome of Ville DeFee and Elder Mage Rumplestiltskin."

The mage stepped forward and offered his hand. "Everyone calls me Stil."

Flint shook Stil's hand and then Rome's.

"So to what do I owe this lovely and most recent visit?" Cinder asked. "Two times in a week, after not seeing you for years. Things must be rough."

"I need your help."

"Of course you do. Where is your bear friend?"

Flint opened the door but the alley was empty. "I shoved him out when I heard Rome coming. I was trying to spare him from being arrested. We arranged a meeting point, in case we were separated." Flint looked from Rome to Stil and back to Cinder. "And I do need your help. And possibly his." Flint pointed to Stil.

"Mine?" asked Stil. "What a treat. What's the problem?"

"There's a girl trapped in a tower."

"Oooh," said Rome with a smile. "Sounds like a fairy tale."

Flint glared at him. "It's a mage tower."

Stil frowned. "A mage tower? How did she get trapped in a mage tower?"

"Her father put her there. He said it was for her safety."

Stil frowned. "The High Mage decreed that mages aren't allowed to have children."

"I know that," said Flint. "Which is why I think she's being forced to stay there. He put an armband on her with a red stone. I've seen a similar stone before, and they weren't used for good. On top of that, there have been men seen at the tower of late and I don't think their intentions are altogether of the congenial sort. I need to get her out."

"Wait. You want to take her from a mage tower?" asked Rome.

"Yes."

"You know what could happen to you if you and she get caught, don't you?" asked Stil. "I'm not trying to sound conceited here, but a mage is not someone you want as an enemy."

"I understand, but I have a feeling it will be worse if I leave her."

"What would it take?" Cinder turned to Stil. "To break the spell binding her to the tower?"

Stil shrugged. "Depends how strong of a mage he is."

"He rides a dragon, if that makes a difference," said Flint.

All three turned to stare at him.

"What did you say?" asked Rome.

"That's not possible." Stil shook his head. "Mages and dragons don't mix."

"Really? Tell that to my arm." Flint rolled up his sleeve.

Cinder stepped forward and lay her hand on the bandages. "What kind of injury is it?"

"Acid."

She nodded and placed her palm on his arm. A pink light glowed from her palm and flowed under the bandages. The itch that had taken up residence over the past day left him.

She removed the bandages. The skin remained pink, but healed.

Words failed him. On a whole he avoided magick whenever possible. But in the last week he'd seen it do amazing things.

"Thank you," he said. "Look, I don't know who this mage is. All I know is that he wears a blue robe, he rides a dragon, and he's keeping her locked in a tower. Now can you help me or not?"

Stil shook his head. "A blue robe means the highest of our order. His magick is beyond me. I'm sorry."

"What if we combined powers?" Cinder suggested.

"No," said Rome. "It is forbidden. Mages and fae do not mix magick."

"We must help her."

"No." Rome shook his head.

Cinder laid her hand on his arm. "Please, Rome."

Rome chewed his bottom lip and stared at Cinder. "No," he finally said. "I won't do it."

"Rome—"

"But." He interrupted her. "I won't stop you and Stil."

Cinder smiled. "Thank you."

Rome's gaze drifted to Flint and then Stil. "I'll await you in the shop. I can't be a part of this, but I will keep watch."

Stil nodded and Rome stomped through the curtain onto the shop floor. The front door locked and the lights dimmed.

"Well," said Stil. "Let's get to work."

KLAUS, CRAIGEN, AND PAUL STOOD HIDDEN IN THE SHADOW OF the tree line, watching the tower. Klaus pulled an apple from his pack and bit into it.

"How long are we going to wait?" asked Paul.

"As long as it takes," said Klaus.

"What if Flint is still in there?"

Klaus shrugged. "Doesn't matter. We go in, take what we want, we get out."

"Look!" Craigen pointed.

Klaus shifted his stance and looked at the uppermost window of the tower. A large white owl emerged on the sill and took off into the night. Klaus's heart quickened its pace. "Well, well, well," he said with a smile. "So there is a way in."

"A small way by the looks of it," said Paul.

"Yes, but our man Craigen is pretty small, aren't you?" Klaus clapped Craigen on the shoulder.

The look on Craigen's face made Klaus shiver. He yanked the man close. "You go in. You get what we need. You get out. No funny business. And leave the girl alone. Do you understand?"

"Of course. Get in, find the goods, get out."

Klaus' gut told him this was a bad idea. Craigen had never been the reliable one. But if he wanted any chance of keeping Belle, he needed to do this. Klaus nodded and a rat-like grin curled across Craigen's face.

The smaller man slung his pack over his shoulder and headed out to the glen. Klaus took a bite of his apple and chewed slowly, watching the rogue make his way to the side of the tower.

He was doing this for Belle and Chloe. And when he returned with enough money, he was going to make it official. He was going to marry Belle.

ZELLE STOOD AT HER WINDOW AS LOCA FLEW OUT INTO THE night sky, wishing more than anything that she could be out there with him. She tracked his snowy form until it disappeared into the trees. Breathing deeply, she took in the warm fragrant night air. She wondered if it seemed sweeter now that she truly wanted to leave her tower.

Her thoughts turned to Flint for the hundredth time since he'd left. The doubt that he was going return shrouded her every thought. She couldn't hold out hope that he would. And even if he did, how would he get her out?

She'd spent the last day and a half trying to figure out a way herself. Her father was powerful. Zelle would say, from all that she'd read about mages, that he was too powerful. She'd never read about a mage dragon rider. As far as she could tell, dragons stayed far away from mages. And the amulet he wore was that of immense power. She didn't know what it did, because she'd never seen one in any of her books.

She grasped the cuff on her right arm. The gold band shone, engraved with words she didn't know. The deep crimson stone in the middle oozed magick. She tugged at it but the band held fast. In the past she'd tried using oil to loosen it, tried losing weight to see if it would slip off, tried to pry it open with a knife. Everything had failed.

She gazed into the stars and wondered where Flint was at that moment. Was he off drinking away her memory? Or perhaps he had no need to. Perhaps she was already forgotten. That couldn't be true. She'd seen his feelings. Deep inside he felt something for her, even if he couldn't say it. And she felt something for him too. A connection she could not deny. Even if he didn't return, Zelle had made up her mind. She could stay in the tower no longer. Being near Flint, talking to Dax, had awoken in her a need to be free- no matter the consequences.

She turned from the window and headed down to her library. One way or another, she had to find a way out.

"CINDER!" CAME STIL'S PANICKED VOICE.

Flint moved forward to catch her as she swayed on her feet.

"Don't touch me," she said, her voice weak. "The contact will break the spell."

Flint stopped. The acrid smell of burning flowers filled his nostrils and he coughed.

Rome rushed into the storeroom. "Stop," he commanded.

"I can't," said Cinder. "If we stop it could explode and kill us all. We have to finish."

They'd been at it for close to an hour.

Cinder and Stil stood over a short dark bottle of dust. Green light poured from Cinder's hands into the bottle. Stil locked his eyes on Cinder and chanted words Flint couldn't understand.

Rome grumbled in rage.

"Stop that," Cinder said through gritted teeth. "You're going to upset me and I won't be able to control it."

Rome stopped pacing and looked at Flint. His gray eyes brewed like storm clouds. "If anything happens to them, I'll kill you myself."

Flint blinked but said nothing. Mages and fae were not supposed to mix magicks but he'd had no idea it could have such deadly consequences. He didn't care about himself. He would gladly die for Zelle. But he didn't want to see Cinder hurt. Or Stil for that matter. Rome, well, he could fend for himself.

"We're almost there." Cinder's magick turned from green to yellow. "Just a bit more."

Rome chewed his lip and crossed his arms over his chest.

A flash of light burst from Cinder's hands and bright red sparks flew from her fingertips. There was a pop and sizzle and then red smoke emerged from the bottle filled with dust. Stil stopped speaking and Cinder's magick went dark. She fell to the ground in a heap.

Rome rushed to her side and lifted her. "Cinder, are you all right?"

She nodded mutely.

"If anything happens to her—"

"Yes, I know," said Flint. "You'll find me. I get it." Flint knelt beside Cinder. Her breathing was slow and her eyelids drooped.

"Take the dust. Sprinkle it around the outside of the tower. Go to the door and say the words on the parchment. I've done all I can," said Cinder.

"Thank you." Flint took her hand. "I owe you, Cinder. I owe you my life."

Cinder shook her head, "No. You don't. But if you want to repay me, let me help your friend, the bear. The magick radiating off him is immense. When he's ready, tell him to come see me and I'll see what I can do, to help him find his true form."

"We would never ask that of you," Flint said.

Cinder shook her head again. "It would be my honor. I have a feeling there's more to him than just a simple shapeshifter. He possesses a power that's locked deep inside."

"I'll tell him what you've offered." Flint looked up at Stil. "Thank you, as well. If there is ever a time when you are in need, I'll do whatever I can to aid you."

Stil smiled and held out his hand. "That is a promise I shall hold you to, Flint Gwyn of Westfall."

Flint shook Stil's hand and then stood to collect the bottle of dust.

"Take me home?" asked Cinder.

"Of course." Rome stood with her in his arms. His angry gaze locked on Flint. No matter how Cinder protested, there was something between her and Rome. But how deep those feelings went, Flint wasn't about to ask.

Flint threw on his cloak and the group walked into the alleyway, parted ways and took off into the night.

CHAPTER TWELVE

Z elle stirred the leftover soup while it warmed and nibbled a slice of cheese. Thoughts of how to get out of her tower occupied her mind. She'd spent only a minute looking through her books before her stomach growled. She hadn't eaten since that morning. She planned on spending the entire night searching for an answer. And every waking moment from here on out, unless Flint returned with good news.

The sound of a chair falling over upstairs pulled her attention. She looked up. Her eyes glued to the ceiling. Had she left the curtains open? The wind didn't sound that strong. She swallowed hard, placed the soup ladle on the counter, tiptoed through the kitchen, and peeked around the corner.

Sucking in a deep breath, she stepped out into the eating area and around the table to the front room. Movement by the stairs caught her eye and Zelle's heart nearly stopped.

"Hello, beautiful maiden," said the man named Craigen.

Panic scratched at Zelle's brain. She glanced around quickly. "How– how did you get in here?"

"A little birdy showed me the way."

Loca. The bar from the window in the aviary. Why had she never thought of that before? Why had her father not thought of it? Probably because the space was so thin, he didn't think anyone would be able to scale the tower and fit through. But someone had.

Craigen smiled, revealing small sharp teeth. His hooked nose was off center and his dirty brown hair hung limply to his shoulders.

"You– you shouldn't be here. My father will be very angry. He's a powerful mage–"

"That never comes at night. Only during the day, and only every three to five days. And if memory serves me correctly, he was just here yesterday." Craigen took a step toward Zelle and licked his lips.

"Please." Zelle stepped behind the table. "Take whatever you want."

"Yes." Craigen nodded his head. "I intend on taking what I want."

Zelle's knees wobbled. "My– my friends. Flint and Dax. I am expecting them any time."

Craigen shook his head and stepped toward Zelle. She moved around the table to the opposite side.

"They won't be coming. And even if they do, it won't matter. They can't get in. Both of them are too large to fit through the bars."

"Don't do this," said Zelle. "My father has a chest upstairs, full of jewels. I'll show you where it is if you promise to leave and not return."

"But I want a pearl. A pearl with amethyst eyes, skin like alabaster and a voice like an angel."

Her gaze shot to the door. They circled each other around the table. His greedy gaze scanning her body making her flesh crawl without him even touching her. When she reached the side closest to the front room, she ran. She threw the door wide, just as Craigen caught her by the waist. She screamed into the night that she couldn't touch, and heard shouting and footsteps approaching.

"Help! Help me, please," she screamed.

Craigen dragged her from the doorway. She stomped on his booted foot with her heel, but it did no good. Two men appeared in the opening and she prepared to scream for help again, but stopped short. They weren't Flint and Dax.

"Craigen, I told you not to touch her," said Klaus.

"Sorry, boss, but I just can't help myself with this one."

"You fool!" yelled Paul. "Let the girl go and get out of there."

Craigen let go of Zelle and she ran for the stairs. She glanced behind to see him close the door. The shouts of the other men followed her. She raced up the stairs, but Craigen caught her by the ankle, causing her to trip over her gown and hit the steps. There was a cracking noise as her armband collided with stone steps. Craigen climbed on top of her. She kicked out and connected with his hip. He toppled downward and she staggered to her feet. The whole right side of her body throbbed with pain. Her hip shot a jolt of agony down her leg when she tried to put weight on it. Slowly, grabbing the railing she hobbled up to the library.

She'd just gotten the door closed when Craigen's boots hit the steps. Her father couldn't put locks on any of the doors?

She whimpered and backed away as the door flew open once more.

His eyes were wild and his nose bloodied from the fall. His aura was the deepest shade of red she'd ever seen, dotted with a murderous inky black.

Zelle backed up as Craigen advanced. "Please. Don't," she whispered.

He struck her across the face, throwing her to the ground. Her head hit the rug covered stone floor and her vision blurred.

He scrambled on top of her, his rough hands roaming her body. Yanking at her gown he ripped the bodice down the center.

No, she couldn't let this happen. Zelle's mind snapped into action.

"Stop." She grabbed him by his hair and tried to yank him off. He pinned her under his weight. His mouth scoured the tops of her breasts like her scrub brush.

"Stop!" she cried louder. She beat on him, tearing and gouging and pinching and doing everything she could to push him away.

Then his lips were on hers. His sour breath filling her mouth. Vomit crept up her throat and her stomach roiled. She sucked in his breath and though he tasted terrible, her limbs gained strength.

His tongue probed her mouth, his hands grabbing and squeezing her flesh.

A tingle zapped her from her armband. A memory stirred of the dead dark skinned man with white eyes and she breathed Craigen in. His tongue stopped moving and his groping hands slowed.

She grabbed him by the skull and locked his lips on hers.

He breathed in through his nose. She sucked the breath out of him through his mouth. Over and over she sucked his breath into her. Her armband crackled again and pain shot through her head for a moment but then stopped.

She continued to suck in his breath. Over and over, until he stopped breathing all together. Purple mist swirled over her body, covering them both. His arms went slack and Zelle found herself holding him up easily. She opened her eyes.

He stared at her, frozen in terror. Anger exploded inside her. She pushed him off her and leaned over his immobile body. She sucked in one last breath. A white coil of essence swirled out of his mouth and into hers. She fought to keep from laughing at the joy it brought her. His face went ashen and his eyes glazed over. Purple mist surrounded Zelle, glowing and wafting off of her in a way she'd never seen before. Her head lightened and her limbs tingled.

She stared into the unblinking, solidly white pupils of Craigen. Giving him a shove, he flew across the room and hit the wall on the opposite side with a crash. Books rained down off the shelf onto his head.

Zelle got to her feet, energized. Her body hummed with magick. Closing her eyes, she threw her head back, and took in everything around her. A smile played across her lips, until an image of Craigen's white eyes burned into her head. Followed by image after image of men's faces with white eyes. So many, they were too quick for her to register. Guilt and pain hit her in a flurry of images she didn't understand. A battlefield, dead men; hundreds, thousands.

Zelle cried out and backed into the couch. A knowledge washed over her. She'd done that. She'd killed all those men.

Craigen stared at her with cloudy eyes.

"Craigen?" she whispered.

She inched her way forward. Her throat so dry she couldn't swallow. She was mere feet away when she bent down to him.

"Craigen?" With a trembling hand she pushed him. He didn't move. Mist trailed her as she moved. This wasn't possible. She couldn't have done that.

A pop sounded from her armband and she raised her sleeve. The red stone in her cuff had cracked in two. Red sparks fizzled and sputtered inside and then slowly the stone went dark.

"What the hell?"

Zelle looked up. Klaus hung from the windowsill.

"What did you do to him?" he shouted.

"I– I didn't–" Zelle shook her head. "It wasn't my fault."

Klaus's expression hardened and he reached above the sill and swung himself up. Zelle screamed and ran for the stairs. Taking them two at a time, she made for the aviary.

"Loca!" she cried. "Loca!" Her heart pounded in her ears a she neared the aviary door.

Throwing it wide she scanned the room. Her birds all slept but Loca was nowhere to be seen. Zelle raced to the window. Klaus had already made his way up from her bedchamber window, toward the aviary.

"Loca!" She picked up the bar, ready to put it in place. She scanned the sky. "Loca, come!" she screamed.

Klaus was just a few stones below her. A cry escaped her lips. "Loca, please!" she called.

A white blur shot toward the open window.

"Loca! Hurry!"

Klaus was one stone below. His hand would be on the ledge any moment. Zelle watched in horror as his hand shot onto the sill. He hoisted himself up as Loca darted over his head, making him duck. Loca screeched and flapped his wings in Klaus's face. His hands slipped and he fell several inches. Loca continued to beat about Klaus's head, scratching at his face, until Klaus lost his grip and fell, hitting the grass with a thud. Zelle peered out over the ledge. Paul bent over Klaus's form. He looked up at her as Loca hopped from the ledge up onto Zelle's shoulder. She gathered him close and wet his feathers with her tears.

"Good boy."

Klaus lay immovable for several minutes, before he roused, shook his head, and sat up. His gaze moved up the tower to the window. His fury slapped her from all the way down on the ground. She snapped the bar back into place. The magick resealed over the window and Zelle stepped away.

Her heart beat as fast as Loca's. Loca leaned over and preened her hair. She shook from head to toe. Backing into the corner of the aviary, she slid to the floor.

She was a murderer.

CHAPTER THIRTEEN

F lint had barely slept. After meeting up with Dax they'd taken off toward Zelle's. They'd trekked through most of the night until Dax had forced him to stop and rest. He'd allowed them only four hours, and then they'd eaten and continued on.

Something in Flint's gut gnawed at him the whole way. It was stupid. She'd been fine for how many years? But seeing those men outside her tower made him more anxious than he was willing to admit.

By mid morning, they arrived in the glen. Flint stopped and stared at the tower for several minutes. An uneasiness skittered over his skin. They moved carefully toward the tower. Reaching it, Flint circled the building once. No sounds emanated from inside.

"Zelle?" he called.

Silence.

"Zelle?" The hairs on his neck stood on end.

"Something's wrong," Dax said. "I can smell it."

"What is it?" Flint asked, trying to tamp down his rising fear.

"Men. Men and death."

Flint flew into action. "Zelle," he yelled as loud as he was able. "Zelle, it's Flint!" Pulling the bottle from his bag he opened the stopper and quickly sprinkled the dust around the perimeter of the tower. Reaching the front door he stopped and did as Cinder had instructed.

He retrieved the parchment from his bag, his hands shaking so badly that he was barely able to focus on the strange words written on it. At the end of the last sentence a strong wind rushed through him at the tower, blowing the door wide. Flint approached the entrance and lifted his hand. It went through effortlessly. He'd done it!

Scanning the room, he noticed an overturned chair, and the couch had been shoved askew.

"Zelle!" Flint ran for the stairs. He reached the library landing in two strides, threw the door open and stopped. A man lay crumpled on the floor under a pile of books. Flint looked for Zelle, but there was no sign of her. He turned and ran into Dax, who blocked the doorway. Flint pushed him aside and rushed to Zelle's room. It was empty and undisturbed.

By the time he made it to the aviary, he was out of breath. He stopped just outside to steady himself for what he might find. He grasped the handle and opened the door. Pushing inward it swung open with a creak. The birds chattered noisily.

"Zelle?" he tentatively called out.

There was no response.

"Zelle?" Flint said again. His voice was barely a whisper.

He swallowed down the terror etching its name into his chest. A light purple haze emanated from a dark corner. Squinting, Flint could just make out her form huddled there. He raced toward her, sending the birds flapping around the room.

"Zelle."

Loca screeched, fanning his wings in Flint's face.

Zelle didn't move.

Flint fell back, as the bird continued to beat his wings, claws outstretched.

"Loca, easy. Easy." Flint raised his arm at the bird. The bird stopped screeching, but continued to beat Flint away from Zelle. "Easy, boy."

He put up his hand, deflecting the bird. Finally, Loca retreated to Zelle's shoulder.

She stared off into space.

Flint scooted forward, his eyes on Loca. He reached out, slowly and set his hand atop Zelle's warm, soft skin. At his touch the purple mist that surrounded her intensified.

"Zelle," he whispered. "Zelle, it's Flint."

He rubbed her hand with his thumb. Her dress was torn down the middle, her light skin showed from her neck to her naval.

"Flint?"

She gazed through him, like she didn't see him. Blood crusted on her lip and nose. Anger twisted in him like a spike as he realized what had happened to her.

"Zelle, I'm here. I'm right here." He inched closer and she blinked several times. He reached out and touched her bruised and bloodied lips.

"The men came back," she said. Flint's heart squeezed at the monotone level of her voice. "I opened the window for

Loca to go out. One of them squeezed through. He attacked me and I… I…"

Her eyes filled with tears and Flint grasped her by the wrist, pulling her close. She let out a horrible cry. Her slender arms clung to him. He gathered her close. He'd kill them. Klaus and the other one were dead men. As soon as Flint found them he would show no mercy. Loca moved from Zelle's shoulder to his perch high above.

"I killed him," she sobbed. "I killed that man."

Flint held her tighter. "It's all right. It's going to be fine. I'm here. I'm going to take you away where no one can hurt you again." Flint hated himself for lying to her. It wasn't all right. It was most likely never going to be all right for her again. Not a sweet tender soul like Zelle. He knew all too well the pain and guilt of killing. Even killing those who deserved it. He wouldn't wish that pain on anyone.

"Zelle, we need to get you out of here."

She looked up with clear, bright eyes.

His heart shuddered. The purple mist swelled off her skin, surrounding him. Her scent overpowered him, her gaze drew him in.

"What are you?" he asked.

"Flint! You better get down here!"

Dax's voice broke through the spell Zelle cast over him. He got to his feet, pulling Zelle up as well. An ear-shattering roar sounded from outside the tower. Zelle's eyes went wide with terror.

"Father."

ZELLE AND FLINT RUSHED OUT TO WHERE DAX STOOD ON THE stairs.

"In my chamber." She pointed to her room.

"I won't leave you to deal with this alone," Flint said.

Zelle shook her head. "He has to be here for something specific, he shouldn't be long."

"No." Flint shook his head. "It doesn't matter. I broke the spell."

"What?"

"I broke the spell on the tower. You aren't bound here anymore. That's how I got in."

She hadn't even noticed. She pounded on her head with her fists. Think. This wasn't what she wanted. She'd hoped not to have to confront her father. But now it was inevitable. She looked down and pulled her gown closed.

"I need to change." She ran into her room before anyone could protest. Flint and Dax followed her in. "Hide in the bathing room." She pointed.

"Zelle—"

"Please, just do it." She couldn't meet Flint's eye. She didn't know what to think, or do.

They moved to the bathing room and closed the door.

"Zelle?" A call came from downstairs. "Zelle?" Father's tone was urgent.

She threw off her ripped dress and ran to her wardrobe, grabbing a sage green one. The band on her arm remained dark and broken.

"Zelle!" The voice was closer, moving up the stairs.

She knew the moment he entered the library because his scream of her name became frantic. Zelle yanked the dress over her head and tugged it into place around her body. Her father burst into her room, as the gown brushed her toes.

His face held terror she had never seen before.

"Zelle! Oh my dear, what happened? Are you all right?" He crossed to her in a few large strides, moving with an air of confidence she had never seen him use before. She blinked several times at the sight of him. He'd grown younger in the last few days. His gray hair now brown, his wrinkled leathery skin, younger and peachier. Zelle's mouth went dry. He looked like a man in his fifties, instead of his seventies.

He reached out and touched her face. "Zelle, your lip is bloodied. Say something."

"A man got in through Loca's window," she croaked. "He attacked me."

Her father's eyes softened. "Oh my darling daughter, did he hurt you?"

Zelle couldn't get over the fact that her father's appearance had changed so drastically. She scanned the only face she'd seen for years. Every intricacy that she had memorized in detail had morphed into something new. Something foreign.

His brows furrowed. "What's the matter? Are you in shock?"

"I'm shaken," she managed.

"Why don't you sit and I'll get you a drink." He pushed her down onto her soft bed and headed for the bathing room.

"No," Zelle almost shouted. Her father turned, wide eyed. "I mean, I don't want a drink. I want to go."

"Go?"

"Yes. I don't feel safe here anymore."

"I'll double the spells. I'll bar up the bottom windows so no one can climb up. Unfortunately, you'll have to get rid of Loca but—"

Zelle hopped to her feet. "No. I want to leave."

"Leave for where?" Her father looked confused.

"Into the world. I know you have been protecting me, but after what happened... I need to get out. See Fairelle. Live a life, maybe get married. If the time comes that I am in danger, I will come to you. But I won't bother you otherwise. I know you are powerful in your community and you can't have anyone know about me, so I'll stay away." She was rambling, but she wanted out. More than anything, she wanted out.

He scanned her bedroom. "Why was the door open?"

"What?"

"The front door. It was open when I arrived. You said the man came through Loca's window. So why was it open, and how come I didn't have to use the portal to get in?"

Zelle's hands trembled and she locked them together. "Please, Father," she pleaded. "I want to leave with your bless-ing." Her smile was weak. His gaze drifted over every surface of her room and finally lit on the bathing room door. Zelle swallowed hard. "Father—"

He shot her a look so venomous that she closed her mouth. He threw the door wide. A hiss escaped him and he took a step back.

"You!"

"Father, let me explain."

Flint walked out, followed by Dax. "You must be Zelle's father."

Her father said nothing. He simply stared at the two men.

Zelle's heart pounded. She'd never seen her father like this before.

He stood, staring, not speaking for several minutes. Finally, he pulled a small pouch from his robe and began to chant.

"No," Zelle said.

"What's going on?" asked Flint.

"It's an amnesia spell," Zelle cried. "Father please," she pleaded.

Her father continued on with his spell. He opened the pouch and the dust inside glowed blue.

"Run," Zelle yelled.

"No." A hard look came over Flint's face. "I'm not leaving you with him."

"Go," Zelle screamed, "Please."

Flint stepped close to her father and grasped his arms, shaking the mage. "I don't know who you are, but I know you aren't Zelle's father. And I'm not going to let you keep her any longer." Flint shoved him roughly, breaking the man's concentration and sending him to the floor.

"Flint!" Dax stepped forward. "Stop."

"Yes, Flint," her father said, getting up. "Listen to your bear friend. He of all people should know what happens to those who mess with my kind."

"What do you mean by that?" Dax asked.

The man's gaze traveled to Zelle. "It seems our time together has come to an end, my dear. But don't worry, I'll be seeing you very soon. You can be sure of that. We are family after all." His gaze moved to Flint. "As for you, you'll never see her again."

Before Zelle could move, her father said three short words, blew dust into Flint's face, and then disappeared.

Flint cried out and fell to his knees. Dax ran to the window. Fader the dragon roared and beat his wings. Zelle rushed to Flint.

"Flint! What is it?"

"My eyes," he cried.

"Dax get some water," Zelle ordered.

Dax ran out of the room.

"I'm here," Zelle said. "I'm here, Flint. We'll take care of this."

Flint moaned and writhed in her arms. Panic overtook her. What had just happened? Her sweet old father had been young, and he'd attacked them in a way she'd never thought possible.

"Shhh…" she cooed, wiping his hair from his forehead. "I'm right here."

Dax returned with a pitcher and a rag. He knelt and placed the pitcher on the floor next to Zelle. She snagged the rag and plunged it into the water.

"Here." She pushed the rag at Flint's hand. He grabbed it and wiped it over his face, rubbing at his eye sockets.

"Slow," Zelle said. "Don't hurt yourself."

"It already hurts," Flint snapped.

Zelle swallowed down the sting of his words. He scrubbed furiously. She grabbed his hands. "Stop! You'll make it worse."

"How the hell would you know?"

She gasped.

"He doesn't mean it," Dax said gently.

"The hell I don't!"

"That's enough," said Dax in warning. "She's trying to help."

"I don't need any help." Flint jammed the towel into his face.

Zelle's anger spiked and she ripped the rag from Flint's grasp.

"Hey!"

His eyes flew open and Zelle had to hold back her horror. He stopped moving. His mouth opened and closed several times, but he said nothing.

The pit in her stomach grew several sizes. His eyes were

red as blood where they should have been white and where they'd been brown they were completely black. The skin around his eyes was bright red and blistering.

"I... I can't see," Flint whispered. Zelle and Dax stared at each other for a minute. A bloody tear leaked from the corner of Flint's eye. "Why can't I see?"

"It's fine." Zelle rinsed the blood-stained rag and wet it again. Gently she touched it to Flint's face and rubbed around his eyes. "You need to rest."

Another bloody tear flowed down his cheek.

"Close your eyes," she said softly. He blinked several times and then obeyed. Zelle dabbed the rag over his raw skin. He lay motionless as she worked. Her hands shook but she refused to allow herself to cry. "You need to rest," she said again. She looked at Dax. "Help me get him to the bed."

Dax mouthed, "We have to get out of here."

She nodded her understanding and motioned toward Flint.

Dax grabbed Flint by the arms. He staggered to his feet and Dax moved him to the bed and lay him down. Zelle got up, picking up the pitcher and rag and sat next to Flint. She placed the rag over his eyes. He groaned and she got up and walked to her vanity. Inside she pulled the vial her father had given her. She hated to give Flint anything that her father had brewed, but she'd taken it hundreds of time with no ill effects.

"Drink this." She sat next to him once more.

"What is it?"

"Something to help with the pain and to help you sleep."

He rolled on his back and she lifted it to his lips. He gulped it down without so much as a wince, and then he rolled away again.

He lay silent except for his labored breathing, which

evened within a few minutes and then fell into a rhythmic rise and fall.

This spell was bad. As powerful as her father was, reversing it was not going to be easy. If it was possible at all, which she doubted.

CHAPTER FOURTEEN

Z elle left Flint to rest and went downstairs a short time later. She closed the bedroom door with the memory of Flint's black eyes staring at her. She couldn't understand what had happened with her father. His anger had been such a shock that she'd been unable to think of little else in the last hour.

Down in the library Dax rushed about picking up books and shoving them into his and Flint's bags.

"We have to leave. Only pack what you absolutely need. We can get you everything else."

She went down a mental list of things to take but her body didn't move.

"Zelle, we can't stay here. It isn't safe. The magical wards are gone, anyone can get in and your father will most surely return. He has too many of his books here to just let them rot."

Her gaze traveled to the ashy skinned dead man lying in the corner with all but his face obscured. She swallowed and dropped onto the couch, her head in her hands. How had this all happened?

"Hey." Dax's voice was gentle. He crouched in front of her and took her palms in his. His bright blue eyes held strength and kindness. "He didn't mean to speak to you like that."

"I know."

They stared at each other for a moment.

"He's not going to get better," Dax finally said. It wasn't a question.

She wanted to lie and tell him that Flint would be fine in a few days, but the truth was, she had no idea.

"I know this is sudden but we really have to go. I need you to be strong and pack your things. Then we'll get Flint outside and I'll carry him. It'll be mid day soon and we need to be as far away from this place as possible by nightfall, in case your attackers decide to return."

She gazed into Dax's blue eyes and wondered what memories someone had locked away inside him.

"Zelle, I need you to do this."

She shook her head. "Right. Sorry. I'll go pack."

She stood and headed for the stairs. This wasn't the departure she'd hoped for.

ZELLE LOOKED OVER HER BIRDS. THE CREATURES SHE HAD cared for and loved for the past years. It was time for all of them to fly. No longer time for complacency. They would leave here and find their own way, just as she would. She took in the scent of feathers and seed and closed her eyes for a moment, remembering each bird in turn.

Her gaze drifted high into the rafters to Loca. The bird

watched her from the darkness. His bright yellow eyes staring at her like he didn't know her.

Dax came up at that moment. "I have our bags."

She nodded. "I'll change and grab my things and then I'll be ready."

He squeezed her arm. "I'll get Flint."

"How are we going to carry him? We have no horse," she said.

"Leave that to me."

Zelle walked to her room and Dax lifted Flint from the bed and helped him down the stairs as she went to her wardrobe and pulled it wide. She removed a lavender dress with silver trim and her long, deep blue cloak.

Stripping off her green dress she flung it to the floor. She stripped off her bloomers and threw them to the floor as well. She stood naked in front of her vanity and gasped. With the cuff broken, her true form stood before her. It felt familiar and foreign all at the same time. Her face had not changed only her ears. She touched the tips, which now were quite pointed and stretched far beyond a human's. She tried to cover them with her hair to little avail.

An intricate silver design swirled over her chest and abdomen. She ran her fingers over them and was bombarded by the memories of being tattooed as a child. Her name and rank in her society.

She looked at the cuff bracelet and anger rose within her. She grabbed it and pulled, but it didn't budge. She breathed deeply and stared at her nails. They had lengthened three times the size they had been and were razor sharp. She sliced into her arm where the cuff sat, sucking in a breath at the pain. Blue blood trickled from the wound as she cut around the top and bottom of the cuff. She twisted it and the band slipped sideways, causing the cuff to clatter to the floor, revealing her own sacred silver arm tattoo. She stifled a cry when she saw it.

The face of a handsome man with tanned skin and eyes such a mixture of colors you couldn't say what they were, floated into view. *Khazidhæ.*

Memories assaulted her. Her home, her family, her name. All things that had been hidden from her by magick. Anger blossomed inside her, bright as a field of sungolds. She needed to get to Khazidhæ. She needed to find him. He would avenge what had been done to her by Rasmuss.

She'd been stolen. Locked away and imprisoned. The thought shocked her to the core. She fell against the wall and crumpled to the floor. Rasmuss had used her. Violated her magick and turned her into someone that she wasn't.

She'd been made into a complacent servant as void of free agency as the priestesses in her father's temples. Zelle pulled herself into a ball and sobbed. How had she forgotten who she was? How had she forgotten her family? Where she was from people bowed at her feet and paid tribute. Here she'd scrubbed floors like a serving wench. How had she let herself be turned into someone so lowly? Who was she?

The crying ceased in an instant. She was not this. This was unbecoming of who she truly was. She brushed the tears from her face and got to her feet. Turning to her mirror she stared at the woman before her and let her anger take over once more. She would find Khazidhæ and she would have her revenge.

ZELLE WALKED TO THE AVIARY, HER SMALL BAG OVER HER shoulder. She'd only taken one other dress, her hairbrush, a few healing items and the cuff bracelet. She covered her ears with her hair as much as possible and pulled her cloak over her head. She only needed one other thing.

She stood in the doorway of the aviary, looking up high.

"Loca," she called.

He stared at her but didn't move.

"Come, Loca, we must leave."

Again the bird simply stared. He saw the change in her. Her chest squeezed at the thought of leaving him, but if he wouldn't come to her, she had no choice.

"Good bye, old friend."

Loca squawked and took off out the door to the floors below.

She walked slowly down the stairs, trepidation tracing her steps as she made her way to the exit. This was surely the last time she'd be in this tower. For as much as it had been her prison, it had also been her home.

She stood at the front door and looked out. What did the world hold for her? She swallowed hard and trampled her fear. She would not be the cowering girl Rasmuss had made her.

She stepped onto the soft grass, feeling it between her toes for the first time. The warm soil molded to her feet like shoes. She lifted her face to the sky and breathed deeply the scent of freedom. It was a memory she would never forget.

"How long has it been since you've felt the grass?" asked Dax.

"I've never touched grass before."

He gave her a quizzical glance and she smiled.

Flint sat, half awake, propped against the tower, Loca perched on his shoulder. The sight made her gut clench. It hurt that Loca trusted Flint instead of her.

"I'm going to transform now and I'll need you to help Flint get on my back."

"Transform?"

"To my bear form."

Did she know Dax was a bear shifter? She couldn't remember. She scanned his frame, wondering what he looked.

"I'll need you to carry at least one bag as well," he said. "I can put one on Flint, but not both."

"That's not a problem."

Dax proceeded to remove his clothing. She turned to gaze out at the woods as he did. The sounds of his bones snapping made her stomach churn.

He snorted and nudged her arm with his nose. She turned to find an enormous, creamy bear standing next to her.

She couldn't help gaze into his hazel eyes. "You're amazing." She ran her fingers through his soft fur.

He tried to tell her something and then lumbered over to where Flint waited.

"You know how dumb I feel riding you like a pony?" asked Flint.

Dax growled.

"Come on," said Zelle. "Let's get moving." She helped Flint to his feet. Then she slung a bag over his shoulder, disrupting Loca's perch and sending him fluttering to the ground. She led Flint to Dax's back and he climbed on and lay flat against Dax's spine.

"Hang on here and here." She moved Flint's hands to grip Dax's fur. "You can tell how he'll move by his shoulders."

Dax looked at her and she picked up the other leather bag and swung it over her shoulder. It was heavy, but she could manage. She caught his eye and nodded.

He started off toward the wood at a slow pace. Loca flew

to Flint's back and perched on him as if he was a footstool. Flint held tightly to Dax and she walked behind them, scanning the area for danger.

They must look quite a sight, she thought. A white bear, a blind man, an owl, and her. But looks were the last thing she was concerned with.

SIX HOURS PASSED BEFORE THEY FINALLY STOPPED TO REST. They'd been in the woods the whole time and had yet to come upon another person. Her feet throbbed from not being used to the rocky terrain. More than once she'd cut herself on a stone or thorn, but the pain spurred her on. Reminding her that she was free.

Over the past hours, in the silence of walking, she'd remembered everything. Who she was, how she'd gotten into the tower, and what she'd done. All of the good in her life; the pain and the sorrow. Centuries of lifetimes and she finally remembered them all.

Parts she wished that she hadn't remembered. Like the loss of her mother, the hardness of her father and lastly the man she'd shared a bed with. But other things she couldn't imagine living another day without. Her room back home. Her magical abilities. Her brother.

She helped Flint onto a blanket that she'd spread on the ground as Dax wandered off.

"Can I get you anything?"

Flint looked up at her and at the sight of his face she raised her hand to touch him but then stopped.

"Something to drink."

His aura was clouded with physical pain and anger. She brushed the hair from his sightless eyes.

"Here." She removed her waterskin and untwisted the top. She placed her hand under his chin and tipped the water into his mouth.

He took several drinks and then she replaced the cap on the skin. She made to stand but he grabbed her hand and held onto it.

Flint was a warrior and where she was from, warriors were held in the highest of regard.

"Can I get my clothes?" Dax asked from behind a tree.

He was human again. She closed her eyes and handed him his clothes.

"We should eat," he said.

She pulled open a bag and removed three apples and a brick of cheese. He took them from her and tried to hand them to Flint, but Flint rolled away and refused to eat.

Dax shook his head and handed the portion back to her. "Save it for later."

He sat next to her on the mossy ground and they chewed their food in silence for several minutes.

"I've been thinking," said Dax. "What your father said—"

"He's not my father." Her voice came out harsher than she'd anticipated.

"I apologize. But what he said, about me knowing how it feels to have no memory, what did he mean?"

"I have no clue. Do you know him?"

Dax shook his head. "I don't remember anything from before I awoke as a bear."

She tore off a small piece of cheese and chewed it. "So you've not always been a bear?"

"I don't think so. I've been searching your books, trying to see if I could find something to jog my memory of who I used to be. I've caught glimpses. Bits and pieces, but nothing substantial."

"Where are we going?"

Dax's gaze traveled to Flint and he lowered his voice. "To Sage's, maybe Adrian's. Those places are safe for all of us. The biggest problem is going to be getting Flint to agree."

"But he needs his family now more than ever," she whispered.

"He won't see it that way."

"How could he not?" Was he that stubborn? The answer was all too clear.

"Flint is the strong one. The protector. He feels responsible for everyone and everything. He won't want them to see him wounded."

"Even if it could save his life."

"Especially if it could save his life."

She didn't understand. She would give anything to have her family near her now, taking care of her.

THEY CONTINUED ON, WALKING LATE INTO THE NIGHT. WHEN the bright golden moon rose high in the sky and Loca took off to hunt, they stopped. Dax built a small fire and they ate bread and dried meat. Again Flint refused food and instead went straight to sleep.

She and Dax spent hours talking. She had yet to tell him who she was, but she'd told him that she'd regained her memories. And he hadn't pried. But he had determined that if anyone could help her, it would be Sage the vampire king. She was leery, but what choice did she have? Without Rasmuss, she had no way to get home. She could go down to the mage lands and begin laying waste to everyone until he agreed to help her, but that wasn't what she wanted.

She wanted Rasmuss's head on a platter. She wanted to suck the life out of him and watch him fall. But that was going to take help. Help she didn't currently have. There was only one who could help her achieve her goal.

Zelle awakened to Flint's screams. She hopped up as Dax roused. A crash sounded from the other side of the fire. Flint staggered about and bumped a tree, hitting his head.

"Dammit," he roared.

"Flint!" A head wound was the last thing he needed. She moved to him quickly, wrapped her arms around his waist and pulled him away from the tree.

"Stop it," he growled. "I don't need your help. Let me be, woman." He pushed at her arms and stumbled toward the dying fire.

Dax got to his feet.

Her chin quivered at Flint's tone and something inside her roared to life. She took a deep breath and rounded on him, slapping his face.

"Flint Gwyn, I'm trying to help you. Stop being such a big baby. If you don't want my help, fine. Stumble around until you fall into the fire and kill yourself. Or wander into a ravine." She was immediately sorry for her words, but she refused to back down.

Dax looked on in silence.

Flint's chest puffed out like he was about to yell at her. She waited for his venom but it didn't come. "I need to urinate," he said.

She suppressed a smile and softened her voice. "Well then, let's get you to a tree." She stood next to him until his chest deflated and he put an arm over her shoulders. She laced her fingers into his and wrapped her arm around his waist. Dax nodded and lay down on his blanket once more.

Taking slow steps, she moved him to a tree several yards from camp

He stared at her with his completely black irises. "This part I can do myself."

"I'll just be over here. Let me know when you're done."

FLINT STARED INTO HAZY BLACKNESS. ZELLE'S SLIGHT FORM fuzzed in and out of view when the fire silhouetted her. Twigs snapped under her feet as she walked away. He swallowed hard, trying not to cry again. The pain had dulled to a light burning, but nothing worse than what he was used to. Pain was a common companion in his life. The blackness wasn't.

He'd been able to see shadows in his dim gray vision as they'd made their way through the woods. The edges of his view were brighter than the rest but he still could hardly see a thing. He scanned his surroundings, trying to find something he could recognize, but it was too dark. The bite of the chilly air told him that it wasn't just his vision causing the darkness; it was past midnight. Reaching out, he touched the rough bark of the tree in front of him, opened his breeches and tried to position himself so he didn't piss on his boots.

He tried to process his current situation. He was in the woods, away from home, with only Dax to help him keep Zelle safe, and he couldn't see.

His heart sank. This wasn't possible. He'd always been the one people depended on. If he couldn't find a cure for his eyesight, how would he function? What would he do? He refused to be anyone's burden.

He closed his pants and fumbled with his belt, trying to buckle it. He swallowed. She didn't deserve this. To take care of an invalid. It wasn't fair for her, now that she finally had her freedom.

A twig snapped to his right. "Do you need some help?"

No. "My belt," he said softly.

Her special scent of lilac and fruit wafted toward him. She pushed him against the tree trunk and touched his waist. He placed his hands atop her shoulders. Despite everything he'd been through, his body responded to the nearness of her. His arousal spiked when her hips rubbed against his thighs.

He sucked in a breath and her hands stopped moving. He wanted more than anything to kiss her. To feel her comfort, her touch.

She laced her fingers behind his neck.

"Zelle, don't."

"Don't what?"

"Don't do that." He turned his head away and the feel of her warm breath hit the side of his neck.

"What? Put my arms around you? Or don't do this?" She pulled his head down with a strength he didn't know she had.

Her lips locked on his and her tongue skimmed his teeth. A moan escaped her and he crushed her to him. Her tongue mingled with his. Heart pounding his head fought for conscious thought as desire ripped through him. He needed her. Wanted her. His kisses became more aggressive and she reciprocated.

There was no denying it. His feelings for her were real. She brought him peace in a way he'd never felt before. She soothed his demons and made him want to be a better man.

Her hand slipped from his neck as he planted hot wet kisses on her mouth and then trailed them down her neck. She moaned his name and his need to bury himself inside her spiked. Her fingers trailed down his chest to the front of his breeches. He sucked in a harsh breath and moved away from her.

"Zelle," he breathed. "Zelle, don't—"

This wasn't right. He didn't want it like this. Not with her. He wanted to be with her properly. To love her and pleasure her the way he'd never done with a woman before. The way she deserved. Not in the middle of the forest against a tree, with Dax a ways off by the fire.

ZELLE'S BODY HUMMED WITH THE NEED TO BE WITH HIM. To bring him happiness. To give him release.

She reached for him, but he moved away from her and stumbled on a tree root. She knew he wanted her. She could smell it on him. A fresh wave of desire settled over her, and with it the need to feel him inside her.

"Why?" she asked.

"Because I don't want this." He ran his hands through his hair. His darkened eyes staring straight ahead.

Her heart dropped.

"I mean, I do. I want you. I just don't want it to be like this."

"Like what?" Anger and frustration mixed inside her and tears threatened to spill. She wanted to be soft and sweet the way he liked her, but her true nature demanded respect for who she was.

"Like this." He gestured around. "Against the tree in the forest. Besides, Dax isn't too far off."

"I don't care where we are. I just want you." She reached for him but he backed away at her touch.

Zelle huffed and wiped a tear from her eye. Her body shook with anger and rejection. She breathed in and out over and over, trying to calm the rage that built inside. Rage that she hadn't felt since being trapped in the tower fifty years before. Anger that had been forced out of her by Rasmuss' magick. It swirled inside like a tornado building strength with each passing moment.

"Zelle." His shoulders slumped and he took a step closer to her. "I can't take care of you. I can't protect you. I'm no good for you. You deserve better, especially now."

"You don't know that," she spat. A thick mist wafted off her skin, surrounding her, but she didn't care.

He shook his head. "It's purely selfish of me to have you when I shouldn't. If I didn't deserve you before, to be with you now would surely be a curse to you. I'm blind, Zelle."

"We'll fix it."

"Don't lie. Between you and I, we don't lie. Whatever he did, it's permanent and you know it. He promised I'd never see you again, and I won't."

"I'll find magick to fix you. Magick like what you used to get me out of this tower."

He shook his head. "It's not possible. I don't profess to know everything about magick but I know even it has its limits on what it can heal. My eyes are mutilated. I feel it every time I blink." He took a step toward her. "You deserve more. You deserve someone good, like Dax."

Her head pounded. The mist swirled off her skin so dense it obscured her vision. Her blood pulsed in her ears cutting off ambient sound. Her heartbeat wildly making her body quake. A feeling of dread overcame her and the needed to get away.

"Zelle—" He stepped closer.

She couldn't think straight. The mist wound snug as a winter blanket. It twisted and coiled, constricting her breathing. Memories flashed of the last time her mist had grown too thick. Panicking, she tore off into the woods. She couldn't let this happen. She needed to get as far away as possible.

Flint yelled after her, but she didn't stop.

"Zelle, what's the matter?" Dax called.

Running as fast as she was able, she passed rocks and bushes, flowers and a creek. She stumbled over a tree root and fell to the ground. The mist churned white-hot. She had to get up. Her head pounded and her skin burned.

She gulped in a huge burst of air. Terror dripped down her body staining her thoughts with images of the dead birds in her hands, and dead men strewn across a battlefield.

Zelle got to her feet and continued to stumble forward. She tore at her throat and clawed at her body willing the mist away but it choked her of all sense of reason. The mist wound tighter and tighter. Everything went silent and suddenly her muscles snapped stiff. Her mouth opened in a silent scream as her neck snapped back forcing her to look into the sky. She couldn't hold back any more.

A wave of white lighting shot from her body, arcing out in all directions. It rippled through plants and brush, blackening everything it touched. Trees toppled to the ground. Rocks split in two, and flowers withered and died at the touch of the powerful magick. Zelle focused on the stars unable to move until finally she crumpled to the ground.

Nameless faces flashed through her mind. *A white castle surrounded by blood red trees and the ground made of ash. Khazidhæ. A woman with snowy white hair and eyes of amethyst like her own. Hundreds of men. All with white eyes and all dead. Lying on a battle-*

field, lifeless. The image of Rasmuss walking up to her, a smile on his face.

"Very good, my Rapunzelle. Very, very good." He clamped the gold armband on her. *"That was so good, and now you shall help me."*

"I will never help you, Rasmuss."

"Oh my dear, you will. You will."

Zelle's eyes flew open and a yelp escaped her.

"Zelle?"

She sat up. Dax ran toward her, his clothes ripped and scorched.

He knelt beside her and touched her back. "Are you all right?"

"No." Her eyes flooded with tears and her body shook. "I remember."

"Remember what?" His face held concern and confusion.

"I'm not supposed to be here. He stole me and made me do things. Horrible things."

"Who is he?"

She shook her head and sucked in a ragged breath. "Rasmuss."

"Where did he steal you from?"

"Shaidan. My name is Rapunzelle. I'm a daemon."

CHAPTER FIFTEEN

F lint paced between the trees. He hadn't wanted to upset her, but he couldn't just sleep with her in the forest. And now she'd run off and Dax as well. He rubbed his neck, the black shadows in his sight raising his trepidation. For the first time he really wondered what his life would be like from then on out. He'd need help for everything. No longer would he be free to do what he wanted, when he wanted. For the rest of his life he would be forever dependent on others for help. His soul sagged at the thought. Standing in an unknown forest, in the middle of the night, he was as helpless as a babe.

This was his fault. She was so innocent and fragile and he had forced her to leave her one sanctuary, her tower. He had to get her to safety. He owed her that much. Then he would figure out what to do with his own set of problems.

Something moved to his left and the hairs prickled on his neck. He breathed deep, listening to the sounds of the woods.

He had no weapon and for the first time in his life, fear crept up his spine.

"We're back." Dax grabbed Flint by the arm and led him to camp.

Flint blew out a breath and almost cried out in relief. "Where's Zelle?"

"She's a few yards off."

"I need to talk to her."

Dax sat Flint down on his blanket. "That's not such a good idea right now, friend."

"Why? What did she say?"

Dax sighed. "You two need to talk, I agree, but not now. Give her some space. She's been through a lot."

"Dax, please. I didn't mean to…" Confusion churned Flint's head like a storm cloud. Dax was probably right. If he talked to her tonight, he would just make it worse. "All right," he finally said.

Flint touched Dax's tunic and part of the sleeve fell away. He ran his fingers over Dax's arm.

"What happened to your tunic?" He inhaled. "Why do you smell of smoke? Did you encounter a dragon?"

"No." Dax removed Flint's hand. "Get some sleep. I'll wake you in a few hours so we can move on."

"Sure." His heart sank with each thought of Zelle. The image of her beautiful face and purple eyes was burned into his mind. "You go on. I'll just wait here."

Dax sighed. "You can be a pain in the ass all you want. We're still going to take care of you." Out of the corner of his vision Flint watched Dax's shadow move past the bright fire-light and disappear.

Flint stared into the dusty dull gray of his new life. Memories of Zelle's beautiful eyes, his only companion.

. . .

153

Hours later Dax shook him awake. He opened his eyes praying he could see again. But the shadows that had taken up residence still remained.

"Someone was in the woods last night and I had to chase them off. The sooner we move on, the better." He placed something in Flint's lap. "Here. It's bread, fruit, and cheese. Water is on your right."

Flint wished for the first time in days that he had more than water to drink. Mead, perhaps, or something stronger would be nice. Suddenly the desire to get drunk and pass out washed every other thought from his mind.

"Thank you, Zelle." He raised his voice, not knowing where she was.

"She's not here," Dax said.

Flint's brows furrowed and he directed his vacant gaze at Dax. "Where is she?"

"She took a walk to the stream to clean up." He hunkered down in front of Flint. "Look, I shouldn't be telling you this. It's not my place, but you need to know something."

"What?"

"Zelle was kidnapped by Rasmuss and held in that tower. She isn't his daughter."

Fiery rage burned through Flint and he clenched his fists. "I'm gonna kill him."

"Yeah, well that can wait. For now we need to get her to safety. She needs help. Help we can't give her."

"Where's she from? We can take her there."

"It's not that simple."

"Then explain it."

There was silence for a moment. "I think it would be better if you hear the story from her. But in the meantime, the only place I think she might find what she needs is in Tanah—"

"No." He couldn't even bear to hear the name of the place.

"Flint—"

"I won't have her going there. That's the last place in Fairelle I would take a tender soul."

"There are things you don't know. Things I think it would be best if Sage—"

"I said no!" Flint stared in Dax's direction. He didn't need to see Dax's face to know the look on it. The exasperation. His jaw clenching right along with his fists as he bit back words he really wanted to say. Flint had seen that look on Dax's face a hundred times in the past half year.

Footsteps crunched away from where he sat.

"Dax—"

"Stop!" Dax's rushed footsteps pounded back. "You have no idea what is going on right now. I know you are scared and I know you don't want your family to see you like this, but there are things bigger than you at stake. And the truth is, Zelle needs you more than ever, but you did something to push her away. You're such a selfish bastard and you don't even know it. All you ever think of is yourself. Your pain, your loss. You never think of anyone else. Do you know what I would give to know who I am and what I wouldn't do to be near my family if I had one? You have no clue what it means to really lose your loved ones, Flint. Sure you've lost people, but Snow and your brothers are still alive and they want you to be in their lives. Me? I have nothing. Not even a memory of those I lost. So just shut your mouth, eat your food, and do what you're told. And if you don't like where we go, then feel free to take off like you always do. But until then, you're no longer in charge. I am."

Dax's words stung, mostly because they were the truth. The truth he'd kept deep inside. The truth he'd never wanted to face. The truth of his life. For all that he claimed to do for his family, he hadn't thought about how the deaths of Snow or Kellan or Mother and Father had affected anyone else.

There was silence for a long time and then Dax's joints cracked as he stood. "We need to keep going."

Dax walked away again, swearing under his breath. Flint didn't move for several minutes. He listened to the sounds of the forest and categorized memories in his mind. The crinkle of his mother's eyes when she smiled. The color of Snow's dress. The sheen of his horse's coat when they came home from battle. All sights he would never see again. He tried to find them. All the memories he wanted to keep, he filed them all away for future nights of loneliness.

Finally, he ate his food. When he finished he hung his head in his hands and stared into nothingness.

Flint awoke to the sounds of voices.

"Time to go." Dax moved around and Flint heard the rustling of the satchel and clothing.

"Dax, I'm sorry."

"You don't need to apologize to me." There was a sizzle as something wet hit the coals of the fire. Steam washed Flint's face.

He wanted to say something to make it better between them. "Cinder said for you to come see her when we finished here."

"What?"

"When I saw her last. She said you held a powerful magick and she wanted to help you."

Dax was silent for a minute. "Let's get you and Zelle to safety and talk about that after."

Flint nodded.

"Food's packed," Zelle said.

"Morning, Zelle." Flint forced a smile.

There was no response.

Her soft footsteps came close and he shot his hand out, catching her slender wrist. A hiss escaped her lips and she pulled away.

Flint swallowed. "Zelle. I'm sorry. I didn't mean to hurt your feelings yesterday."

"You didn't."

A shudder traveled through him. The edge in her voice sliced through him like his slayer's sword. He took a deep breath. Her scent of lilacs and fruit had deepened. A musky undertone aroused his senses.

He cleared his throat. "Well, whatever I did, I'm sorry. I was only trying to protect you."

"I don't need your protection, but I thank you for your kindness." Her footsteps moved away from him. "I'll awaken Loca, and then I'll be ready, Dax."

"Good."

A chill ran through Flint. Something had happened between Dax and Zelle. Jealousy stuck in his chest and clung to his bones. Flint swallowed it down and forced himself to keep a level head.

Dax was too honorable to have touched her, but if they were getting closer, that was a good thing. She deserved someone like Dax. Even though he didn't have his memory, it didn't take a genius to see that Dax was a man of both means and propriety. He could give Zelle what she deserved. Love and protection.

157

The thought made his stomach sour. Dax was right; he was selfish. Even in his present state he still wanted her for himself.

ZELLE WALKED TO THE HIGH TREE THAT SHE'D SEEN LOCA perch in the night before. Her body and mind fought for control. She wanted to go to Flint and help him, but she also wanted to punch him in the nose for the way he'd been acting. She couldn't imagine what he was going through, but she knew what it was to no longer be the person you thought you were. Everything inside her was so mixed up. The Zelle that Rasmuss had made her into was not the woman she'd been for centuries. She wasn't meek and timid. She was strong, the strongest woman in her realm. Royal, cherished and feared.

Trained to protect herself, she held powers that even she hadn't fully explored. The same magick that Rasmuss had been draining from her for the past fifty years. Anger narrowed her gaze and she clenched her fists.

"Loca," she called, spotting the bird. He ruffled his feathers, but didn't come down. She tempered her anger, cleared her throat and tried again, assuming the same soft voice Rasmuss had given her. "Loca." She forced herself to smile and held out her arm for the bird. He shifted his weight and looked down at her. "Loca, come," she said as sweetly as possible. The affection she felt for the animal was as real as anything she'd felt before. That was something Rasmuss' treachery would not rob her of.

He fluttered down on her arm and stared at her. She didn't move him to her shoulder, but walked with her hand outstretched. She stopped near Flint who looked beaten and sad. Zelle swallowed her sympathy forcing herself to be strong.

He was a strong man. One of the strongest she'd met. All of her babying would do him no good. In the end he would resent her for it. It was possible for them to make a life together, but only if he allowed her in and asked for help without feeling weak for doing it.

As if hearing her thoughts he looked up, his eyes black as ever. Guilt swept over her at the sight of his handsome face. Scarred and forever sightless. It was her fault he was blind. He'd been trying to help her. The sight was made worse by the knowledge that she couldn't heal him.

"Call Loca," she said.

"What?"

"Call Loca. I can't leave him and he doesn't trust me right now."

"Why wouldn't he trust you?" Flint's brows knit together.

"Just call him. He'll come to you."

"Loca." The bird propelled himself off and landed on Flint's shoulder. Moving in close he nipped Flint's ear and then settled down and closed his eyes.

"What's going on?" Flint asked.

Zelle swallowed down the pain of seeing her beloved pet trust someone else. How could she tell him the truth? That she was a kidnapped daemon? He was a vampire hunter. And with the way he felt about his own sister and Sage, who knew what he'd feel for her.

After they took him to his family and he was safe, then she'd tell him. If she told him now he might refuse to go with them. And she couldn't be responsible for his death. As selfish as it was, she wasn't willing to risk her own either. When they reached safety, she'd try to find a way to contact Khazidhe. He'd know what to do.

CHAPTER SIXTEEN

O nce again Flint's vampire slayer healing abilities came through for him. Out in the sun the shadows and light had better contrast. He could make out Dax's form moving around, though he couldn't see any details. Like a charcoal drawing, everything registered in shades of black, gray, and white. He wanted to keep exercising his eyes, hoping that it would force his sight to come back, but the light seared through them, and caused a pounding in his head. He pulled up the hood on his cloak, and covered his face.

"Ready?" Zelle touched his hand, startling him. Loca hooted softly in his ear.

"I'll walk in front of you so you can step where I step. It'll be easiest that way." She placed his palm on her shoulder.

"I'll walk beside you, in case there are any branches or anything else," said Dax.

"Thank you." He didn't know what else to say. His fingers skimmed the velvety fabric of her cloak. She laid her hand atop his and moved forward. He followed, stumbling at first but after several minutes they fell into a rhythm and she released his hand. He continued to hang onto her, not wanting to lose contact for reasons that had nothing to do with tripping or falling.

"Where are we going?" he asked.

"North," Dax replied. "Zelle, let me know if you tire and I'll guide Flint."

"I will."

Flint's pride took a jab, like a naughty child being led along by his parents. He should be the one out front making sure they were all safe, not Zelle. Dax was capable enough, but if they were attacked, he wouldn't be able to protect all three of them. Fear skittered over Flint again and then a feeling he was all too familiar with. Shame. He didn't like it, but what choice did he have? He wasn't in charge.

AFTER SEVERAL HOURS WEARINESS FATIGUED FLINT'S LIMBS AND sucked him down towards the ground, so they rested.

"How long is the travel?" asked Zelle.

"A couple of days. We'll stop tonight at an inn near Ville DeFee."

"Those are the fae lands right?"

"Yes," replied Dax. "Then we'll continue on. To Westfall."

Trepidation filled Flint at the thought of going home. Would his brothers welcome him? They'd likely hire someone to take care of him, but he wouldn't allow that. He'd do it himself, of that he was determined.

"The wood is more beautiful than I had imagined," Zelle said. "The colors are brighter than I expected. It makes me miss home."

"Don't worry," Dax said. "We'll get you there."

Confusion swarmed him. "Where is your home?"

There was a long silence and he thought she might not answer him.

"I lived somewhere else before the tower."

Joy for Zelle swept over him. "I didn't know that. Does that mean you remember?"

"Yes. We should move." The leaves rustled as Zelle got to her feet. Flint looked up at her and watched her fuzzy dark form move away.

So many questions flooded his mind. He opened his mouth to ask.

"We should, if we intend on making the inn by night fall," said Dax.

Shut out again. Flint sighed.

He stuffed the rest of his food into his mouth and stood. The thought of being at an inn tonight strengthened him. The fruits and breads that Zelle ate were fine, but he needed meat and potatoes to fill his belly, and if they made the inn, he would have it.

Flint knew the sun was setting by the chill in the air and the long shadows that streaked the world in darkness. Loca took off every once in a while to stretch his wings, and then return minutes later to Flint's shoulder.

They walked out of the cocoon of the forest and onto a clear space with a fine dirt road. The smells of civilization hit Flint. Scents he'd never noticed before surrounded him. In the forest it had smelled of damp wood, leaves, and moss. Out on the road he caught the stench of sweat, dirt, vegetation, and dung.

He gripped Zelle's shoulder though he no longer needed

to. The flat, compacted road was worn down from years of traveling horses and wagons. Only the occasional rock hit Flint's boot. And though they were small, it jarred him every time. Every touch seemed heightened now that he couldn't see. Every smell stronger. Every sound crisper.

"See those lights," Dax said. "That's where we're headed."

"Good. My feet are not accustomed to this terrain."

"Aren't you wearing shoes?" asked Flint.

"I have none. I never needed them before."

How could anyone have walked that far with no shoes?

"I can give you mine. They'll be big–"

"No thank you. I'm fine."

He wanted to insist, but he had no right. The feel of the grass, leaves, sticks all of it had to be so new for her. Just as he had to relearn everything without sight, she was seeing many things for the first time.

His heart longed to have her share with him what she felt and saw. To see the wonder and joy in her face as she discovered Fairelle.

Very little had been said about anything since they'd left the tower, he realized. She had remarked on few things during their journey but not many. Even to him, though he'd traveled all over, he discovered new things all the time. New trees, flowers, buildings, patterns in the sky, the clothing people wore. It all varied from place to place. Yet, she'd not mentioned any of those things. Flint found that odd. She'd said she'd been kidnapped. But maybe she already knew Fairelle. If she'd remembered where she was from, perhaps she had been accustomed to seeing new things where she was from.

The smell of a cooking fire made Flint's stomach rumble. He licked his lips. Soon they would eat real food and he would sleep in a bed.

THEY REACHED THE INN FIFTEEN MINUTES LATER. DAX ENTERED first, with Zelle next. She kept her hood down, so no one could see her face. Flint walked behind her, his hand still on her shoulder.

The sounds of riotous laughter and chatter mingled with the scent of body odor, meat and cheap perfume. She glanced at the bodies pressed into the large room. Men slapped shoulders and spilled alcohol. Women with large breasts spilling out of their dresses brought food and drink or sat on the laps of the drunk men. Zelle was both disgusted and aroused at the sight of such blatant sexuality. She would need to be vigilant, that she didn't lose control of her desires.

"Evening, Dax," said a large man with deep brown skin and black hair.

Zelle took him in. He was powerfully built like Dax and Flint, his dark muscles showed beneath his unlaced tunic. His breeches covered solidly built legs and his left arm sported a tattoo of some sort.

"Bryant." Dax inclined his head. "We need lodging for the night. One room."

"Two rooms," Zelle said.

Bryant's gaze traveled to her face and he smiled. "Well, well, well, what have we here?" He stepped closer.

Flint's grip tightened on her shoulder.

"And what, lovely creature, is your name?" Bryant lifted her hand and kissed it.

"Rapunzelle," she replied. "But you may call me Zelle." A husky tone emanated in her voice. She needed to be careful.

"Zelle. What an exotic name for such an exotic creature," he smiled again. "Might I offer you something to eat?"

"We'll eat in our rooms." Flint raised his head slightly.

Bryant's gaze went to Flint and his smile faltered. "Lord Flint. I'm sorry. Of course, if you prefer to eat in your rooms I can have something brought up."

"I do prefer it," said Flint.

"I would prefer to eat down here," Zelle said. It was dangerous to be out amongst so many humans in this type of environment, but she couldn't help but want to stay a bit longer. It had been years since she'd been in the company of so many people. And Bryant's aura told her that he was trustworthy.

"Zelle." Flint's voice was low. "It has been a long day. I think it would be better if we all ate in our rooms and got to bed. We have a long journey tomorrow."

Zelle picked up Flint's hand and held it for a minute. The feel of his fingers entwined with hers made her skin tingle. She searched his tired and now scarred face. She wanted to take him in her arms and tell him how much she cared but he'd made it clear the night before that he didn't want her in that way. He wanted to help her. Find her safety. But that safe place would not be at his side.

She placed Flint's hand on Dax's shoulder.

"You and Dax head up. I'll remain down here with Bryant for an hour or so. I'm positive he'll make sure nothing happens to me, won't you, Bryant?" She walked to Bryant's side and beamed up at him. The sweet musky scent of desire wafted off of him.

"I swear with my life," he said sincerely.

"Zelle, please–"

"Good night, Flint." She refused to look at his downcast eyes. He tried to hide the fact that he couldn't see and it pulled at her heart. "I'll say good night when I come up."

"I think I might join you for that meal as well," said Dax.

"Feel free to," replied Bryant. "You are welcome to as well, Lord Flint. If you care to join us."

"I don't." His voice had turned cold as the stone of her tower.

She had the feeling that though she couldn't see past his hood, he was staring directly at her.

"Then I'll send up Leah with your food in a few minutes. I know she's a favorite of yours," said Bryant.

Zelle stiffened at the insinuation. The thought of Flint with another woman made her want to explode like the night before. She had no right to feel that way, but it didn't stop her gut from clenching and her having to bite the inside of her cheek.

"Have her bring several bottles of ale as well."

"Of course."

Dax led Flint across the crowded room and up the stairs. Suddenly, at the loss of contact, all she wanted to do was run into his arms. She was being childish and proud. Flint had helped her and even though he may not want her the way she wanted him, he didn't deserve to be so readily dismissed.

"Your dinner, my lady." Bryant smiled down at her.

She paused and watched Dax and Flint round the stairs and move out of sight. Finally, she returned Bryant's smile and allowed him to lead her to a small table in the only section that wasn't crowded.

ZELLE HAD SAMPLED THE BEEF, PORK, AND LAMB. POTATOES, coatage, sweet plen, and sugarbread. She'd had a glass of mead, and the fuzziness in her head made her laugh a bit too much at Bryant's jokes. Dax was also enjoying himself. His eyes crinkled in the corners when he smiled and his booming laughter infected them all. But for all the new experiences and delightful company, through the entire meal she found her gaze wandering to the staircase and her thoughts drifting to Flint, who was not alone in his room.

When she could stand it no longer, she excused herself from the men's company, claiming the tiring walk. Bryant's face drooped at the prospect of letting her go, but he graciously kissed her hand and allowed her to leave.

Dax caught up with her at the bottom of the stairs. "Flint wants me to stay with you tonight, if that's all right."

"Why? I can protect myself."

Dax bit his lip and refused to meet her eye. "That's not it."

Zelle stared at him for a moment as he ran his hand over his head.

"He's not alone," she finally said.

"No."

"The whore, Leah."

Dax nodded.

Anger boiled inside her to the point that she dug her nails into the railing scarring it. "Very well."

"Our room is the second one in the hallway. Flint's is the first."

Zelle nodded. "I bid you good night."

"I'll be up soon. I need to speak to Bryant about something first."

"Take all the time you need." Her vision wobbled as she took the stairs slowly, anger burning brighter with each step. She hit the landing and paused. There were eight doors all together. She came to the first door and stopped. A giggle sounded. Zelle turned to go, her heart breaking with the knowledge of what was happening inside.

"Oh, Flint," a woman moaned.

Zelle's anger burst and she threw open the door without even touching the surface. Flint had a woman pressed against the wall, facing away from him, her dress hiked up to her hips. He was fumbling with getting his belt off.

Zelle rushed forward and yanked him away.

The stench of alcohol clouded him.

"Hey!" the woman cried. "What do you think you're doing, missy?"

"Get out," Zelle said.

"Zelle, stop."

Zelle slapped Flint, rocking his head to the side. "Do not speak to me, *Xihuli*."

He stumbled and landed hard on the small bed.

"You can't treat Flint like that."

Zelle rounded on the bar wench. Her large breasts jostled under her low-cut chemise. "Get out, or prepare to fight for your life, little girl."

Leah wagged a finger in Zelle's face. "I don't know who you think you are, but this is my sale."

Zelle grabbed Leah's finger and bent it backward until it cracked. The woman dropped to her knees and cried out.

"Sale? Woman, do you think I need money to make a man desire me? You have no idea who you're speaking to."

Tears swelled in Leah's eyes.

"Zelle, stop this." Flint rose.

She turned in time to see him reach for her, but she stepped out of the way, releasing Leah. Her anger swirled around her in a bright magenta mist.

Leah climbed to her feet, grabbed Zelle from behind, and pressed a knife to her throat. "This is my business and I would leave before you get hurt. *Little girl*."

"Leah," Flint warned. "Don't touch her."

His face had gone hard. Even through his sightless, drunken haze, he was ready to protect her. Zelle elbowed Leah in the stomach. The woman dropped her knife and doubled over.

"Zelle! Are you all right?" Flint took a step forward.

She grabbed Leah by the throat, pressing her against the wall. Leah clawed at Zelle's arms as Zelle squeezed her airway shut. It surprised Zelle how weak human women were. So fragile. So easily broken.

Leah stared in terror. Within seconds her eyes glazed over and Zelle moved close.

"Zelle, what's happening?" Panic etched Flint's voice as he swung his arms wildly.

Zelle moved her mouth to within inches of the other woman's and breathed in. Leah's eyes widened and she exhaled. A crackling sound emanated as white essence floated out of her. Zelle breathed in again, as more essence snaked out of Leah's mouth. Zelle's head buzzed harder than before. The third time she breathed in, a choking gurgle sound tore from Leah's throat.

"Zelle!" Flint shuffled forward. "Zelle, where are you?" His hands collided with her spine. He gripped her cloak and yanked. She broke eye contact with Leah.

Leah shook her head and coughed several times. Flint wrapped his arms around Zelle's waist and he lifted her off the ground.

"Let go of me," Zelle yelled.

Tears leaked from Leah's eyes and she raced from the room gasping and choking.

"No," Flint retorted.

"Because you want to screw her?"

Flint's grip slacked and she twisted to face him. His shoulders slumped and he swayed where he stood. Loca floated in through the open window and landed on a dresser.

"No. Not because I want to screw her."

"You will screw a whore for money, but not me? Why?"

"No, I won't screw you," Flint said. "It isn't like that."

"It isn't? Or maybe I was just in the wrong position." Zelle grabbed Flint by the arm and tugged him to her. She stepped up to the wall, twisted to face the smooth ashen wood and pulled him in close behind her. "This. This is how you like it, yes?"

"No." Flint backed away. "No, that isn't how I like it."

"But that's how you had her. Pinned against the wall. And before in the aviary, it wasn't like that. I can give it to you in that position if you want. I've never tried that one."

"Stop, Zelle."

"Tell me, why not me? Are my breasts too small?"

"What? No."

She stepped up to him, pressing her body into his as he backed away.

"Am I not as pretty as she?"

"No. I mean, yes. I mean. No! You're much more beautiful." He continued to back away.

Her jealousy knew no bounds. It wasn't part of her nature to be denied. She was made for love, for lust, for sex. She fed off it, ate it up. It was who she was. The fact that the man she wanted was able to resist, her enraged her beyond belief. With Rasmuss' spell broken and the cuff gone, there should be nothing keeping Flint from wanting her.

She shoved him backward until he fell on the bed. He laid there, his dark eyes wide with confusion.

She should let it go. Just let him be. But she couldn't.

Something inside her wanted him to be hers. She flicked her fingers at the door and it shut at her command.

Climbing on top of him, she straddled his hips, grinding into him. He grabbed onto her waist and moaned. His arousal was more than apparent.

She leaned down and breathed in the scent of his neck. The desire he let off made her body ache to be touched.

"Why?" she whispered in his ear. "Why do you want the whore pinned against the wall so she can't see you, and not me?" Her lips lingered over his skin, the craving to taste him filled her mouth made the mist swirl brighter.

"I do want you," he said. "I want you more than anything. But I can't."

"Why not?"

"Because I'd ruin you and you deserve better."

She stopped moving.

"I have sex with whores against the wall so they don't look at me. So they don't see me and I don't see them. With them all I have to give is a few coins. But with you, all I see is you. And all you see is me. With you… I'll pay with my heart."

Her breath caught and arousal lit a wildfire in her stomach. Anticipation skittered over her skin and her thighs heated.

She turned his face toward her. His sightless eyes were pained and his body taut beneath her. His hands skimmed under her cloak. She rocked her hips against his, grinding into him through their clothes. He moaned and grabbed onto her hips through her dress.

She leaned in and placed her lips to his, still rubbing against him. "All I want… is you."

She kissed him tenderly skimming her tongue over his bottom lip and then sucking it into her mouth.

He wrapped his arms around her and crushed her to him.

Her lips burned as his pressed hard against them. Her tongue plunged deep into his mouth. She threw her cloak to the floor without losing contact and then trailed her hands under his shirt, jerked it over his head, and tossed it aside. He sat up and kissed her breasts through her dress, his lips finding her sensitive peaks and making them wind tight with desire. He skimmed his hand under her dress and lifted it over her head. He kissed over her breasts tasting them in turn and making them harden with desire. She raked her fingers through his curls and pulled his mouth to hers again.

"Flint." Surrounded by mist she needed release. "Flint, make love to me," she moaned.

He flipped her on her back and this time he settled between her thighs. He pushed his breeches down to his ankles, and ran his hands up her legs.

"Where are your bloomers?"

"I don't wear them," she said breathless. She ran her palm down his cheek and then down to his scars. She remembered each one in turn from having felt them before. Finally she traced her fingers over his arm where it had been healed. The mist thickened around her. So strong.

Their mouths met once more, his hard slick chest covering hers. His thick soft chest hair delighted her sensitive skin and he bent in and spread her thighs with his own. He rested his hips on hers, then broke their kiss and looked at her with his sightless eyes.

"Are you sure?" His voice came out seductively husky and soft.

"Make me yours."

She gasped as he slowly joined their bodies. She moaned as he filled her completely. He blew out a long slow breath and then kissed down her throat. They lay joined for a moment as he licked his way down to her breasts and the beating rhythm of him inside her pleasuring her in ways she had forgotten were possible.

She rocked her body with his, until the bed shook. She licked his neck and scars. Her warrior. The mist built with every thrust of his hips. She grabbed onto his shoulders, her nails digging into his flesh. Her mist, a dark sexy hue of magenta grew thicker and thicker around their joined bodies, encompassing them in a cloud of unbidden desire.

He kissed her again and rocked deeper. Yearning wound tight inside her as she pushed closer to the edge. His breathing quickened with his pace as waves of ecstasy overtook her. He stared at her, unseeing, and his muscles bunched before he roared her name. She refused to look away as her body exploded.

White light burst in a shower of sparks around them. She panted, the euphoric feeling overtaking her. The greatest sense of release settled over her, bringing with it a bone numbing peace. Her body quaked as Flint kissed up her throat and across her chin to her lips. Their mouths met in a warm blending. Soft and gentle. She pulled him close and ran her fingers down his sides, until he chuckled.

"I love you," he whispered.

Zelle stopped moving, her smile faded. "What?"

"I love you," he said again.

She swallowed hard as realization of what they'd done cleared her head like a strong wind. Yesterday she would have given anything to hear those words from him. But today... Today was different. Today she was someone else. Someone she hadn't told him about.

"Flint... There's something I have to tell you. Something about myself."

"I don't care," he said. "I don't care about your past. Or who you were. I just care about here, and now. And our future. I never thought I would love someone. And I know we haven't known each other long, but when I'm with you I feel things that I've never dreamed I would. I love you, Zelle."

She closed her eyes. All she had ever wanted in her life was someone of her own, to love and be loved. A male who loved her for her and not for what she was. But this man, the one she had opened her heart to, was the one man who was bound to turn away from her when he found out the truth. It was going to end badly for both of them, she realized. And them having sex wasn't going to be enough to keep him at her side when she told him the truth.

Her heart skipped a beat, but then she kissed him.

For today she could feel this, be this, own this. For that night, she could be just Zelle, the girl in the tower. And he could be Flint, the lone traveler who had saved her.

She caressed his cheek and her chest squeezed. "I love you, too."

CHAPTER SEVENTEEN

Flint woke the next morning with Zelle wrapped in his arms. After they'd made love, they'd held each other, with him stroking her arm and her swirling her fingers over his scars, until the drink had overtaken him and he'd passed out.

He lay for a long time, listening to the sound of her breathing. Her leg wrapped over his, her hair fanned out across his chest. He visualized the color of her eyes, the shimmer of her hair, the light blush of her cheek.

In a vain attempt to forget about Zelle and what she meant to him, he'd allowed Leah to stay after she'd brought him food. After finishing the first bottle of liquor, he'd thought of nothing but Zelle. Even while having Leah pressed against the wall he'd visualized Zelle's face, but it had done no good. Zelle had smelled different, felt different, spoken different. Honestly, if Zelle hadn't burst in when she had, he would have sent Leah out anyway. It had taken him less than a minute to realize that he'd never again be able to have sex with a woman without wishing she was Zelle.

Whatever Zelle had attempted to do to Leah the night before, he was certain it was the same thing she had done to the dead man in her tower. But he was afraid to ask. Afraid that knowing would ruin what they had.

He brushed his knuckles across her cheek and up her neck over her ear. He ran his fingers over the edge of it and swallowed hard. It was longer and pointier than it should be. How had he not noticed before that they were so long?

"Mmmm… Flint." She rubbed his chest and kissed his arm.

"Morning." He swallowed the lump that threatened to choke him.

She kissed his chin. "You need to shave again."

"I probably do." He extricated his arm from under her head. "Do you know what time it is?"

She sat up. He hated being an invalid. He couldn't even tell time anymore.

"The clock says it's about eight."

"We should probably find Dax and get going." He threw his legs over the edge of the bed and his feet hit the cool wooden floorboards. There was a rustling of fabric and then light flooded his face. He winced as pain shot through his head. A dark form moved across the room.

"Does the light hurt?"

"A little." He rubbed his eyes. The skin beneath his fingertips was pebbled and sensitive to the touch.

"Mayhaps some dark glasses might help."

"Perhaps." He nodded. Gerall employed a glassmaker. He supposed he should find out who the man was. "Do you know where my clothes are?"

"Here. Let me help you."

She leaned over him, her fragrance spiking his interest. His tunic pressed against the top of his head.

"I can get it," he said too harshly. He swallowed and tugged the tunic down.

"Maybe you forgot who's in your bed this morning. I'm not the whore."

He bit his cheek.

"Believe me, I'm well aware of who you aren't. I'm just not sure I know who you *are*."

"I beg your pardon?"

Why was he always putting his foot in his mouth? "Nothing. I'm sorry. I had too much to drink last night. It makes me grumpy."

"No. Go ahead and say it. I came in here last night and attacked your female friend and now you... what? Think I'm a murderer?"

"No that's not it. I don't think that."

"But you think I'm different. Or maybe you're regretting having made love to me, or telling me you love me."

Flint cursed under his breath. Leave it to Zelle to always say what she thinks. "No—"

"It's all right. Mayhaps we are both regretting it this morning."

Her words were a slap to the face. Her shadow moved away. He reached for her but missed. "Zelle—"

"I'll return to my room to dress and send Dax over to get you some food."

"Zelle, wait." Flint stumbled to his feet and tried to get to the door, but hit the end of the bed with his knee. He grabbed it, hopping on one foot. "Dammit!"

The door closed with a bang and Loca squawked. Flint fell

on the bed, grabbing his leg and massaging his knee. Why couldn't he have just let her help? What did it matter that her ears were different or that she had a jealous streak? Hell, he'd never had a woman fight for him before and, frankly, it was the nicest thing anyone had ever done for him.

She'd been kidnapped. Something had obviously happened to her. It changed her somehow. That had to be it. The mage Rasmuss had done something to Zelle while she was in the tower.

Flint rubbed his knee. If it was the last thing he did, he was going to make Rasmuss pay for what he'd done to Zelle.

"I AM NOT SITTING IN THE BACK OF THAT," FLINT GRUMBLED. Loca's claws dug into his shoulder. The bird tugged his ear before ruffling its feathers and settling down again. The first day of having Loca so close had been strange, now it was just irritating.

"You have no choice," said Dax. "We need to move fast and this was all Bryant could get."

"Fine." Exasperation dripped from Zelle's voice. "I'll sit in the bed of the wagon. You sit in the front with Dax."

"Zelle, that's not what I meant."

"If it's the only way to get you to get in the stupid wagon then I'll do it."

There was a groan and creak from the springs of the wagon as Zelle propelled herself into it.

"Would you care to drive too?" Dax asked.

"Very funny."

"Well, you seem to have forgotten who's in charge, so I just figured you might want to do the driving."

Flint grumbled. He walked forward, arms out, until he hit

the back of the wagon. He pulled himself up, until a firm hand hit his chest and pushed him off. Loca screeched as he stumbled backward, but caught his balance.

"Oh, no. You made such a big deal about not sitting here. You don't get to change your mind now," Zelle said. "Dax, take him up front with you, please."

Flint sighed. She was mad again. Her mood fluctuations were going to take some getting used to. "Zelle, I'm sorry I'm being so pigheaded."

"Yes, you are, which is why I prefer to sit by myself. Dax, if you would, please take Lord Flint up front."

Flint stiffened. She hadn't been so formal with him, ever. And her referring to him as Lord kicked him right in the stones. He wasn't the Lord of anything. His father was. Erik was. Not him.

"Come on." Dax grabbed Flint by the arm.

Flint allowed himself to be led to the front of the wagon. Loca hooted just as he tripped over a branch.

"Sorry. Forgot." Dax helped hoist him into the seat.

"Right."

He grabbed the railing, panic settling over him at the feeling of being so high off the ground and unable to grasp anything but the small wooden bar on the side of the wagon. Loca pitched sideways and fluttered off his shoulder momentarily. Flint suddenly wanted nothing more than to be sitting in the wagon bed, but his pride prevented him from begging Zelle to allow him. Once settled, Loca returned to his shoulder, and Flint tugged the hood over his head.

The seat wobbled as Dax hefted himself up and Flint grasped the side and back of the seat as much as he was able.

"Ready then?" Bryant's voice came from Flint's left, near Dax.

"Yes. And thank you again for the wagon," Dax said.

"Don't mention it. I would do anything to help Miss Zelle."

Flint's chest tightened.

"Do come and visit me again. I would be most happy to take you out to a proper dinner next time."

"I would enjoy that very much." Zelle's voice was soft and seductive. It sent a chill up Flint's spine.

"Let's get moving," he said roughly.

"Good bye to you as well, Lord Flint," said Bryant.

Flint nodded but kept his head down. He'd had quite enough of Bryant and the inn for the time being. Dax slapped the horses with the reigns and they lurched forward. Flint held tight, trying to keep his bearings.

FROM THE VANTAGE POINT OF A WINDOW IN THE INN, KLAUS watched as Flint Gwyn, the female, and the large fair-haired man pulled away from the entrance. The woman sat in the bed of the wagon, her head bowed low. Flint assumed the same posture in the front, with an owl sleeping on his shoulder. Something was wrong with the picture, but Klaus couldn't put his finger on what it was.

"See, boss," said Paul. "I told you I saw them. It's her, isn't it? The one who killed Craigen."

It was her.

The night before he'd been approached at his hideout by Rasmuss. He'd informed Klaus of Flint taking his daughter. He'd described the girl and told Klaus to get her back at any price. Due to the venom spewing from Rasmuss, Klaus had failed to mention the fact that he'd seen the girl in her tower several times. But there could be no mistaking the girl's description. Flowing silvery hair, pale skin, purple eyes. In that moment Klaus had been grateful he'd not been able to get into the tower. He didn't want to be the one on the other side of Rasmuss's wrath.

Klaus hadn't had dealings with Rasmuss since Sage had killed Terona and taken the throne of Tanah Darah. He didn't know Rasmuss well, but he did know one thing; Rasmuss had money and lots of it. Hordes of it. Mountains of stolen gems and jewels and gold at his disposal. And Klaus wanted it. Needed it. Because of that, he didn't bother to ask why Rasmuss wasn't going after the girl himself.

"Should we follow them?" Paul asked.

"We'll wait. They're heading north. They'll be easy to track."

"But if he makes it home we'll have his brothers to deal with," said Shamus.

"They won't make it that far." Klaus watched the wagon plod out of sight.

"Are you sure you still want to do this?"

Klaus turned his gaze on Paul. For all of Paul's muscle, he had no brains. "I'm sure we need Morgana's influence and money. And I'm sure that I don't want to turn down Rasmuss either."

"I'd rather turn him down than fail him."

Klaus looked at him hard. "Then we'll just have to not fail."

ZELLE KEPT HER HEAD DOWN AND HER MOUTH SHUT. SHE wasn't sure how everything had gone so wrong so quickly that morning. Over the past day her memories had returned, and so apparently had her temper. She'd never cared before because her temper had always been useful and gotten her what she wanted. But now who she was and who she'd been for the last fifty years collided in a jumble of emotions that left her dizzy.

Daemon males were not as fragile as human males, not by half. Neither their egos nor their bodies broke with a sharp word or sword. It took more to upset a daemon male. Probably due to their harsh upbringings.

Even so, losing her temper with Flint gnawed at her, leaving a hollowness in her breast. He'd done nothing wrong, said nothing wrong, per se, but the tone of his voice had indicated he regretted what they'd done. There had only been one man before Flint and he'd enjoyed their time together immensely. Much more than she ever had.

They had been together only because her father, her real father, had decreed it, not because she loved him. Memories of her time in his arms, his bright orange hair and loving eyes, pushed into the forefront of her mind. She pulled her cloak tighter around her and tucked her feet under herself. She didn't want to think about him. For as much as he had adored her, she had not loved him. Their pairing had been by decree only, not by inscription of the heart. The complete opposite of how she felt for Flint.

She hadn't lied when she'd told Flint she loved him. She did. Which made what she had to do that much harder.

Zelle sighed and rubbed her forehead. She needed home. The essences and lusts here were too tempting. And the magick holding her more carnal self at bay was gone.

Khazidhæ's face etched into her mind. His tanned skin and bright, colorful eyes. His large, muscular build and deep booming voice. Her chin quivered. How she'd missed him. But worse was how she'd not even known she'd missed him until the last twenty-four hours. She wondered if he believed she was still alive. Had he looked for her? They weren't allowed to come to this plane unless called upon. Which begged the question, how had Rasmuss been able to kidnap her and transport her here?

The wagon bumped and Flint's hand landed on her shoulder, grabbing on to her.

"Sorry."

She reached for his hand, but he'd already pulled away.

On both sides of the road small huts dotted the sprouting grain fields. Men and women worked through the fields, tilling the ground or tending to the crops.

Her hips ached and she shifted her weight. It didn't help. She looked up at the sun high in the sky. It had to be close to noon.

"Can we stop soon for a break?"

"There's a place close by," said Dax.

"Are we near Marissa's?" asked Flint.

"Yeah."

Zelle's jealousy stampeded through her like a herd of horses at the sound of another woman's name on Flint's lips. She needed to stop. Jealousy was both childish and unbecoming a female of her status. Her father would have told her as much, forcing her to her rooms for a period of contemplation if he'd been there.

She continued to watch the grain sway in the breeze as they passed. A head stuck out in a spot, and then another as someone ran through the field parallel to the wagon.

"Did you see that?" Zelle asked.

"What?" Dax slowed the horses.

"Over there." She pointed.

"What's going on?" asked Flint.

"I don't know." Dax reined the horses to a stop and scanned the fields. "Someone's running through the field."

"Children?"

"Men."

A shiver raced through her as she made out three distinct figures tracking them.

Zelle's heart raced like rabbit. "Go. We need to go."

Dax slapped the reins. The horses took off and Dax slapped them again, urging them faster. Zelle looked for something to hold on to. The only thing she found was the front seat. She grasped the railing and Flint grabbed onto her at the same moment. Their fingers entwined as they lent each other meager support.

The men running through the field picked up speed.

Dax snapped the reins and the horse took off at a gallop. Zelle held her breath as they pulled further and further away from the men, leaving them behind.

CHAPTER EIGHTEEN

The wagon halted. Flint's senses were on high alert, but useless. If someone was chasing them, he could do nothing to protect Zelle. If she hadn't specifically asked for them to stop for a rest, he would have insisted that they keep moving without pausing, despite the intense pain to his back and hips from bumping around. But he hadn't wanted to do anything else to upset her. She held his hand for close to an hour, her fingers locked in his, giving him an inkling of hope of her forgiveness, but in the end she'd pulled away, leaving him only with his thoughts and regrets.

Dax hopped down from his side and the wagon seat bounced. Flint waited to be helped, when a spike of pride hit him without warning. He wasn't a babe. He could do it himself. Throwing his leg over the side he reached for the step on the side.

"Flint, wait for me." Dax's footsteps slapped through the dirt.

Flint felt for the step below him and put his weight on it. Grabbing the side, he stepped off and landed on the ground.

"Dammit, Flint!"

"You could've hurt yourself." Zelle came up beside him.

"I am no child."

"Then you should stop acting like one," Zelle retorted. She tugged him close and wrapped her hand around his arm.

"You don't need to do that."

"Have you been to this place so many times you know your way around here, too?"

Flint clenched his jaw. He was sure Zelle was referring to Bryant's inn– and Leah.

"Let's go." She propelled him forward.

Loca hooted and nipped his ear just before he hit a large rock with his foot.

"Careful." Zelle sounded unrepentant.

"Maybe you should just leave me with Loca."

She threw his arm down. "Maybe I will."

Inwardly Flint kicked himself as Zelle walked away. She'd been trying to help. Again. But he had to learn to do this stuff for himself. He couldn't keep relying on others for everything. He needed to learn to take care of himself. He might as well start now.

"You want help?" Dax asked.

"I can do it."

"If you say so." Dax's steps crunched away from him. Their voices floated back to him in hushed tones.

He tried to make out their words but couldn't. A bird cawed in the distance and a beehive buzzed off to his left. The wind whistled as it blew across his face. The space that surrounded him was open with nothing to block out the breeze.

He stepped forward and Loca nipped him, as his foot struck the rock again. He moved around it and after a few steps Flint realized he had no idea in which direction he was headed.

He visualized Marissa's house. A large stone gate, with a pond to the right, a garden to the left. If he walked through the gate, he would head up the path to the front door. Problem was, he had no idea where Dax had stopped the wagon. He could be walking toward the gate, straight toward the pond, or into the garden.

Flint blew out a breath and rubbed his face. He couldn't ask for help. Not after making such a fuss. Not that it mattered. He realized that he could no longer hear either Zelle or Dax. Were they even outside anymore or had they already gone in?

Loca nipped his ear.

"I know, I know," he grumbled. "Great. I'm speaking to an owl."

"But is the owl speaking back, is the question."

Flint looked up and breathed deep. The scent of rosewater filled him.

"Aunt Marissa."

Slender arms wrapped around his chest and pulled him in tight. "Hello, big man."

Flint allowed himself to be held before relaxing and wrapping his aunt into an embrace. She was tall and thin. Thinner than he remembered the last time he'd hugged her. Or maybe he'd just never noticed before. His mother's only sibling, Marissa had always been kind and a bit strange. A duchess, after the death of her husband, she had preferred a life of solitude.

She pushed away from him. "I hear you've gotten yourself in a spot of trouble."

"No more than usual."

She clucked her tongue. "Oh, Flint. Look what you've done to your lovely eyes." Her soft wrinkled hand touched his face.

Flint didn't want her pity, but the contact soothed his loneliness and reminded him of his mother.

"So, do you want to continue walking toward the pond? Or will you allow me to help you inside?"

Dammit. Taking a deep breath he said, "Help would be nice. Thank you," he added as an after thought.

She linked her arm into his and turned him to the left. "There's a small rock by your left foot. There's a large log to the right. If you reach out your right hand, you can feel the gate."

Marissa continued to call things out to him, telling him what to be wary of. The warmth of the sun changed as he passed under the arch for the gate. The shadows changed as well. Once he was inside, large trees darkened the area leaving him feeling more secure and less out in the open.

The smell of gingerbread and coffee wafted out the front door as they stepped up on the porch. Flint smiled at the smells he associated with his aunt. Loca leapt from his shoulder, most likely to the alcove above the door.

"I see he would let *you* help," said Zelle from up ahead.

Flint heard the clink of silver and knew that Dax and Zelle were already seated at the table.

"Watch out for my–" Marissa's voice broke off as Flint bumped into something and glass crashed to the ground. "Vase."

"Sorry."

"It's all right. It was a present from my mother-in-law. I never liked it anyway." She laughed.

If he was this way with Marissa, how would he be at home with his brothers? Bumping into things. Breaking his mother's china. Ruining her good linens. He didn't want them to see him like that. He didn't want anyone to see him like that.

"Let's get you something to eat. You seem to have almost wasted away since the last time you were here."

Marissa moved Flint through the front room to the dining area. He imagined the layout in his head as they shuffled across the floor. She planted him into a seat at the table and he hung his head.

"Here." She placed a fork in his hand. "Your cup is to the right, your napkin to the left. The plate holds–"

"I got it. Thank you," Flint said roughly.

"Don't you take that tone with me, young man. If you act uncivilized you can eat with the scullery maids."

Flint clenched and unclenched his jaw. Marissa had done nothing but be kind to him. Especially these last few months. Allowing him to stop by. Providing a room and food when he was tired of drifting. Never asking questions or prying. She had no reason to bear the brunt of his anger.

"I apologize, Aunt Marissa."

She leaned in close. The smell of rosewater filled his nose again and made him ache for his mother's comfort.

"I know, lovey." She kissed him on the top of his head. "Eat. Then we'll go for a walk in the garden before you leave."

"Thank you for your hospitality," Zelle said. "The food is delicious."

"You are most welcome, dear girl," Marissa replied. "I'm going to go check on a few things and I'll return soon."

Marissa's soft footsteps drifted toward the kitchen.

Flint stabbed his plate and hit nothing. He tried again, and again he his nothing. Moving the fork around he spilled things onto the table, cursed and threw down the fork. Reaching for his cup he knocked it over as well.

"Dammit." He tried to pick the cup up and knocked something else over. A chair scraped against the floor.

"Let me help you," Zelle said in a soft voice.

"I can manage."

"You might manage knocking over everything on the table, ruining the tablecloth and then getting a few small bites in your mouth, but honestly, why waste the effort?"

Her voice wasn't harsh or irritated. It held a sympathetic quality, but none of pity. And... she was right. Flint sighed. "Thank you."

The chair next to him slid out and Zelle's scent wafted towards him. His arousal grew at the nearness of her. The feel of her hand sliding into his lap with his napkin made his body tense and his arousal grow larger. He coughed. Her palm lingered on his thigh and then brushed away. Memories of the taste of her soft skin, the feel of her petite body underneath him as he'd buried himself inside her had his skin prickly and sensitive.

"Flint."

"What?" The memory burst at the sound of his name. A fork pressed to his lips. He opened his mouth and took a bite. His stomach growled as he chewed the pork roast.

"Here." Zelle took his hand from his lap and placed his fingers on the plate. "This is the roast, I'll cut it for you. Here are the potatoes, and the vegetables." She guided his hand forward and touched a basket on the other side of the plate. "These are rolls. And this is your cup." She ended by wrapping his fingers around the goblet. The slide of her velvety touch messed with his head and he couldn't remember a single thing she'd just told him.

He traced the cup with his fingers and then lifted it to his mouth. He missed, but rolled it to his lips. The sweet mead warmed him going down.

"Would you like me to continue?"

Absolutely. "I think I can manage. Thank you."

"I'll go see if I can help Marissa, and wash up, possibly."

Flint gingerly placed his cup on the table and reached for a piece of bread. He caught the rustle of her cloak as swished out of the room. He looked in the direction but in the dimly lit room, he could see nothing.

"You want to tell me what happened between you two last night?" asked Dax.

Flint swallowed hard, nearly choking on a piece of bread, and shrugged. "I don't know what you mean."

"Don't play coy. Leah came running down to Bryant crying and screaming about how Zelle tried to kill her."

Flint shook his head. "It was a misunderstanding."

"It didn't look that way. She had bruises on her throat and her coloring was close to ash. I had to give her money to calm her."

Flint nodded but said nothing. It explained why Bryant hadn't come banging on his door the night before. Bryant never allowed rough treatment of his girls.

"Zelle spent the night with you, I take it."

Flint stiffened but said nothing.

"Be careful with her Flint. She's not what you think she is." His voice carried a warning, but not malice. "Underneath that sweet face is an iron will and a dangerous creature."

"Dangerous how?"

"Don't get me wrong, Zelle is as good as they get. And as good as you will ever be lucky enough to receive. But she isn't

Leah. You can't just have your way with her and then drop her at the next village."

"I am well aware that she isn't Leah."

"Then heed my advice on this one, brother. Let her go." The pleading in Dax's voice made Flint's hair stand on end.

Zelle wasn't anything like the whores he'd been with. But it wasn't Zelle Dax should be worried about. Flint had opened his heart and body to her in a way he hadn't with any other woman. At this point, he was more worried about himself being hurt than her.

FLINT WALKED ARM IN ARM WITH MARISSA THROUGH HER fragrant garden. His senses were assaulted by the smell of roses, plumeria, phlaxel, and bitterburn. All of them mixed in his nostrils and reminded him of his mother's and grandmother's gardens. The memories of running through them with his brothers and sister when they were children filled him with an inexplicable ache.

"She seems a nice young woman," Marissa steered Flint to the left a bit.

"Who?"

Marissa chuckled. "You know who. The beautiful and exotic young Zelle."

"Oh. Yes."

"I saw the way she tended to you. And the way she tracked you when I brought you in. She was most distressed to watch you flounder by the pond."

"Um..." He had no idea what to say. So much had changed in the last two days. *She* had changed.

"You're scared," Marissa finished.

"Scared of what?" Flint's cloak snagged on a rose bush and Marissa had to untangle him.

"Of feeling for her."

"Why would I—"

"Oh, please." She steered him to the left again. "I know you, Flint Reagan Gwyn. You are just like your father. So scared to hurt and possibly ruin a beautiful young creature. He was the same way with your mother. All blubber-mouthed and goofy smiles. The way you would be if you weren't so angry at the world. I know you think you aren't a good person because of what your father made you do and what has happened to you, but you're wrong. And your father was wrong for having put that burden on your shoulders. How long has my sister been in the ground?"

Flint swallowed. "Twelve years."

"And your father?"

"Five."

"And for all that time you have taken upon you the responsibility of your family."

"Erik is the Lord of Westfall."

"But you are the lion at his door. You protect everyone. Why not give them a chance to protect themselves, and in the process find some peace and happiness for yourself? Why does it all have to be your responsibility?"

"Because I made a promise to my father."

"Yes. A promise you have fulfilled."

"Have I?"

Marissa sighed and stopped. Her shadow fell in front of him and she took his face in her hands. "You are not responsible for the deaths of your father and brother. You are not responsible for the choice Snow made. Gerall, Hass, Ian, Erik, Jamen, they need you. Not to protect them, they just need you.

193

It's time to let go of the past. Forget what your father made you. Maybe this new affliction will show you that. Perhaps it is a gift from the gods in disguise."

"It isn't a gift."

"Not now. But if you let it, it will be."

Flint didn't want to learn to find the gift in what Rasmuss had done to him. He wanted to find the bearer and kill him. This was not done by the gods. It was done by a man.

ZELLE AND DAX WALKED SEVERAL PACES BEHIND FLINT AND Marissa, allowing them space. She couldn't hear what they were saying, but they were deep in conversation. Dax pointed out every kind of flower, but her gaze was on Flint's form.

"Be careful," said Dax suddenly.

She looked over and caught his eye. "Of what?"

"Him." Dax gestured with his head.

Zelle shifted her cloak. "Why do you say that when he's your friend?"

"Because I care about him. And I care about you. Flint has things in his past that keep him from forming attachments. You're a nice girl who's been through a terrible ordeal. I don't want to see you get hurt anymore than you already have."

"Nice girl... mmmm..." If only he knew the things she had done. "I understand about his past. He's killed people. It's written all over him. But he isn't a bad person."

"No. He isn't. But he isn't normal, either. He's seen many things, done many things—"

"He's a warrior with a protector's heart. Those kind of men often struggle with the things they do to keep their families safe. I've seen that first hand." Zelle's mind traveled to Khazidhæ and her heart squeezed. She needed to see him.

"Just... be careful."

"I thank you for your concern, Dax. You are a true friend." A movement in the distance caught Zelle's eye. A person raced through the garden. Before she could make a sound, someone grabbed her from behind, and pressed a cold blade to her throat. She gasped at the feel of the metal on her skin.

"Hello, beautiful."

Dax spun around to a sword aimed at his chest. An inhuman growl escaped him. Her gaze traveled to Flint and Marissa. Marissa's eyes had gone wide. She spun away from Flint just as a man appeared with a weapon aimed at her as well, leaving Flint to stand alone.

"What's going on?" Flint called. Loca screeched and landed on Flint's shoulder.

"Well, well. Hello, Flint."

Flint's entire body tensed. "Klaus." He lowered his head, raised his hood to cover his face, and took a casual stance as Klaus approached.

"And how are we this fine day?" Klaus asked.

"Perfectly pleasant until this intrusion. To what, may I ask, do we owe this visit?"

"You have something I need to return."

"Something of yours? I think I not."

Zelle's heart beat faster as Klaus's gaze fell on her. She swallowed hard and sucked in a deep breath, her nails lengthened.

"We have been asked to retrieve the girl."

"By whom?" A hard edge crept into Flint's voice.

"That, I am sorry to say, I am not at liberty to discuss."

"You can't have her," Dax growled.

"Oh, but I think I can. I have you out numbered four to... well from the looks of Flint, you're the only one capable of fighting."

"Not by half," Dax roared. The man behind him quavered as the air surrounding Dax shimmered and shook.

Dax's clothing ripped as his limbs extended and white hair sprouted all over his body. Zelle had barely blinked before he was down on all fours, his giant mouth roaring at everyone.

"You." Klaus smiled.

Dax turned on the man with the sword. With a swipe of his paw, he rendered the man's arm immobile. The man dropped his sword, turned, and ran, trailing blood behind him.

"Dax, get Zelle!" Flint yelled. Loca took off, talons out, scratching at the face of the man who held Marissa.

Marissa cried out and ducked from her captor's hold. Flint swung wild and connected, hitting the guy square in the jaw. He doubled over and Flint gave him a kick to the gut.

Dax rounded on the man holding Zelle. The blade pressed harder into her throat.

"Don't or I'll kill her."

She was propelled backward.

"If you hurt her I'll rip you apart with my bare hands," yelled Flint.

Marissa ran to Flint's side, taking his arm. Loca landed on his shoulder again. Zelle was yanked from behind, causing her to stumble. The knife cut her throat and a strangled cry escaped her. This was not happening. She wouldn't let it. Mist swirled around her. Anger raced over Zelle's body and settled in her chest. This was not allowed. Men as low as this were not permitted to touch her. Not ever.

"All we want is the girl. Let us go and we won't hurt her,"

Klaus said. "I know she's beautiful, Flint, but really? Is she worth dying over? Because something tells me that you aren't doing so well, despite that hood covering your face."

Zelle glanced around. A high wall surrounded the garden. The only way out was past Flint and Dax. Not very smart of their attackers.

The man prodded Zelle forward, past Dax, who growled and backed up a step to make room. His eyes tracked her every move.

Zelle smiled. "I'll be all right, Dax. I can handle myself."

The man snorted in her ear. "You killed Craigen, but I bet you won't be so tough with two of us."

They neared Flint. Marissa had moved behind Flint by several feet.

"You know I'm going to kill you, Klaus. You don't deserve Belle and Chloe, and if it's the last thing I do, I am going to make sure they are safe and as far away from you as possible."

Klaus's face changed. He pulled something from his belt and aimed it at Flint.

Zelle screamed Flint's name.

As a blast sounded, Zelle grabbed Paul's arm and bit as hard as she was able. Paul let out a holler and Dax slammed into him.

He toppled backward with Zelle tumbling atop him. His knife flung to the ground and Zelle saw her chance.

She flipped over and faced him. Her mist pooled about her as she locked gazes with him and breathed in. His eyes widened and his mouth opened in a silent scream as he fought for air. Fury raged through her as over and over he exhaled and she inhaled. She was tired of human men thinking they could take advantage of her. Treating her like a prize sow to be bought or sold or molested at leisure. No more would she allowed them to see her as such. She would show them what happened when they messed with Rapunzelle of Shaidan.

Zelle stabbed her elongated nails deep into the man's abdomen. He flinched as blood bubbled from his lips.

"You are unworthy to touch me," she whispered.

Everything around her went silent as she sucked out every last breath he held and his face turned gray. When he stopped moving, Zelle sprang to her feet to find Dax and Klaus locked in a heated battle. Anger seeped through every one of her pores. She rushed to break them up.

The cuts across Klaus' chest dripped blood and his weapon had disappeared. He eyed her and then finding he was alone, he backed up a step.

"Stop," she commanded.

Klaus's gaze locked on hers.

"Zelle," Flint called. "Zelle, don't."

She walked to Klaus. He backed up a step but then as she locked her gaze on his, he stopped moving. Up close she saw what she'd missed on his face from high in her tower. His nose was too pointed and his eyes too close together. His gaze held hatred and malice. She placed a palm on his chest. "This is what you wanted from me, right?"

He didn't speak, only looked on, incapable of moving.

She moved her mouth to within inches of his and tasted his sour, salty breath upon her face. She breathed it in.

"Marissa, go inside," Flint said.

Marissa headed off toward the front door.

Zelle sucked in another of Klaus's breaths and his eyes went wide. The feel of power rushed through her. She smiled, enjoying the way it tickled her insides. "You see, I'm not as sweet as you thought, am I?" She traced her fingers up and down his chest trying to decide if she should suck him dry or shred him to pieces.

Dax knocked into her, pushing her away. She rounded on him. Klaus was her prey. Dax's hazel eyes connected with hers and he shook his heavy head, chuffing at her. Klaus stumbled out of her grasp and fell sideways. Zelle rounded on him and advanced. Sucking him dry it was.

Klaus reached behind him and produced the weapon he'd dropped. Zelle paused but then continued forward. Dax stepped between them and stood up on his hind legs, shielding Zelle with his large body. Zelle tried to step around him but Flint caught her arm and held her in place.

Klaus got shakily to his feet, pointing the weapon at them. "This isn't over," he said. His gaze drifted to Dax. "The next time we meet, one of us is going to die."

Dax roared his reply.

"Run, Klaus," Flint said. "Because when next I see you, it shall be *your* last."

"You have no idea who you've made an enemy of, Flint Gwyn."

The trio stood where they were. Klaus backed out of sight until he hit the tall grass and ran till they could no longer see him.

Zelle ripped from Flint's grasp. "You should have let me kill him. Why did you let him live?"

Flint stiffened. "I wasn't letting him live as much as I was saving you from killing him. I know what you did to Craigen and that man over there hasn't hit you yet, but it will. I meant to spare you the pain of doubling it, when it does."

Zelle's head buzzed and her body hummed light and powerful all at the same time. She needed release. Needed to purge her energy. "Trust me, you have saved me nothing." He had no clue what Rasmuss had made her do. To innocent men. She would not have felt bad about Klaus. Not ever.

For a moment she wanted nothing more than to feel Flint between her thighs, making love to her hard and fast, giving her the release her body craved. She touched his chest, swirling her fingertips in his soft hair.

Flint licked his lips and placed his hand on hers, making her meet his gaze. "We should get moving. It's obvious Rasmuss is after you," Flint said. "Dax, let's get you dressed."

Dax nodded his shaggy head and lumbered to Flint's side. They stood there, staring at each other for a long moment. She could see on his face he wanted her as much as she wanted him. But finally he squeezed her hand and then let go. Grasping a handful of the bear's hair he held on as Dax led him to Marissa's house.

The sounds of Flint and Dax's footsteps pounded on the ground as they moved toward the house, further and further away from her. Her heart thundered and tears threatened to unleash as frustration wound tight inside her choking her from the inside out.

She remembered what Khazidhæ had taught her and breathed in deeply. She closed her eyes and cleared her mind, concentrating on her breathing. A squawk caught her attention and then Loca's heavy, familiar form gripped her shoulder. He nuzzled her neck and picked at her hair.

She continued her breathing until the mist dissipated and nothing was left but a hollow numbness in her chest. She opened her eyes and reached up to pet Loca, but he took off before she touched him.

Zelle stared at Paul's body that lay strew on the ground like discarded garbage. She'd sucked him dry, just like Craigen. The feeling left her jittery. Memories of what had happened the last time she'd had that much power inside her for too long flooded back. She couldn't let that happen. She couldn't risk hurting anyone else.

Her thoughts turned to Khazidhæ and she swallowed hard. She needed to get to him.

He was the only one who would know what to do to help her. If he didn't kill her for what she'd become, first.

CHAPTER NINETEEN

F lint's body warred with itself. Part of him wanted to
lock Zelle in her tower and keep her safe from the
world, while he made love to her. Worshipped her and
doted on her every need. And the other part was so afraid of
what she was becoming that he dared not even touch her.

She's killed two men and tried to kill two more- the fragile
woman he'd met in the tower that had been terrified to find
him inside. Yet, somehow in the past week she'd become something else. Or maybe she always was and she hid it well. She'd
tried to tell him in the tower that she was in there for a reason.
Maybe the reason wasn't to keep her safe– but everyone else.

"Well, it seems Dax and Zelle are already in the wagon."
Marissa entered the bedroom where he'd spent the night
barely able to sleep.

"I'm sorry again, Aunt Marissa. I know yesterday must
have been terrifying."

She chuckled and slipped her arm into his. "I have seen a
great many things in my life. I was once the adventurous youth

and your uncle was quite tolerant of my flighty ways. But I must say, I've never, in all my days, seen anything like what Zelle did. She's rare indeed. She possesses a magick that may just make her a target of evil designs."

"She already is, I'm afraid."

"Then you must do everything in your power to keep her safe."

That's what he wanted, but it seemed that more and more Zelle and Dax were the ones keeping him safe and not the other way around.

"I'll try my best."

"You want something to be a lion for? Be a lion for her."

Flint swallowed the lump in his throat. His feelings were jumbled. He'd spent all night trying to figure out what he wanted and needed- but he still didn't have an answer.

Marissa kissed his cheek. "Let's get you on your way."

"You're sure you'll be safe when we're gone?"

"I can handle myself. Besides, now that I know that there might be danger, I will raise my defenses for the next couple of weeks."

"What defenses?"

Marissa chuckled again and patted his cheek. "You don't think you're the only one with special friends, do you?"

FLINT SAT IN THE WAGON BED AS IT BOUNCED ALONG. ZELLE sat next to him, the nearness of her making him tingle with anticipation. Her scent threatened to consume him, warm and musky with a hint of floral. Warmth radiated off her skin like an inferno. Every one of his senses was heightened and all of him took her in.

Zelle began to hum, her voice permeating the air. Between

the bumping of the road, the sounds and smells of Zelle, and the constant lack of sleep, Flint found himself becoming drowsy.

Zelle reached out and took Loca from his shoulder, her face passing close to his own. Then she tugged him down and lay his head in her lap. She ran her fingers through his hair and sang softly.

Her touch made Flint's body pay attention. Her voice swam in his head, calling to him. Soon her fingers traced his cheek and down his chin.

She turned his head so he faced her.

Her warm breath hit his face as she bent in close. She ran the soft pad of her thumb over his lips before she touched her own to them. His arousal sprung to life at the taste. She kissed him tentatively; her languid tongue mixing with his pulled a moan from him. He wanted her. No matter how he denied it. No matter how he tried to stay away. Nothing could save him from the feel of her, the smell of her, the taste of her. She was special in a way he'd never known. Precious like a rare gem. To be guarded and kept safe.

She pulled away, but lingered inches from his face. "Sleep," she whispered.

She kissed him once more and then sat back and sang again.

FLINT HAD FALLEN ASLEEP IN HER ARMS HOURS AGO. SHE STILL stroked his soft brown hair, her mind focused only on one thing. Flint. She'd spent the night tossing and turning in her large lone bed trying to understand what was happening within her.

When she'd thought Klaus was going to harm him, the need to protect him had become overwhelming. A sinew deep nature that she was helpless to resist. Protecting them both had been her only thought. No matter what it cost.

Something was changing inside her. The feelings inside her were more than lust. They were more than just caring. They were the something Khazidhæ had warned her about and protected her from for a thousand years.

It was too late to go back, though. What's done was done. There was no changing her feelings for Flint. No taking them back. Not with who she was. Like it or not, her soul had made a decision.

"How much farther?" she asked.

"A ways. Things might get bumpy as we go over the Demonlands," said Dax.

Zelle swallowed hard. So close to home, yet a whole world away.

"There's no one there but the guard that protects the rift. Sage has a domicile there, but it's hidden by fae magick. Other than that, no one goes into the Daemon Wastelands. No one will see us pass through."

From what she'd been taught, when the rift had opened a thousand years ago the fae and mages had come in and decimated everything in an attempt to close it. They had managed to kill everything in the area, but hadn't been able to close the rift.

"You still think we're doing the right thing?" They hadn't told Flint their plan to get to Tanah Darah, bypassing his home. He wouldn't be happy about their decision, but they had no choice. Flint needed his family. And she needed to get somewhere that she could be safe as well. In Fairelle, there were very few places she would be safe from Rasmuss.

"He's not going to be happy about it, that's for sure. But he needs this. We all do."

Zelle nodded. She just hoped when she arrived that they'd let her stay. At least until she could get to Khazidhæ.

ZELLE AWOKE WITH A BUMP. THE SKY WAS EBONY AND THE AIR chilly. She looked around. An enormous midnight colored castle loomed above her. Inside lights illuminate various windows like hundreds of tiny eyes staring out at her. The ominous sight made her shiver. A memory flashed into her mind. *A beautiful woman leading her into the castle through a hidden entrance. Terona.*

The memory faded and a chill trickled down Zelle's spine.

Dax jumped from the wagon and stretched. "Wait here. I'll go first and try to explain."

Zelle nodded. Flint stirred when she touched his hair again. He breathed deeply and yawned. Anxiety snaked around her. He wasn't going to be happy about being deceived.

"We've stopped. Are we here?"

"Yes."

"I've been asleep all day?"

"You have."

He smiled up at her and ran a finger down her cheek before dragging himself over to the edge of the wagon and lowering to the ground. He growled as he stretched his muscles.

"Oh man, that's stiff." He rubbed his shoulder. "It's cooler than it should be for this time of year."

He took several steps and then stopped. He lifted a foot and stepped it down on the ground again. Gravel crunched beneath his boot. His brows knit together as he crunched carefully several more times. He turned to Zelle.

"Where are we?" His voice held a cold note that slammed into her.

"Flint!" a woman cried.

A raven-haired beauty ran from the castle door, followed closely by several men. Flint stiffened and turned his vacant eyes upon her.

Zelle wanted to hold his hand and be by his side as he faced his family, but this was something he had to do alone.

"Flint!" the woman cried again racing to his side. "Flint. Oh my gosh, you're alive!" The woman flung herself into his arms. Peppering his face with kisses. He stood immovable as the men surrounded him and embraced in a large group hug. The aura of happiness swirled around the group in a vibrant spectacle of colors. All except for Flint, who wore the deep blue and red aura of betrayal.

Murmurs of well wishes, love, and happiness floated from them. But Flint kept his vacant stare solidly on her. She covered her head with the hood of her cloak in an effort to distance herself, but it didn't work. Finally the group backed up a step and followed his gaze.

The woman from the group moved closer to the wagon. "Dax said you're Zelle. I'm Snow, Flint's sister. Please, come down with us."

Snow smiled revealing pearly white teeth. She held her hand out and Zelle scooted to the edge of the wagon. Flint offered her his hand as well. Zelle looked at it tentatively for a moment and then slipped her fingers into his hard calloused ones.

He jerked her off the wagon so abruptly that Loca

squawked and took off into flight for a moment before settling on Flint's shoulder again.

"You knew," he whispered in her ear.

His strong arm had her pinned in so tight that she couldn't move away.

"You need your family."

Flint growled. "We'll talk about this later." He slipped her arm into his so she could lead him. Zelle stepped up to the group who watched them with great intent.

"Hello." She bowed her head.

"Welcome," said a large blond male with broad shoulders and a winning smile. "I'm Erik." He put out his hand. Zelle stepped forward to take it, but Flint pulled her back. She looked up at Flint but he stayed stoically silent. Zelle's temper flared and she ripped from his grasp.

"Hello." She offered her hand.

"I'm Gerall," said a tall thin man with glasses.

"We're Hass and Ian," two giant brawny twins said in unison.

"Welcome," said Snow again. "Why don't we get you inside, it's chilly out and you must be tired from your journey."

"Thank you." Zelle stepped to Flint. His jaw muscles worked hard. She ran her hand down the length of his arm before linking her fingers with his and pulling him forward.

"Steps," she whispered when they had reached the bottom of the castle. Loca nipped his ear.

Flint slowed and reached out with his foot. He stepped up solidly.

"Railing to your left."

His hand shot out and grasped the stone. Together they ascended toward the door. Snow passed them and rushed up the stairs. A tall man with long blond hair and pale skin stood waiting with Dax. She could only assume that the man was Snow's husband Sage, the king of the vampires.

The group drew closer to the entrance. Snow pulled Sage into a hug. He watched them with indifference, then stepped back as they entered.

Sage aura remained a gray mask of uncertainty.

"Thank you for having us," Zelle said.

Sage looked at her and smiled. "Any family of Snow's is family of mine. Whether they like it or not." His gaze traveled to Flint, but neither man said anything more.

Every surface of the grand entrance hall was covered in black stone. Portraits lined the walls on either side of the wide space. At the far end of the room several couples watched the exchange. Zelle pulled Flint further into the hall to stand next to Dax.

The brothers piled in and stared at them. The silence and tension in the room was so thick Zelle thought she might drown in it.

"Zelle, you must be tired. Can I show you to your room?" Snow offered.

"Thank you. I would–"

"She stays with me," Flint said.

Everyone exchanged a look.

"Flint," said Dax moving toward them. "Let Zelle stay in her own room."

"No." Flint pulled her closer.

"What do you think, we're going to flirt with her?" Erik joked.

Flint removed his hood. Zelle witnessed the looks of surprise on his brothers' faces. Snow gasped.

All around his brothers wore expressions ranging from

horror to sadness. One of the twins turned from the group and kicked at the ground swearing softly.

"Yes," Flint said.

"Flint, please don't," Zelle said softly.

"It's true and you know it. They can't help it, can they?"

"Please," she whispered. Though she was sure he hadn't made out the entirety of the situation, it was obvious he'd caught on to some of it. Specifically the way she couldn't control the fact that men desired her. However, in the presence of his family and so many people she had no desire to argue.

"I think you should let go of her." Erik stepped forward.

Loca hooted and Flint tensed.

"It's fine," Zelle said. "Your brothers won't hurt me."

"That's not what I'm worried about," he replied.

The accusation slapped her. "Just because I was courteous to Bryant and his hospitality doesn't give you the right to treat me like *your* friend from his establishment," she whispered through clenched teeth.

He was afraid *she* would do something. After everything they'd been through.

Everyone stared at them as Flint looked down at her. She didn't want to do it there, in front of everyone. Tell him the truth about who she was. Her gaze traveled to Dax. He'd told her she'd be safe there. That they would help her. She had to trust that his words were true.

Zelle faced the group and pushed back her hood. The gasps from the brothers were audible. The fragrant lust that filled the air had mist swirling around her fingers within seconds.

"No," Sage said suddenly. "She can't stay here." He moved forward quick as light and stood inches from Zelle, his aura belying both his rage and terror.

Loca screeched and flapped his wings between Sage and Zelle. Flint struck out with the flat of his palm and knocked Sage away. "Don't touch her."

Dax growled and stepped closer. "Easy," he warned.

Snow rushed forward and grabbed Sage by the arm. Loca screeched for several more seconds.

"How can you say that? They are guests in our home. Dax said she needs our help."

"No, she doesn't." Sage scoured Zelle's form. "She's perfectly capable of taking care of herself. I don't know how you got here, but I don't want you on my lands. You are not welcome."

"Sage!" Snow gasped.

He turned to Snow. "Can't you see, Love? Don't you know what she is? To have her here will bring destruction on us all."

"What are you talking about?" asked Flint.

She hadn't expected anyone to realize what she was. She'd thought she had time to explain. "Flint, I wanted to tell you–"

"She's a daemon," Sage spat. "A succubus."

She hung her head but then pride rippled up her spine and she lifted her chin, meeting Sage's gaze. What she was held no shame.

"So what?" Snow said, her voice firm. "She doesn't look like she's here to try and take over."

"But she will. One way or another. They whip men into a frenzy for her affection and cause them to kill each other. If she stays, nothing but death will follow in her wake. And how do we know she isn't related to Terona? I saw someone in the mirror."

"I'm not like that," Zelle said. "That's not what I want."

"Are you still a virgin?" Sage asked.

"Sageren." Snow's fangs descended. "That's enough."

"Answer me!" Sage demanded.

Zelle's eye twitched. "No."

"Then it is inevitable. Once a succubus has been with a man, her appetite begins. She will crave every man within this castle, and they her in return, until finally it drives her mad with lust."

"That won't happen to me," Zelle said.

"Won't it?"

"No," she said firmly. "I saw what it did to my mother. What it turned her into. And I refuse to be that. But it's more—"

Sage shook his head. "It doesn't matter. No matter how strong you think you are, nature always wins in the end."

"It wasn't so long ago that we would have all said the same of you, Sage," replied Snow.

"She needs your help," offered Dax. "She hasn't done anything but help both myself and Flint. She saved our lives."

"I won't send her away," said Snow. "You boys will just have to keep to your rooms, or go home until we figure out what to do. But Zelle stays." Snow marched over to Zelle and locked arms with her.

Sage's gaze fell heavily onto Snow. "Snow—"

"No!"

Sage's fangs descended into his mouth, their sharp points reaching almost to his chin. Snow bared her fangs at him. "Sageren, I said no."

His eyes narrowed and then he roared in rage and flew from the hall so fast that Zelle barely saw him disappear.

Zelle blew out a long breath. The brothers still stared at her and suddenly she was too self-conscious to even breathe. She replaced the hood.

ZELLE AND THE TOWER

"Do I have a room, Snow?" Flint's voice sounded distant and cold.

"You can pick anything in the west wing that Erik and the rest have not taken over."

Zelle moved to Flint's side, but he turned from her. "Dax, will you take me?"

Dax placed Flint's hand on his shoulder.

"We'll all go." Erik gestured to the others.

Gerall grabbed Hass and Ian and pushed them forward from where they stood, gawking.

Zelle watched him disappear through a door with the rest of the men. Her heart broke with every step Flint took away from her.

"We have room for you, too," said Snow.

"I thank you for your kindness, but I'm afraid your husband is right. Despite what I said, I'm not sure I can control what's inside me. At least not without help."

"Then we'll get you help."

Zelle shook her head. "There are only two people who can help me. One is the man who imprisoned me to steal my magick. And the other doesn't even live in Fairelle."

"Then we'll just have to bring him here."

"I don't know how."

Snow winked. "I have an idea I might. But first, you and I are going to sit down and have a nice cup of tea, and you are going to tell me everything."

CHAPTER TWENTY

F lint's heart broke as he moved away from Zelle. A
succubus. A daemon. He'd known she was different.
Magickal even. He'd thought maybe part fae, part
mage. But a daemon. How was it possible? How had Rasmuss
gotten her here? Not that it mattered.

He played and replayed Sage's words in his head. How
many men had she been with, how many had she made love
to? Made to feel the same peace that had rooted inside him
and twisted him up. Made them think they were safe and
cared for, only to have it be a lie so she could control them.
How many? Dozens? Hundreds? Thousands?

He was being a self-righteous hypocrite. He'd lain with whores
who did the same thing, hadn't he? Paid them to make him feel
special. And none had ever made him feel half what Zelle did. But
there was a difference with Zelle. He loved her. Or… she made
him think he did. Had she been playing with him the whole time?
Was what he felt even real or was it all a trick of magick?

"Flint?" It was Gerall.

"Hey." Flint still sat in the same spot Dax had plunked him on before giving him a piece of his mind about his treatment of Zelle and then leaving.

"I have food," Gerall said.

Flint could smell roast and potatoes. "Set it down... somewhere." He gestured around, not knowing where anything was.

Gerall set the tray down and then a chair scraped across the floor toward the bed. They sat in silence for a long time.

Finally Gerall said, "I missed you, brother."

Flint choked down emotion. "I missed you, too."

"It was wrong of us to let you go," Gerall said. "Erik feels responsible for..."

"Me being blind? Don't be stupid. It was my choice, my fault."

They sat in silence for a few minutes longer.

"Does it hurt?"

Flint shook his head. "It did at first but now I feel nothing. Even the skin around my eyes seems numb."

"Can you see anything?"

Flint shrugged. "Shadows here and there. Nothing when there's no light present. I thought perhaps I would need your eyeglass maker to get me some glasses, but now..."

"You should still see him. Maybe there's something he can do."

"For him to be able to do something he'd have to have something to work with. I'm no fool. I know there's nothing he can do for me."

"And you think this is permanent?"

Flint snorted. "A mage threw magick dust in my face and

215

told me I'd never see Zelle's face again. Do you think he was wrong?"

Gerall didn't reply.

"Where's Jamen? I didn't hear him."

"Oh." The jovial sound in Gerall's voice peeked Flint's interest. "He and Scarlet were married several months ago."

"Married?"

"It's a long story, but needless to say, she took him back and they're expecting a child."

Flint's heart squeezed with both happiness and jealousy. He forced a smile on his face. "That's wonderful. I'm happy for them. So they stay in Westfall and you stay here?"

"We've taken turns staying here for the last few months for the most part. At first things were pretty quiet, but there were a few problems in Westfall—"

"Problems?"

Gerall's hand fell on Flint's knee. "Don't worry about that now. Just try and get acclimated and then we can talk some more."

"So you don't hunt anymore?" Flint asked.

"Not so much. Every once in a while we might get a report of a vampire hunting in human lands and we check it out, but things have been quiet. Peaceful even, with the vampires. There is a vampire girl missing from a wealthy family but Erik has taken to looking for her."

"Peaceful..." Flint mused. Zelle was his peace. But how could he trust what he felt?

Gerall stayed silent for a moment. "You care for her."

"Who?"

"The succubus."

He stiffened. Gerall wasn't usually the one to judge.

"How can you, knowing what she is?"

"I know now," said Flint.

"You mean you didn't before?"

Flint shook his head. "I knew there was something different about her, but that's all. I mean, you didn't know what she was either till Sage told us. None of us has ever seen one."

"I just figured that you two had been spending time together for a while."

"Only a few weeks."

"Do you love her?"

Flint ran his hands over his face. He'd always been truthful with Gerall. Between the two of them, they had no secrets.

"I don't know." Flint hung his head and dropped his hands between his knees. "When I'm around her I feel warm, home. I've never felt that before, ever. Not even when mother and father were alive. Is that because I love her, or because of what she is?"

There was a knock on the door.

"Can I come in?" asked Hass.

"And me?" asked Ian.

"Sure," said Flint.

"What about me?" It was Erik.

"Yes, everyone can come in, already." Flint failed to keep the irritation from his voice.

He rose from the bed and Loca screeched as his brothers moved closer. "Easy boy." Flint felt Loca's wings flapping, so he held out his arm for the bird to land on. It was strange how attached they had become to each other.

"What's with the bird?" asked Ian.

"It's Zelle's. His name is Loca. He's been helping me."

"Helping you?" asked Gerall.

"He nips my ear if I'm going to trip and he thinks he's a dog or something, when people get too close."

"I thought he was going to claw Sage's eyes out," said Hass.

"Oh man, can you imagine if we had two brooding brothers shuffling around blindly in this place?" asked Ian.

"That would be a pain." Erik chuckled. "I don't know how we're going to deal with this one." Everyone laughed and Loca squawked as Erik pulled Flint into a hug. "You know I'm kidding you, big baby. We'd do anything for you."

Flint's chin quivered as the bodies of his brothers pressed in on his. Loca fluttered off as pairs of large arms wrapped him in a hug. He'd missed this.

The pain of everything he'd been through came crashing down on him and for the first time he let them see him weep. Tears streamed from his eyes as his brothers held him, allowing him this moment of pain. Great sobs wracked his body until there was nothing left.

When he finished they stepped back and he wiped his tears. "Great, now I really am a big blubbering baby."

"Well, you sure smell like one," said Hass.

"You could definitely use a bath and some new clothes," said Gerall.

"Come on. Let's get you fed and bathed. Then we can figure out what to do from there."

"Do about what?" asked Flint.

"About Zelle. Snow isn't going to be able to keep Sage tamed forever."

KLAUS FIDGETED AND SWALLOWED HARD WHILE HE AWAITED THE arrival of Rasmuss in the deserted castle Rasmuss used as a hideout.

Rasmuss wouldn't be happy that he'd failed to bring Zelle. Klaus replayed the words he planned to speak as he paced in the cold stone room. The surface of the mirror shimmered and glowed brightly. A tall woman with pearlescent hair falling to her thighs and bright amethyst eyes stepped out of the mirror. The resemblance to the girl Zelle was striking. Though the woman was older, she was just as beautiful. Morgana.

Klaus's body shook. If Morgana was there, that meant Rasmuss had already been alerted to his failure.

She scanned the room before she sniffed the air. "Ahh-hhh… The memories these walls hold." She smiled.

"Queen Morgana, I am so pleased that you could come." Klaus' body tensed. He tried to remember the excuse he'd been practicing to tell Rasmuss.

Red mist swirled around her and the long blood red gown she wore clung to her form as if made from the mist. Her scent intoxicated and delighted Klaus.

"Yes." Her eyes lit on him, looking him up and down. "I'm sure that you are. Where is Rapunzelle?"

"About that." Klaus swallowed. "She was with a man named Flint and another–"

"Where is she?"

Her heated gaze penetrated him to the core. He found himself unable to think of nothing but bedding her.

Morgana frowned. "You don't have her."

"I'm sorry. I thought it would be easy, but I didn't antici-pate them being so strong. If it had just been Flint Gwyn we would have been successful. But there was a shifter. A bear–"

"Silence." Her voice hissed through the room whispering

into every corner. Her eyes blazed crimson and furious. Her nails lengthened as she paced in front of the mirror. She stopped suddenly and turned her gaze upon him. "Did you say a bear shifter?"

"Yes. A white bear."

A large smile spread across her face revealing sharp white teeth. She laughed. "You really have outdone yourself."

Klaus blinked rapidly. "So, you aren't mad?"

"Mad?" Her brows knit together as she slithered toward him, her hips swaying. The red mist grew thicker the closer she drew. She reached out with a long nailed hand. "Of course not, my darling. You have brought me something I want even more than Zelle. You've brought me news of my beloved Kondak."

Her heavenly scent invaded his mind. "Dax? The bear?"

"Of course. I've been searching for him for years." She ran her fingers over his lips, her gaze fixed on them. "And you brought me this news. So there is only one thing I can do."

"What?" Klaus's voice was horse with desire.

Morgana moved in until their bodies touched. Her left hand cupped him, making him stiffen. She pressed her lips to his, her tongue plunging into his mouth.

This was wrong. He loved Belle. He wanted to marry Belle.

Morgana stroked him through his breeches. He moaned and crushed her against him. She chuckled and kissed him harder.

Again his mind told him to stop. But just like all the other times he'd cheated, he didn't listen.

CHAPTER TWENTY ONE

"This used to belong to Sage's stepmother." Snow stepped into a large dusty room and Zelle's gaze traversed every surface. It looked like Terona had been accumulating mage supplies for decades. Books and jars, potions and dusts. Everything one needed to create a spell. A scent caught Zelle's attention. A familiar perfume that delved richly into a musky aroma.

"So do you think anything in here might help you?" Snow asked.

"If I can figure out what I'm supposed to do, yes."

"What *are* you supposed to do?"

Zelle tried to remember what she'd been taught and what had happened to her. She remembered a pull in her gut that she could not refuse. She'd followed the sensation that had lead her out of her castle and out to the fields beyond. Hundreds of soldiers had tried to stop her from going. Eventually several had run off to alert Khazidhæ.

She had rounded a hill and in the middle of a field stood a

portal, along with a man she hadn't known. Rasmuss. The men had tried to stop her but Rasmuss had used a spell on her and caused her mist to grow and grow until it exploded, killing all the soldiers. Then he'd pulled her through the portal to Fairelle.

"I'm not sure what I need to do. I was on the other side of it last time. And I don't necessarily want to pull someone through as much as I need to contact them." She didn't even know if that was true. She wanted revenge. Of that she was sure. But did she want Khazidhæ to come here? If he did would he'd want to take her home. Was that even her home anymore?

Snow laid her hand on Zelle's shoulder. In the past hour Zelle had shared more with Snow than she had with any other being, ever, except Khazidhæ.

"Well, let's start looking through the books. If we don't find something here, Sage's father accumulated a vast library we can look through."

"Thank you. For helping me."

Snow smiled. "Of course. I would do anything for someone who needs help. Especially when that someone is the love of my brother's life."

Zelle looked over at Snow. "What did you say?"

"Come now. Surely you must see it. The way he attends to you, protects you. I've only ever seen Flint act that way with our family before. Never has he even brought a woman home before and there was only one he ever mentioned when we were younger, but it was short lived. For years I feared he would never let anyone close."

Zelle's cheeks heated. "It's most likely what your husband said. It's an effect of what I am, and of us having made love."

Snow cleared her throat. "Well, um..." She cleared her throat again.

"Was I not supposed to say that? Flint tells me I say things I shouldn't."

"No, it's fine," Snow waved her hand. "I just... Let's get started shall we?"

"I'll start over near the table."

Snow nodded.

A BOOK LAY FLAT ON THE TABLE, OPEN TO A PAGE ABOUT LOVE spells. She flipped page after page. All the spells in the book had been written by the same hand. Some had comments or notations in the margins. Everything from control spells to fortifying spells. Each complicated and intricate in their own right. But for someone like Zelle, who had never cast a spell before, they were near impossible.

"Find anything?" she asked Snow.

"I don't think so." Snow closed the book she'd been reading.

"From the looks of these books Sage's stepmother was a powerful woman."

"Her name was Terona. She was a daemon, like you. But... nothing like you."

Terona. "She was a daemon but doing this kind of magick. That's strange," Zelle said.

"Why?"

"Daemons have their own magick. It's innate. All of this is alchemy. Mage magick. Magick made through the essence of other objects and beings. Everything has an essence. If you take that essence and capture it and combine it with other essences, you can change the things around you. That's what the mages here in Fairelle do."

"How do you know that?"

"Rasmuss, the man who captured me taught me a bit about alchemy."

"Who was Rasmuss?" Snow curled her legs under her.

Memories of the old man who had cared for her and shown her love collided with the images of the younger man he truly was. The anger and flash of dust as he blew it into Flint's face—

"I don't know. He said he was my father, but he lied. I don't even know if Rasmuss is his real name."

"Do you have family where you're from?"

Zelle looked at her hands. "Yes."

"And you want to get back to them."

Did she? "They probably think I am dead." It wasn't really an answer.

"Flint was gone just nine months and I wanted to die from missing him."

Zelle did want to see her family. But if they did, they'd want her to come home. And going home meant leaving Flint.

SNOW SHOWED ZELLE TO THE LAST ROOM ON THE END OF THE west wing so she could rest before dinner. Apparently they'd arrived mid Vampire day, though it was the middle of the night.

Zelle had been in her room for only a few minutes when there was a soft knock at the door.

"Come in," she called from where she sat, exhausted, in a large chair.

Dax popped his head in. "Hey."

"Dax." She smiled. "Come in."

He found a second chair and dragged it close to where she sat. "How are you?"

"I've been better. I've been worse."

Dax nodded. "You have to excuse Sage. He's only just gotten his home back and he is afraid of dividing it with any kind of war."

"I'm aware that I cannot stay here forever. I want to try to contact someone from my plane."

"If you want to go home we can take you to the portal."

"No. That, I'm not as sure about at the moment. I want to see my family, but, what I really want is revenge."

"And if you go through the portal you can't come back."

"Correct." The thought made her shiver. There was no in between. She couldn't have both. There were things about Fairelle that she'd come to love. The food, the sights... people. But she needed to make sure her family was all right. She needed to make sure that they were happy...

"Do you remember what Rasmuss did to get you here?"

"I remember how I got here but not how he did it."

"In the book I took from your tower it describes how the four brothers originally called the Djinn from your plane."

"It did? I must have missed that part. Too bad I don't have the book."

"I do."

She sat up. "You do?"

"It was interesting." He shrugged. "I took it. I apologize."

Zelle leaned forward, her body riddled with excitement. "What does it say?"

"I'll get it." Dax rose and headed for the door.

"How's Flint?" she blurted.

Dax paused before heading out. "He won't speak to me."

Sadness and guilt hit her at the thought of Flint. He hadn't even turned in her direction after finding out what she was.

Maybe she should go home and leave him be. Then with the support of his family he could go on with his life.

She looked down to find her hands swirling with purple mist. Taking a deep breath she tried to calm the mist away.

Dax returned moments later, carrying the book and leaving the door open.

He thumbed through the pages. "Here." He turned the large volume toward her.

According to the record the first brother drew an inscription on the ground. Then, standing inside the circle, he called forth the daemon by name and offered his own blood as sacrifice. She recognized the inscription and symbols. They were daemonic. *First I call, Then I bind, Do my bidding, You are mine.*

"I can do this," she said. "I just need something to write with."

"All right."

Zelle and watched Dax as he rifled through a desk. "Why are you doing this? Why are you helping me? Are you afraid of me as well?"

Dax stared at her. "No. I'm not afraid of you Zelle. I've seen what you are. You're a good, kind person. I don't believe for a second Rasmuss could have made you that person if you didn't have it inside you already. And I'm helping you because I understand. If I remembered where I was from, I would do anything to get back there."

Dax walk out of the room to find her something to write with. A knot of anxiety mingled with a burn of hope in her chest. If she did this she'd see Khazidhæ. Tears threatened to spill onto her cheeks.

She pushed the table, couch, and chair out of the way. She was rolling up a rug when someone stepped into the room.

"Let me help you with that," said Erik.

Zelle looked up to find a pair of bright blue eyes staring at her. She stepped away from him, her heart pounding.

"Redecorating already? You haven't even been here a day." He laughed and rolled the rug for her.

"I... I need the space." She wasn't sure what he wanted.

"You planning on dancing or something?"

"A spell."

Erik propped the rolled rug in a corner. "What kind of spell?"

She crossed her arms over her chest. "Why are you being so nice to me?"

"Why shouldn't I?"

"Because it isn't normal."

He smiled and one eyebrow arched up. He crossed his arms over his broad chest and stood with his feet planted slightly apart. His posture reminded her of Flint. The two were completely opposite, yet in that moment she saw that without a doubt they were brothers.

"It's not normal to be nice?" Erik said.

"I'm a daemon. My kind almost destroyed Fairelle. And you are a vampire hunter. Snow told me you killed Terona, not that I blame you. I would too if I had the chance, but I know daemons are not a favorite around here."

"So people keep saying, but all I see is a beautiful woman who needs help."

Her cheeks heated and she stared at him for several minutes. He was handsome, with his light hair and light eyes. So different from Flint. Flint was a good head taller, but leaner. Probably from not taking care of himself for the past few months. Where Erik's face held happiness, Flint's held only pain.

"I'm doing a summoning spell," she finally said. "I need to contact someone from my land."

Erik's brow furrowed. "Why?"

Zelle took a deep breath. "I need to see someone. And… I need to know if I'd be allowed to stay in Fairelle."

"Why would you be banished?" A look of concern crossed his face.

"Because I made love with Flint."

Erik's brows knit together. "I don't understand. Isn't that what Sage said was in your nature?"

"It's not that simple."

"Then explain it to me."

"I…" How did she explain? "My mother was a succubus. She married my father, but she was not a virgin when she did so. Her succubus side had already been awakened. Because my father was not her first, and the man she had been with first was not her husband, the succubus took over. My mother's appetites were… plentiful, to say the least. She took many others to her bed until madness and lust destroyed her."

"And what does that have to do with you?"

"In an effort to keep me from the same fate, my family allowed me to be touched by only one male. In doing so, my succubus would be bound to only him, forever, and I would never desire another."

"So you're married to another?"

"No. Not yet. I was to marry him, but it was never official. It was arranged. I never loved him."

"And you've been with Flint."

"Yes. But with Flint it's different."

"Why?"

The sudden realization that she was talking to Flint's brother made her nervous.

"Do you love him?"

She couldn't voice the words so she nodded. "It doesn't matter. No matter who I'm with, it won't matter. I'll forever seek love with others, trying to fulfill the hole that will grow inside me and eventually consume me. It's more than that though, because I'm not fully succubus. I'm half my father's daughter as well. I am a soul weaver and the energy I consume needs to be expelled in some way. Which was why my father agreed to me sleeping with my intended though we had not yet been married." She gave a sharp laugh. "I was to have been married just two days after I was taken."

"So you need to have sex to expel the energy?"

"Safely."

"And non-safely?"

"I explode in a burst of energy that kills just about everything within a mile radius."

"Well you have Flint to help you with that."

Zelle shook her head and walked to the bed to sit. "I didn't tell Flint what I was. I'm sure the last thing he wants right now is me."

"When is your next burst of energy set to happen?"

Zelle looked down at her hands. The mist had thickened and snaked up her arms. "Within the next twenty four hours, I'd say. I was able to calm it yesterday but that is a rarity. Rasmuss used to drain the energy from me. But without him... Only the person I'm going to call might be able to stop it."

"Then let's get to calling." Erik rubbed his hands together.

. . .

ZELLE DIPPED HER FINGERS IN THE PUNGENT BUCKET OF ANIMAL
blood that Dax had brought her. The scent caused her
stomach to lurch. She took deep cleansing breaths as she drew
the words and symbols on the stone floor of her room with
Dax, Erik, and Snow looked on.

When she finished she stood in the center of the ring and
Dax handed her a blade. She took it, her hand shaking. Her
nerves were getting the better of her. The mist inside pulsed
with life, wanting to be set free. The sensation was all too
familiar, though she hadn't dealt with it in so long.

She pushed up her sleeve and scored her arm. The burn
of the slices traipsed up her arms and she bit her lip. Blood
flowed freely, pooling on the ground.

She spoke the words that she had written. "Khazidhæ, son
of Braxis the Soul Weaver, I call on thee. Show thy face and
come to me. Here to stay in my care. Come now Khazidhæ,
hear my prayer."

Zelle's blood flowed out around her until it hit the painted
words and symbols on the floor. The bright red words and
symbols glowed as her blood mixed with them. She cut again,
deeper, and her stomach flopped while her head lightened.

One corner of the room filled with light and then the area
began to vibrate. The sound of voices and clashing swords
spread to encompass the room. A hole formed, like a window
opening, and in the picture beyond lay her homelands. Bright
red trees sprouted from the black ashy ground. A group of
males stepped into view and her heart shuddered.

A tall, tan-skinned man with long, dark hair secured with a
leather strap talked to a group of soldiers. His black and blue
iridescent armor bore the scars of war.

Zelle's heart squeezed to a stop as tears rolled uncontrol-
lably from her eyes.

"Cutter!"

The man turned at the sound of his name. His bright, fiery eyes tried to focus on her. He took a step closer to the portal. The soldiers near him tried to call him back, but he fixed his gaze on her.

"Cutter, I need you," she yelled into the void.

"Zelle?" he called.

"Cutter, help me!"

His eyes widened and he raced toward the portal at top speed. The men behind him scrambled to chase after him.

She held her hand out to him and stumbled forward from the circle. Her vision blurred and her knees wobbled.

"Cutter!"

Just as he was about to touch the portal, the soldiers pulled him away. Cutter roared in fury and turned, punching the men, trying to knock them away.

Sage raced into the room. "What the hell is going on here?"

Snow went to him quick as light. "She needs this."

"Zelle! Zelle!" Cutter lunged for the portal but his men were on him again. "I'll come for you."

"No!" Sage bellowed. His aura shifted to an inky black.

Zelle fell to her knees and Sage swiped at the symbols on the floor. The portal began to close.

Zelle cut herself again. "Khazidhæ, son of Braxis the Soul Weaver, I call on thee. Show thy face and come to me. Here to stay in my care. Come now Khazidhæ, hear my prayer."

Strong hands pried the knife from her grip and threw it to the floor. A second set of arms picked her up off the floor and dragged her away.

"Stop," Zelle screamed. "Cutter!" She watched in horror as Sage grabbed a pitcher of water from a stand and threw it on the circle. The symbols blurred together and thinned, breaking the spell.

Zelle cried out as tears spilled down her cheeks. She called Cutter's name over and over, but the portal faded and closed.

"It's all right. Zelle, it's all right."

She spun out of Flint's grasp. "You *Xihuli*! You do not know what you've done. I need him!"

"I will not have more daemons in my home." Sage surged forward, moving to within an inch of her face. "You dare try and open a portal to call more daemons through in my home, after I have offered you shelter?"

"Yes," Zelle said, her anger rising. Mist tangled her feet and pounded in her head. "I need him. He is the only one that can help me now. As you pointed out, I am a danger to everyone around me. He could have stopped that."

"Get out," Sage said through gritted teeth.

"No." Snow rushed forward. "Sage, stop this. I won't let you force her out. She has nowhere else to go and I won't have her wandering Fairelle alone. Don't push me on this."

Sage's eyes went from deadly to something else. Desire wafted off him in a huge wave. Snow's mouth twitched and her pupils dilate. She sucked in a deep breath and her lips curled up in one corner.

"We should continue this in private," she said.

"Indeed." Sage turned his head toward Zelle, but his eyes stayed on Snow. "You can stay for now, but if you try this again, you will leave no matter how soft my wife's heart may be."

Before Zelle could blink they disappeared.

"Leave us," said Flint.

Zelle looked directly at him for the first time. His face and hair were damp. His clothes were clean and finely made.

Though he still looked tired, she could see the man he had once been.

Everyone exited, the last one pulling the door closed behind him.

"Zelle," he said, his voice serious. "What were you doing?"

"Calling someone from my world."

"But why?"

"Because I need him."

His posture went rigid. "Do you love him?"

"Yes," she said simply.

"I see," Flint said. "So you intend on leaving Fairelle with him? To go home?"

"I don't know." Blood loss and fatigue sucked her in a downward spiral toward sleep. She located a towel on a table and wrapped it around the worst of the cuts, holding pressure on it.

Flint stayed silent for a long time. "Were you even going to tell me or were you just going to go?"

"I didn't plan this Flint. And I don't plan on going home if I can help it."

"Then what did you plan?"

"I don't know."

Blood covered her dress and feet. She moved to the wash-basin that was filled with water and removed the towel from her arm. The bleeding had slowed. Knowing he couldn't see her, she stripped off her dress and wet the towel, cleansing the blood from her arms and legs.

"You don't want me. Not that I don't blame you. I lied to you by not telling you what I was when I remembered," she said.

"Why do you think I don't want you?"

233

She stopped cleaning herself. His sightless eyes gazed in her direction and desire pricked her skin. "Do you?"

He rubbed his neck. "I don't know what I want, or feel, or believe. How do I know that what I feel for you isn't just part of what you are?"

"You don't." She dipped the towel in the water and rubbed it over her skin once more. "I understand. You don't trust me."

"It isn't you I don't trust."

She threw the towel in the basin and faced him. "What do you want from me, Flint?"

Flint's forehead creased.

"You seem to want something from me, but I don't know what. Is it sex? Do you want sex with me but no attachment, no feeling, like with the whores?"

"Zelle, don't."

"No, I think it's time we get this over with." She stormed over to him. "Tell me. Tell me you only want me because of what you think I do to you. Tell me you don't want anything more than to have sex with me. Tell me you don't care about me, that you don't love me. Tell me, Flint. Tell me what you want."

"I want you!" His lips slammed down on hers. He gripped her hair and pulled her into him. Her heart fluttered wildly at his touch. His lips traveled down her throat and she moaned his name. His hands ran over her body, setting her alight with need.

"You're naked," he said in a moan.

"I was washing." He broke her words off with another kiss. Shivers ran from her waist to her knees. She stepped back, toward the bed and he moved with her, his hands roaming her body. They fell onto the mattress and Flint's fingers trailed down her skin to her most sensitive spot. She sucked in a sharp breath as his thumb rubbed at her, sending desire shooting through her.

"Flint," she whispered. "Flint, I need you."

"Yes." His voice was rough with desire. "You do." He kissed her throat and down over her breasts.

She lay on her back, her legs hung over the side. He knelt in front of her, his soft lips leaving firm suckling kisses on her inner thighs. Her head swam at the feel of him between her legs. He reached up to her hips and tugged her closer to him. As his tongue came in contact with her sensitive wet pool she almost shot off the bed. Flint dug his fingers into her hips as he licked and sucked her, making her body pulse and ache. She fisted her hands in his dark, soft hair, wanting to draw him impossibly closer. As Flint's technique grew faster and more urgent she tensed. Her body growing tighter, like a coil ready to snap.

"Flint," she whispered. "I love you."

The building tension inside her grew and she bucked her hips against him. He slid his fingers inside her and she shattered into a thousand piece, grabbing his head and calling his name through each tidal wave of ecstasy. Her legs shook with fatigue and her arms felt like custard. She opened her eyelids to find Flint's unseeing gaze on her.

She needed him. To feel him inside her.

She pulled on his hair until he rose from the floor and fell on top of her. Their mouths collided again. She rolled him onto his back and stripped his shirt from his body. Making her way down his chest, she kissed every inch of him and then unbuckled his breeches and yanked them off.

His naked body lay beautifully splayed before her. Hard muscles pulled taut over long bones. She kissed up his leg, past his thigh to his hip. Her fingers gripped him tightly as she kissed up his chest to his mouth.

He fisted the sheets until his knuckles went white and his neck muscles strained.

"Zelle," he panted. "I want you."

Zelle guided him inside her and shuddered at the feel of being on top of him. Bending over him she kissed him softly, letting her tongue run over the seam of his lips before sucking the bottom lip into her mouth and then sitting up again.

"I want you, too," she replied.

She slowly pitched her body back and forth.

He grabbed her hips. "Not yet." His jaw clenched. "Wait. Just give me a minute."

Zelle watched his darkened eyes as they scanned over her with the movements of his hands on her body. He traced the line of her throat, the curve of her shoulder, the swell of her breasts, as if memorizing every inch of her. The mist clouded her so thick she thought she would choke.

His hands roamed her skin, making her tremble. She dipped her head and their mouths met. She could wait no longer. She slid down the length of him, hard. The feeling rocking her to the core.

He cried her name and she kissed him hard once more before she sat up and pressed down on his hips again. She worked in a quick rhythm. Neither of them were going to last.

He cupped her rear and guided her. Faster and harder their bodies joined until pain and pleasure mixed. His muscles tensed and his head reared. A moment later her body spasmed and her head snapped backward, a silent scream of pleasure escaped her open mouth. The mist swirled and then broke apart. White sparks showered the bed like lit snowflakes.

Flint continued to move her hips, rocking her through her

climax. When she regained control of her body she bent down to kiss him. His strong arms wrapped around her.

She wanted this. She needed this. Now and forever. To be with Flint.

He rolled with her, onto his side. They kissed, letting their hands caress and touch and feel until his kisses went from soft and gentle to more urgent again. He lifted her leg over his hip. Zelle moaned as his lips trailed down her throat and he thrust inside her once more. Her body rubbed up against his in a friction that only made her more sensitive. She dug her heel into his rear trying to bring him closer.

She now understood what everything she'd read about in the books was all about. As Flint's thrusts became faster and deeper, Zelle smiled. This was what she was meant for.

CHAPTER TWENTY TWO

F lint made love to Zelle half a dozen times in as many
hours, and still he only wanted more. She lay in his
arms, her body draped over him filling him with utter
contentment. Happiness sprinkled over him drenching his soul
and forcing his heart to blossom. Holding her in his arms,
making love to her, only made things that much sweeter.

He loved her. Of that there was no doubt, but he still
wasn't certain that his feelings weren't a product of what
she was.

His fingers traced a design on her right arm, where the
armband had been removed. His thoughts traveled to the man
Cutter that she had been calling out to. She said she loved
him, but how was it possible she loved Cutter yet had made
love with him so many times and in so many ways over the last
hours?

A sharp knock interrupted his thoughts. Zelle sat up.

There was a second knock.

"Where's my dress?"

"I don't know," he replied.

Before they could move the door opened. Flint tugged the covers up to cover them.

"I'm sorry," said Snow. "But Zelle, I need you to come with me."

"Is something wrong?"

"There is a Prince Khazidhæ and his entourage here and he is demanding to see you."

"He's here?" she squeaked.

Zelle slid out of his arms and off the bed. "Who is he? What's going on?" Flint demanded.

"Please hurry. I don't know how long Sage will be able to hold his soldiers back."

"Yes, yes, I'll be right there."

Flint slid over to the other side of the bed and the door closed.

"Here." Zelle thrust Flint's clothes into his hands. "Hurry, we must hurry."

"Who is this Prince Khazidhæ?"

"It's Cutter. He made it through. Damn, this dress is covered in blood. I need something else to wear."

"Did you pack anything?"

Her dark form raced across the room and a bag thudded to the floor. "Yes." She drew close to him and kissed his cheek. "Thank you."

Flint pulled on his tunic and breeches and stood. Trepidation coursed through his veins. From Snow's tone, the arrival of Cutter was not going to be a joyous occasion.

Zelle took him by the arm and led him to the door. "You must not speak. No matter what happens."

"Why?"

"I can't explain now, but please, don't speak."

Zelle opened the door and stopped short. Flint took a deep breath and could smell his brothers' colognes.

"We'll keep you safe," said Erik.

"You don't need to worry about me. You just make sure Flint is safe." She wrapped her arms around him in a tight embrace and then kissed his lips. "No matter what," she said. "Know that I love you."

The brush of her lips caressed his cheeks once more. He made a grab for her, but she was gone.

"Zelle!" Panic rose in his chest. Something wasn't right. "Get me down there."

Yelling floated from inside the large hall like the scent of burning candles. She ran to the huge wooden door with the solid iron handle and threw it open. A crowd of people stood in the middle of a grand room flanked in tapestries depicting battle sequences. A long crimson rug ran the length of the hall to the door where she stood. On the opposite side sat two enormous thrones on a raised pedestal. The metallic scent in the air shot through her teeth like metal filings, making her nerves ache.

Sage and Snow stood next to their thrones on the pedestal with a small fierce looking blonde vampire and a tall male one at their side. Several vampire guards stood at the ready.

Across from them waited a group of heavily armored men, in formation, their leader directly in front of Snow and Sage. Zelle swallowed hard, folded her hands into her sleeves and crossed the room. The door behind her opened and she turned to find Flint and his brothers coming through.

As she drew near the fighters, Snow spotted her. She nudged Sage whose gaze also moved to her direction.

"Ah." He gestured to her. "Here she comes and you can see for yourself, Prince Khazidhæ, that we have neither kidnapped, nor imprisoned her."

The group of armed guards turned. At the sight of her they bowed their heads and dropped to their knees. Cutter turned and his gaze lit on her. She stopped moving.

"Rapunzelle," he whispered. His voice cracked with emotion. "Zelle."

"Cutter." She ran to him and threw herself into his arms. Tears flowed from her like spring rain. She sobbed into his chest as his large arms wrapped her in a protective hug, his metal armor biting and pinching her skin in a familiar sensation.

"Rapunzelle, it's really you. I can't believe it," he said into her hair. He pushed her away and looked her over from head to toe. "We thought you were dead."

She smiled as Cutter wiped the tears from her eyes with his calloused thumb. "You have no idea how I've missed you. How did you get through? The portal closed."

"It didn't matter," he said. "You called to me and some of the guard were with me as well, so we were able to walk through the rift. Not all of them. Only those that saw you. But how did *you* get here?"

"I was summoned and imprisoned. Then fitted with a magick armband, keeping my memories from me and draining my powers."

Cutter's eyes flashed and mixed in a flurry of colors that only he could produce. Amber inside flecked with green purple and even red. A beautiful rainbow which she'd never seen on anyone else. "Who? Who did this to you, sister?"

"Sister?" asked Flint.

Zelle turned to face the group that now stood with Snow and Sage. "Cutter is my brother."

"Twin brother," Cutter added.

"Sire," said a voice from behind her.

Zelle froze. Her gaze drifted to Flint and then she turned away from him. The group of warriors parted and a huge, flame-haired Sagori daemon with bright orange eyes emerged. Cutter turned to look at him.

"Liaos, yes, come forward, of course." Cutter motioned until he stood only a foot from Zelle.

"Hello, beloved." His aura held the yellow of power mixed with orange strands.

"Hello, Liaos." Zelle swallowed the anxiety lodged in her throat.

Liaos nodded to the guard and they took three large steps backward allowing the small group their space. Zelle let go of Cutter long enough to hug Liaos. He kissed her head and breathed her in. His smile fell and his aura flashed bright red. He pushed her away.

Cutter growled and pulled Zelle close, his own aura turning a deadly shade of purple. "How dare you, Liaos."

"She's been with a man." Liaos' eyes frosted.

"How dare you insult the Princess so?"

"Princess?" It was Flint again.

"Smell her, Khazidhæ. She has been spoiled by another, and recently."

Cutter lifted Zelle's arm and breathed it in. She was powerless to keep her hand from shaking.

His eyes narrowed. "Sister. Tell me who did this. Tell me who spoiled you and I shall avenge you."

She lifted her chin. This was one disgrace she would not

allow Flint to bear. "No one has spoiled me."

His gaze searched hers. "Please tell me this happened before you remembered who you were. Tell Liaos you did not do this of your own accord and break your vow to him."

Zelle didn't speak. This was it. The moment she'd dreaded. The moment where he loved her despite what had happened, or cast her aside. She only wished she had more time to explain what she felt for Flint. To help Cutter understand that Flint was the right man for her.

"Tell me who it is, that I might exact my revenge," said Liaos.

Zelle turned her eyes on him. She must protect Flint at all cost. Even if she lost her brother for it. "It is true. I have lain with another. But it has been only one and I am still pure. My mist runs purple still."

"Then there is hope," said Cutter. "There is still time. You can be bound to Liaos. The union is still possible."

"No," said Flint.

Cutter turned to him. "Who are you to speak to me so, human? Do you not know who I am?"

"I think I've followed the conversation quite well."

"Flint, don't." She turned to her brother. "Cutter, please—"

His gaze made her mouth snap shut. Cutter brushed Zelle back into Liaos' chest. Liaos' large hand fell on her shoulder like an iron chain.

She watched on as Cutter approached Flint. His brothers surrounded him, but Flint pushed past them.

"You have lain with my sister. Princess Rapunzelle, heir to the throne of Shaidan. You have spoiled her for Liaos son of Thibonae, Captain of the Royal Guard." It wasn't a question.

"I have," said Flint. "And if she will have me, I will lay with her every night until the day I die."

Cutter's fist connected with Flint's jaw, rocking him on his feet.

"Cutter please." She surged forward but Liaos' hand clamped down harder.

Flint grunted, but didn't go down. His brothers moved in but he threw out his arms to stop them.

"Like I said, I will lay with her every night as my wife, until I die."

Again Cutter's fist connected with Flint's mouth.

Flint spit blood on the floor, spraying Cutter's boots. "You can punch me in the mouth until all my teeth have left me, but my answer will ever be the same."

Cutter flexed and unflexed his hands before his gaze turned on Sage. "I thank you for keeping my sister safe. I am in your debt. If you have a room, I would like to speak to my sister in private."

"Of course," said Snow.

"No," interrupted Sage. "I'm sorry but as you can see, my people are on edge. I would hate for any further misunderstandings with my family."

Cutter's lip curled and his gaze raked over Flint. "This human is your family?"

"He is. And I take responsibility for his actions. Any punishment bestowed upon Flint, is bestowed upon me as well."

Flint's head swung in Sage's direction. The small blond vampire and her tall counterpart stepped between Sage and Cutter. Zelle's heart sank. She didn't want to be the cause of a war between her people and the vampires. She had to stop this before Cutter's temper brought about the destruction of all Fairelle.

When she spoke again, she spoke to him in their native

tongue. *"Khazidhæ, please. Do not harm them, they have done nothing but try to protect me. This was my fault. Leave them be and I will go with you."*

He didn't turn. She stepped forward but Liaos' hand held her back. She looked up at him her anger burning a hole in her chest.

"Unhand me, guard," she said through clenched teeth. As they were not married and Liaos was still only a guard, he was forced to obey.

She moved to Cutter and placed her hand in his. He finally looked at her and his royal stare softened.

"I'll go," she said. *"Leave them in peace and I will make no more trouble."*

"We shall take my sister and return home." Cutter snapped his fingers and his men stood at attention.

"I won't let you take her." Flint stepped forward.

"I'd like to see you try to stop me. *Human.*"

"Wait!" Snow stepped away from Sage. "We have a place in the Wastelands. You can stay there for a few days. A place to calm down and think."

"Snow," Sage began.

She rounded on him. "We have a place."

Sage stared at her for another minute and then sighed. "I can show you."

"I'll go." Dax stepped up. "I know the way."

Cutter looked over Dax. "No."

"He's just a friend," said Zelle. "He saved my life more than once. If it wasn't for him you wouldn't be here. He's the one who found the spell for me."

Cutter's jaw clenched several times and then he nodded. "Fine."

"I'll go, too," said Flint.

"Absolutely not." Liaos threw his arm around her. Her spine pressed into his familiar frame.

Dax stepped up to Flint and placed his hand on Flint's shoulder. "I'll go. You stay here."

Flint's vacant eyes searched Dax's face. "Don't let anything happen to her."

"Never."

Zelle pulled out of Liaos' grasp and faced Cutter. *"I would like to say good bye."*

"No."

Her anger flared and she narrowed her gaze. *"That was not a request."*

Cutter stared at her, but she refused to back down. He nodded curtly and turned to his men. "We'll wait by the exit." The group moved out to the front hall.

When they were gone, Zelle rushed to Flint.

"You don't have to go with him."

"I do. You don't know my brother or his men. Even being vampire hunters and vampires you are no match for them. They are stronger and more bloodthirsty than you can imagine. I'll be all right with them. Cutter would never hurt me. He just wants me safe." She glanced over his shoulder at his brothers. She locked eyes with Erik. "Don't come after me."

Erik's eyes held sorrow, but he nodded.

She reached up on tiptoes and pressed her lips against Flint's. He wrapped her in his arms and kissed her hard. His scent and touch and taste blanketed her. She refused to cry, knowing well she may never see him again.

"Return to me," he whispered.

"I will."

With Dax in tow, she walked out of throne room and into the front hall.

CHAPTER TWENTY THREE

I t took every ounce of Flint's restraint to not follow Zelle. His mind reeled with ideas of what she might endure at her brother's hand. His jaw ached from being punched and he spit blood on the floor once more. Cutter had a mean hook and it had taken all of Flint's strength just to keep standing. But showing weakness in front of everyone was not optional.

"We better get these floors cleaned of blood before we have an even bigger problem," said Sage.

"Sorry about that," replied Flint.

Flint had meant what he'd said. He would take those punches and a thousand more if it meant he could be with Zelle. Over the last hours something had connected between them. Something deeper than love. She was his and he was hers in a way he hadn't believed possible. Without her he was nothing. He'd thought his life was torture before, that had been like playing paper dolls compared to this.

"Flint, are you all right?" Snow placed her hand on his arm.

"I'm fine."

She wrapped her arms around him. He stiffened and then relaxed and wrapped his arms around her in return. The affectionate contact was much needed.

"I have to get her back."

"We will," said Snow.

"We can't promise that," said Sage.

"Sage—" Snow began.

"I don't say that because I don't want to help, love. I meant every word I said about Flint being family. But you don't know what the daemon war was like. My father was there. He told me only the entire elder society of the fae along with the highest mages were able to push them back, and you see what that did to the land. After a thousand years still nothing grows there. My people are weaker than ever. We can't afford a war."

"What do we do?" asked a female.

"Sonya, I don't think you've met Flint."

"Briefly, before he ran off," Sonya said.

Flint stiffened.

"Not helpful," replied Sage. "We'll give them time to get to the Wastelands and then you and Greeg go and make sure they stay put. If they leave, one of you let me know."

"I want to go," said Flint.

"You would do better to stay with us," said Erik.

"I can't just sit here."

"Oh, you won't be," said Ian.

"We're going to feed you, and train. If there's a fight, you need to hone your skills as much as you're able, given your new sight limitation," said Erik.

Sight limitation. An understatement, and a polite way to

describe his blindness. But he could see the wisdom in Erik's words. Even if he did get Zelle back there was no guarantee that Rasmuss or Klaus or someone else wouldn't come after her. Thoughts of Klaus sparked something in Flint.

"Erik. You need to get Belle and Chloe away from Klaus. He's into some dangerous shite. He attacked us at Aunt Marissa's and tried to take Zelle."

Snow sucked in a sharp breath. "I told Jamen he was no good."

"Damn," said Erik. "She only left our estate a few months ago to go back to him."

"Klaus, the human who used to trade with Terona?" asked Sage.

"Yes." said Flint.

"Is Aunt Marissa all right?"

"Yes. She's a tough one," said Flint.

"Who is this Rasmuss?" asked Gerall.

"I don't know. He kidnapped Zelle about fifty years ago and kept her in a tower that she was unable to escape. He put a bracelet with one of those red stone on her arm to keep her there. He was stealing her magick and using it, but for what we do not know. All I know is he's a mage, and high up, from the color of his robe. Plus, he seems to know what happened to Dax."

"Then let's go down there and find him," said Ian.

"It's not that simple. I talked to another mage when I was at Cinder's. A man named Stil. He said there is no Rasmuss in their order. So whoever he is, Rasmuss isn't his real name and unfortunately the only people who know what he looks like are me, Dax, and Zelle."

"What were you doing at Cinder's?" asked Snow.

Flint swallowed. "I was looking for help to get Zelle out of the tower." It was half the truth.

"All right," said Sage. "I need to speak to some people, so we don't have a panic on our hands. Snow, come with me, please. Sonya? I will see you and Greeg in a few days."

Snow hugged Flint again and then let go. Liaos' words burned into his mind. *"She's been spoiled."*

Flint swallowed, remembering the feel of her body on top of his, under his, beside his, and so many other ways. He had to get her back. She was everything. Whether or not it had to do with her being a succubus, he didn't care. He just wanted her. Now and forever.

"WE HAVE TO FIND THEM." MORGANA STUDIED THE AGED MAP of Fairelle that hung on the wall of her room.

"But I still don't understand how." Rasmuss gave a shuddered breath.

The whipping she had given him for having failed to keep Zelle under control still appeared to be wracking his body.

"Patience, darling." Morgana turned and ran her finger down his cheek. "All that essence you have collected over the years from her, did you think it was only to power our amulets and the mirrors?" For all his magical abilities, Rasmuss was not very bright. "It's going to help us take Fairelle for ourselves."

Morgana walked to her workbench and removed a silver bowl encrusted with runes from the shelf. She placed it on the burned and scarred wooden table and produced a scarlet dagger. Sliding the blade across her palm, she dripped blue blood into the bowl then licked the wound before pulling up her sleeve and exposing the ornate golden bracelet with the blood red stone. She pushed a button on the side of the bracelet and the clamps retracted. Plucking the stone from its setting she placed it in the bowl.

She picked up a black lit candle and held it over the bowl.

"Blood of my blood and flesh of my flesh, hear me and let me see thy face."

She touched the candle flame to the blood, producing a flash of light. Amber smoke wafted off the bowl, shimmering and then solidifying into an onyx fog. A group marched into view.

"Khazidhæ," she gasped. "And the royal guard."

"How is that possible?"

If someone knew about the ritual to call daemons, then someone could find out the truth about her, as well. The thought didn't worry her as much as it meant she might have to rethink her strategy.

"Who all knows your true identity?" Morgana asked.

"Flint, Kondak, and Zelle have all seen my older face and know my name."

"Flint is no problem. You blinded him. But Zelle and Kondak could be."

"Then it's a good thing we've found them," said Rasmuss. His gaze traveled to the smoke. "But how did you find them when Terona couldn't?"

Morgana glared at him. "You dare insult me? Terona couldn't do anything but get men into her bed. You think I don't know more than she? I am her mother."

"No, of course not." Rasmuss swallowed.

Morgana surveyed the scene with the group walking through the dark.

"Hunter!" she called.

A strapping young man with piercing green eyes and short blond hair entered the chamber. The jeweled collar he wore shone brightly against his throat.

"Yes," he answered in a flat tone.

"Ready Fader, Thorn, and the others. We ride out in an hour."

Hunter nodded mutely and left. Morgana watched his firm shape depart. How she wished she could compel him to lie with her. He had to be an animal in bed. But her magick only went so far. To be surrounded by such virile men day and night and not be able to compel any of them to be with her left her aching with need. Only one of Hunter's men had ever shown desire in her presence without her even trying. Then there had been Klaus. A mild distraction but not even a fully satisfying one.

She peered into the smoke once more. Dax walked at Zelle's side and jealousy threaded its lethal talons through Morgana's heart at the thought that he may have feelings for her. How many minutes, days, hours had she spent trying to get Dax to give in to her? Even now, five years after his escape, she still wanted him. She would get him back, and make him hers, even if this time it killed her.

A phrase popped into her head. *"And love will make her stay."*

"Did you find my book?" she asked.

"I will."

Morgana gave him a hard look. She needed that book. It was the only one that held all of the prophecies. The only one that told the truth.

"Come, Rasmuss," she said. "Let's bring our family home."

ZELLE'S BODY ACHED. HER MUSCLES GROANED AND TWINGED with each step. They'd walked for hours. Cutter and his men marched without so much as a flinch, but Zelle wasn't used to this much travel on foot. Even though Snow had given her a pair of boots, her feet still complained as if she walked on fiery broken glass.

Dax had offered to carry her once, to which a fight had almost ensued with Liaos. In the end she had refused everyone's help, insisting she could make it on her own.

Everything looked the same in the barren black lands, but Dax walked with purpose and traveled straight to a large jutting black stone. He stopped, stuck his hand around the side of the boulder and yanked it open.

He turned to Zelle. "I'll show you to your room."

Zelle followed him down a long dusty hallway that led into the Earth. The scent of magick and wet rock filled her. Behind her one of Cutter's men lit the lamps as they passed. At the bottom the hall split in two. Dax turned to the right and went down to the last door on the left.

"This is my room. You may have it." He looked over her shoulder to the rest of the group. "There are rooms up and down this hallway and the other direction. Use them. This room," he pointed to the one behind him, "is King Sage and Queen Snow's room. I'll be staying in there."

"I don't want you anywhere near Princess Rapunzelle," said Liaos.

"I'm not near her. I'm in there," Dax pointed. His gaze slid to Zelle's face. "Not in the same room, but close enough to hear her if she has a problem."

His message was clear and Zelle was grateful to have Dax with her.

"What kind of problem?" Liaos asked.

253

"Like your jealousy and anger for a start." Dax didn't even bat an eye at the prospect of upsetting the large demon and Zelle respected him all the more for it.

"Enough," said Cutter. "Zelle, go ahead. I will be in soon."

She locked gazes with Dax. It wasn't that she didn't trust Cutter- she absolutely did- but Liaos was showing colors she had never before seen on him. Mainly green. She tried not to blame him. After all he had just found out that the woman he was supposed to be married to wasn't dead, but alive, and had chosen someone else.

"Shout if you need me," Dax said.

"Thank you." Zelle laid her hand on his arm and then quickly removed it.

She stepped inside the room. A lantern sat on the table nearby. She turned the little knob on the side and it illuminated. The room was comfortable, but cold. A lone wooden bed stood awaiting her with simple but clean coverings. A small chair and dresser finished out the room. There was no finery, only the basics. It made her miss her bed in the tower. At the thought a wave of panic raced through her. She was trapped. Underground and trapped. She closed her eyes and took a deep breath. It was fine. She was fine. She wasn't in the tower. Dax was right next door to take her outside if she needed.

After a moment she sat on the bed, tugged off her boots and flung her cloak to the floor. Her thighs ached from her time with Flint, and her feet oozed from the many abrasions.

She curled into a ball and wrapped her arms around herself imagining Flint's strong arms and warm body pressed against hers. Loneliness shot through her like an ice shard to the soul. She'd known what could happen if they lay together again, but she hadn't cared. She loved him and wanted only him. There was no way she could wed Liaos. Her heart belonged to another. Along with her soul.

A knock interrupted her thoughts. The door opened and Cutter entered void of his armor he looked like they had when he was young in his long emerald shirt and black leggings. So strong, his features so similar to their father's. He closed the door and stood there for a minute before moving to her side and gathering her into his arms. They wept together on the bed, holding each other for a long time without speaking. Finally, Cutter let her go and sat back.

"Sister, I have missed you so," he said, running a finger down her cheek. "The days and nights I spent looking for you. Months even. I wanted to die. Did they hurt you? Mistreat you? Tell me, so when I exact my revenge I can know just how much you suffered."

"I didn't suffer at all."

Cutter raised a brow.

"Truly, I didn't. I was given a cuff bracelet. It covered the spot where your name is tattooed." She lifted her sleeve to show him the scabs where she had ripped off the bracelet. "I didn't remember a thing. Not who I was, or where I came from. Nothing. The magick covered my birthright markings and made my ears more human. I thought I *was* human."

"Human?"

"Rasmuss said he was my father. He altered my memories to keep me complacent and drained my powers every few days. He had me locked in a tower, much the same as I was at home. I was given food, and books, and things to do."

"But why?"

"I don't know. He never was anything but kind to me, until the last time I saw him."

"How did you get away?"

255

"Flint and Dax."

His body tensed.

"Cutter, don't." She took his hand. "Please. You don't know Flint. He's a good man. He never did anything I didn't want for myself."

"How could you? You know better, and now with Liaos–"

"I never loved Liaos."

Cutter searched her eyes. "But you love this human. Flint Gwyn."

"I do," she said. "He is mine. And you know what will happen if I'm taken from him."

Cutter stared at her for a minute and then rose to his feet and paced the room. His strong hands rubbed over his face and through his hair. He stopped and looked at her.

"You know this cannot be. You were promised to Liaos. He has waited over fifty years for you. He never gave up hope that we would find you. Maybe his love for you will be strong enough…"

"I won't," she said quietly. "You know it isn't just his love for me. But mine for him as well. That is the only way to avoid the curse."

"Tell me then, Sister. What do I do? You are Princess Rapunzelle, heir to the throne of Shaidan. You are to be wed to the male heir to one of the most powerful families in our realm. If you were but a mere girl, this would be easy, but you are not. Duty must come first. You know father will say that."

"And what about you? What will you say?"

Cutter's eyes held sadness. "I would say that you are my sister. My twin. Blood of my blood and I only wish for you to be happy. But that will not be. I am sorry. On the morrow we leave for home."

"Cutter, please, do not do this." She rushed to his side and grabbed his arm. "I would not do this to you."

"I know you wouldn't. Which is why it makes this decision all the harder." He released himself from her grip and kissed her head. "Rest. Tomorrow's journey is a tedious one."

Before she could protest, Cutter walked out.

Zelle grabbed her hair and pulled it up by the roots. She couldn't believe this was happening. How could he be so cold?

There was another knock. "Zelle?"

Liaos.

She rushed to the bed, hopped under the covers, and rolled toward the wall before the door opened.

Liaos walked into the room. She caught his scent and shut her eyes tight, trying to keep him out.

"Rapunzelle, I know this cannot be easy on you. Having been pulled into captivity with no memory of our love or our impending marriage. I can only imagine the torments you have been forced to endure." He paused as if waiting for her to say something. "I want you to know that I do not blame you for what you did. I know with your nature you cannot control your urges. I am still committed to marrying you and regaining both your trust and your love. If you will but give it a little time, I know we can get back to where we were before."

How could he have thought all those years ago that she loved him? Did he know no different? She had been kind, but not loving. She supposed in her society that was equivalent.

"It's obvious you are tired, so I should let you sleep. But I wanted you to know that I'm here for you and will do every-thing in my power to protect you."

Even from myself?

He left without another word. She lay with Flint invading

her mind. The feel of his hands on her skin. His lips on hers. The taste of his breath–

It would never work between her and Liaos. That was obvious. Flint was in her soul, and–

Zelle sat straight up in bed. Her soul! She was a Soul Weaver. That was the connection. Why Rasmuss had taken her and drained her powers. Why hadn't she realized it before?

Another thought struck her. Flint. They hadn't been connected before. But now... Zelle smiled. She needed to get back to him. If she did, Cutter would have no choice but to allow them to be together, Liaos or no Liaos.

CHAPTER TWENTY FOUR

Z elle tried to formulate a plan but drifted off to sleep. Hours later she awakened to her stomach growling. When was the last time she'd eaten?

Hunger dragged her from her bed like a snarling beast. The silent halls were dimly lit. She didn't want to go snooping about, but her stomach took on a nauseated feel. She'd never gone so long without food, and though it was less than a day, it felt like a week. She walked to Dax's door and knocked softly. There was no answer. She knocked again. Still no answer.

Zelle turned away when it opened. Dax stood, shirtless, in the doorway. His large chiseled form staring at her, the epitome of manliness. A light smattering of golden curls trailed from his chest to his navel. His brown breeched hung low on his hips exposing the v cut muscles of his hips. Memories of Flint opened the gaping wound in her heart wide once more.

"What's wrong?" Dax scanned the hallway. "Did something happen?"

"I need food."

An expression of relief settled over his features. "Come, I'll take you to the dining room."

WHEN THEY REACHED THE T THAT CONNECTED THE PASSAGE that would take them to the surface a soldier stepped out and blocked their path. A pschyloc daemon. Black of skin with eyes like sungolds and matching nails. Small but deadly.

"Where are you taking the Princess?" he demanded.

"To eat," Dax replied unfazed.

The psychloc looked Dax up and down. "And why are you not properly robed in her presence?"

"I don't mind." Zelle stepped forward.

"It is improper for you to be with a male other than your intended or your family."

"Yes, well, I need to eat, so if you will excuse us." Zelle stepped around the psychloc.

He grabbed her by the arm. "I'm afraid I cannot allow you to go with him."

Dax ripped the daemon's hand from Zelle's arm. "Don't touch her," he growled.

The psychloc's eyes narrowed and his gaze intensified on Dax. His forehead furrowed and a perplexed look came over his face. He was trying to use his mind powers on Dax.

"What are you?" the psychloc asked.

"Dax is my friend. And as your princess I command you to stop trying to invade his mind."

"With all due respect, I don't answer to you, Princess."

"I'm afraid you do," Zelle countered. "The Royal Guard is headed by the heir to the throne, and with my return, Khazidhæ is no longer the heir. I'm sure you wouldn't like to be the one to wake him up and discuss the matter, would you?"

He stayed silent.

"Then you will let us go." Zelle pushed past the daemon and then stopped and rounded on him. "And if you ever lay a hand on me again, I'll suck the life force right out of you and leave your body for your brothers to devour."

The psychloc blanched.

She continued down the hall with Dax. Her father had agreed to allow Cutter to head the Royal Guard, at Zelle's request, since she needed to be shut away from males, but she was the one truly in charge.

No matter what she'd said to the psychloc though, she didn't want to take that from Cutter.

"Keep heading down, we'll be there in a minute," Dax said. "I'm not sure what there will be to eat though. As far as I know, it's been months since anyone was here."

"Well, hopefully we can find something. My stomach is killing me."

THIRTY MINUTES LATER ZELLE HAD EATEN SEVERAL STRIPS OF dried beef, three biscuits that were hard as the rocks surrounding her, and drank two cups of sweet, spiced mead. It wasn't what she had hoped for, but at least it had momentarily stopped the nausea and hunger pains. Dax had eaten twice as much and looked as if he had no plans of stopping anytime soon. Watching him reminded her of having dinner with him and Flint the first day they arrived at her tower.

"You miss him, don't you?"

"Yes." The word stuck in her throat and spurred a well-spring of tears into her eyes.

"Tell me something." Dax wiped his mouth with the back of his hand and then took a gulp of mead. "If you're in charge of the Royal Guard and not your brother, why don't you just order them to leave and you can stay?"

"It isn't that simple. The Royal Guard are just that. Guards. Their job is to keep the Royal family safe. Now that I have made the mistake of telling them I am in charge, I am afraid of what might happen. Liaos is the head of the guard. If he deems it necessary to do something for my protection, he will. Even if it means disobeying Cutter's or my wishes. Besides, I never wanted to take that from Cutter. It's all he has."

"What do you mean?"

She twirled the cup of mead in a circle with her fingers. "Cutter isn't like other royal males of Shaidan. He doesn't want to spend his reign lying with the temple virgins, repopulating our lands. He wants to fight to keep them safe."

"So royals just lay with women all day in your world?"

"Mostly or at least until they marry. It's considered their duty. Each realm in my world has a governor but they are all ruled by my father, the king. The governors' sons have taken on the duty, since Cutter refused. Father wasn't happy about it. But Cutter is more fighter than gentle lover. And there have been enough wars to keep him more than busy." She stared at the cup her heart bleeding for her brother and the duty he was born into yet had not chosen- much like Flint.

"What did you mean when you said your mist ran purple?"

Zelle sighed and relaxed into her chair. "My mother was a succubus. My father is a Soul Weaver. I am both. My mother was a wild youth. Succubi are known for their sexual prowess and desirability. She was betrothed to my father at just the age of forty. Merely a young girl. She loved him instantly, but was bewitched by my father's rival. She lay with the rival and was then cast aside. She didn't tell my father until their wedding night, after he found out she was not pure. Outraged, he locked her away and refused to see her anymore. Having been abandoned by two men, one of which she truly loved, my mother went mad. Soon after Cutter and I were born she took any man that would have her until my father cast her out. Enraged, she vowed vengeance. She died a few years later."

"How?"

Zelle shrugged. "We know not. Her body was brought to the palace for burial, but my father refused it. She's buried in an unmarked grave somewhere."

"And Cutter is afraid that by you being with Flint the same thing will happen."

"Yes. I think he believes that my true love is Liaos. Where I am from love is different than it is here. There it is respect and honor. To them Liaos and I are a perfect match."

"But Cutter loves you."

"He does, but it's different because I'm his twin. Our bond is closer than any in Shaidan. My mother's mist ran red when she went mad. But as of now mine is still purple like my eyes. Pure and untainted."

"Because Flint loves you."

"And because I love him."

"What happens if you go with Liaos?"

Zelle shook her head and closed her eyes. The silence of the room pressed down on her, threatening to cave her in. "I don't know. There is the chance that I could be fine, should I never lay with another again. But if I do... If I am forced to marry Liaos... I don't know what will become of me."

"Then we better make sure you stay with Flint."

Zelle's gaze found Dax's face again. "You are a good man." She laid her hand atop his.

He stared at it. "You know, it's strange to me that I find you attractive but have not felt anything more than that for you. Flint told me the way you affect him."

Zelle's brows knit. "That is strange. And when the psychloc tried to get into your head, he couldn't. I wonder if it has something to do with your amnesia. Maybe it's the same kind of magick that was used on me."

"I wish I knew."

"Are we interrupting?" asked Cutter from the doorway.

Zelle turned. Cutter's posture was rigid, fists clenched. The psychloc from the hallway stood behind him.

"We were just eating. Would you like some?" She pushed a plate toward the edge of the table.

"No." The frost of his voice grated her ears like gravel.

"She hasn't eaten since yesterday afternoon," said Dax.

"And she's done. So she can go to bed. We have a long journey tomorrow." Cutter's eyes stayed firmly planted on her face.

Zelle's anger flared. "You do not need to speak to me as if I am a common *Kenzi*."

"Then you shouldn't act like one."

She was out of her chair in an instant, nose to nose with him. "How dare you speak to me so?"

"I speak to you how you act, Sister."

Her magick sprung to life inside her heating her skin but she kept her voice as calm as his. "I came with you to keep peace and because I missed you, but that can change."

"Do not test me, Sister. I will do anything necessary to see that you retain not only your title but your status as well. I love you more than you can know and will do whatever it takes to get you home. But if you are going to break tradition and lay about with half dressed humans in the middle of the night, even I can't save you from Father's wrath."

Her muscled tensed ready to fight. "I lay about with no one."

"I believe you, but there are others who will not be so forgiving." Cutter's gaze slanted sideways to the psychloc.

Zelle swallowed hard and her stomach soured. It had been so long since she'd dealt with the whisperings of those in her father's court who were trying to gain favor, or bring his down. Her nausea rolled in like a thunderstorm. Suddenly, memories of the intrigue, backstabbing, and cutthroat nature of her father's advisors slammed into her.

"Are you all right?" Cutter reached out and gripped her arm.

"I need air." The walls closed in on her and her nausea grew. "I need air!"

Cutter picked her up and walked quickly with her to the entrance. He passed Liaos' room and the door swung open. "What is wrong with her?"

"She isn't feeling well."

Dax ran ahead and opened the entrance. Zelle jumped from Cutter's arms, just as her stomach lurched and she threw up on the rocks.

"Get the princess some water," Cutter called.

Another wave of nausea hit her and she threw up again. She sniffled, snorted, and cried her way through. Memories bombarded her. The Guard, her tower high above the training grounds and the smells of blood and ash, everything hit her until she was overwhelmed with grief.

Cutter really was going to take her home and there was nothing she could do about it. She was going to have to leave Flint forever. Zelle swiped at her eyes and nose. Red mist wafted off her fingers in a gentle swirl. She sucked in a breath at the sight.

It was happening. Despite what she wanted and what she and Flint felt for each other. Because of her shattering heart, the connection with him would be lost.

"Water." Dax knelt and pushed the cup into her hand.

She looked up from her hunched position to see his eyes widen.

"Drink it," he whispered.

Zelle brought the cup to her lips with a shaking hand. She gulped it down and handed it back.

Dax rose. "I think the stress of all of this has been too much for her. Maybe she should lay down, Prince Khazidhæ."

"I agree. She needs her rest." A nervous note rung in his voice.

Zelle wobbled to her feet supported heavily by the rocks. Cutter glanced at her hands but Zelle hugged herself and tucked them out of sight.

"Let's get you to bed."

A roar and flap of wings tugged her gaze up in the air. All the blood in her body fled from her limbs down to her feet. High above them a dragon circled. It burst out a rock-shattering roar and headed south.

"Rasmuss," she whispered.

FADER LANDED BEFORE MORGANA, WHO LOUNGED AGAINST Hunter's large dragon form and stroked his ear. His brilliant azure scales shimmered in the moonlight. The only time he allowed her to touch him was when he was in his dragon form.

Fader shifted. His wings folded into his body as his form twisted and shrunk until he stood a bare male before her, panting for breath. The sight lit her up inside like a lightning strike. She wished she could run her tongue over his pulsing, slick body.

"I've found them."

"Of course you have." She smiled.

"They are hiding in an underground cavern."

"What do we do?" asked Rasmuss.

"Wait." She stroked Hunter's ear.

"Why? We know where they are."

Morgana blew out an exasperated sigh and turned to Rasmuss. "Because I'm assuming a dragon cannot fit down where they are. We have to wait for them to emerge."

"But how long will that take?"

"As long as it takes." Morgana turned to Fader. "Get us some dinner. And then call the others. We prepare to fight."

Fader shifted and took to the sky.

Morgana smiled. It wouldn't be long now.

FLINT SAT IN THE DINING HALL EATING WITH HIS BROTHERS when the door burst open. Loca screeched on his shoulder and Flint put a hand on the bird to calm it.

"Sage." It was Sonya's voice. "We have a serious problem." The smell of damp clothing permeated the air.

"What is it?" Sage's chair scraped away from the table.

"Dragons."

"How many?" asked Erik.

"Three. But one took to the sky, presumably to gather

others. I don't know who their riders are or what they are doing, but they are watching the lair pretty closely."

"Rasmuss," said Flint. "He rode a dragon called Fader. Did you see or speak to Dax?"

"No," said Sonya. "A group emerged about an hour before we began our return. Princess Zelle is sick. Or at least she was when we saw her."

Flint was on his feet. "Sick?"

"She was carried both out of the shelter and back in by her brother."

"And Dax?"

"He was right at her side."

Fear crept through Flint like a thief in the dark. Zelle was sick and he wasn't there to help. "I need to go."

"You can't," said Erik. "We haven't trained enough and you are nowhere near ready."

"I don't care."

"Greeg is still there," said Sonya. "If there is any movement he'll contact us."

"By the time he does, she could be dead."

"No," said Sage. "He's going to use the pool."

"The pool?"

"I need to change. I am dripping everywhere." Sonya's heels clicked on the floor as she strode away.

Flint cursed under his breath. He didn't like the feeling of being left out. "What's going on?"

"The pool we came through the first time we returned to Tanah Darah," said Erik. "It's a mirror system. We don't know how it works yet, but we found a second mirror in Terona's old room and brought it into the front hall. It can be used as a portal to the pool."

"So Sonya came through the pool?"

"Yes. It's how we've have been traveling between Westfall and here."

Flint remembered the sucking feeling of traveling through the mirror at the bottom of the pool when they had come to save Snow from Terona and Remus. He had no interest in trying it again.

"I can't just sit here and do nothing."

"Good." Sage's cool grip clapped him on the shoulder. "Then you can train with me."

Flint's body complained from his workout sessions with his brothers. But the prospect of sparing with Sage brought a smile to his lips. Energy surged through him.

"When do we start?"

CHAPTER TWENTY FIVE

"Come on Flint, I've seen you fight, you're better than that," Sage said.

Flint growled in frustration. He didn't like being beaten by the vampire. He flipped to his feet and reached for his sword.

"It's by—"

"Don't help him, Snow," Sage said.

The fact that he was failing in front of his family was even worse. He found his sword by his left foot and picked it up.

"Feel the weight in your hands."

"You don't think I can feel it?" he snapped.

"Not the way you should. You used to use your eyes to tell you how far to strike, now you must use the space around you. Listen for the sound of movement. Smell the approaching opponent. Feel the swing of their sword as well as your own. Am I a foot away or ten? Use your other senses to tell you. And most of all, connect with your weapon. A wild swing could send you off balance. Without your sight to tell you where things are, you need to rely on your other senses to tell you what is going on."

Flint didn't like the lecture. He knew how to fight, with or without eyes.

"Go again," said Sage.

Flint took a deep breath and readied his stance. A soft shuffle sounded to his right and he swung that direction. A clink sounded to his left and he swung around.

"Stop moving so much and listen," said Sage.

"What do you think I'm doing?" Flint yelled.

"I think you're paying too much attention to your anger to focus."

"Anger at what?"

"At me."

"Sage, don't," pleaded Snow.

"No. He needs to say it. And he needs to hear it. Your anger helped you before, Flint, because you were wild and reckless in your fighting, making you a great warrior, but from here on out, if you want to be that warrior again, you need to calm yourself and pay attention."

"Nice talk." His anger rose at a quick pace.

"So tell me. Get it out."

"Tell you what?"

"That you blame me for Snow."

"If it wasn't for you she never would have become what she is."

"Flint, I made this choice for myself," she said.

"You made that choice for *him*." Anger trembled his grip and bunched his muscles.

"No." Snow moved toward him. "I made it for me. It's

271

what I wanted. Not because I didn't want you, or Erik or Jamen or Gerall or Hass or Ian or Kellan. But because I wanted this for me." She laid her hand on his chest. "I'm the same person, Flint. My love for all of you hasn't changed. But it has grown to include someone else. I'm sorry that hurts you. I didn't choose him over you. I chose a future that includes you all."

He had no words. His heart was heavy with grief. His thoughts traveled to Zelle. Wasn't that what he wanted her to do? Leave her family and everything she had known to stay with him?

"All right," Flint said. "Let's try again."

Snow hugged him tight. "I still love you, big brother."

"I know," said Flint. "I know."

ZELLE LAY IN BED, STARING AT THE BLANK ROCK WALL. HER tears dried and her body weighing her down, limp and ragged. She stared at the spider web crack that made its way up toward the ceiling. Her gaze tracked the veining until she thought of nothing but the crack. Not her brother, not her father, not Liaos, not even Flint. Only the crack and its possible meaning and existence filled her mind.

She'd barely moved in the last day and a half. The dragons still circled and there was nothing she could do about it except give herself up.

A knock struck her door, but she didn't turn. She couldn't. To turn and talk to someone would mean this was all real. Liaos, going home, father's court, being heir to the throne, leaving Flint. All of it. But most of all, knowing that in the end, she would be doomed like her mother and cast out.

There was only one way to stop that from happening, and Cutter and Liaos were not going allow it. Besides, if she stayed Rasmuss was out there, ready to recapture her and steal away who she was again.

A knock sounded again. She stared harder at the crack and put her hands over her ears. Just allowing her heart to beat and her lungs to suck in air was too much for her. A wave of nausea hit her and she tried breathing through it. She needed food, and not six-month-old stale food. Fresh food. She was starving but the thought of leaving the bed was more than she was capable of.

The door opened and Zelle shut her eyes.

"We need to talk," said Cutter.

She didn't respond. Gone was the brother that she'd known, and played with, and protected for all those years. The man in her room now was the Prince of Shaidan. A stranger.

"We need to figure out how to get out of here. There are more dragons arriving hourly and there is naught to eat. The men are getting restless."

"Then go," she said. "Leave me and go."

"Don't say that."

"Why? Tis better that I stay here as a slave to a man I do not know, than to be taken to a place with a brother who no longer loves me, and married to a man that *I* do not love."

Cutter's boots pounded the stone as he crossed to her, pulling the covers from her and yanking her to her feet. "How can you say that to me? After all I have been through to find you. To save you!"

Zelle pulled from his grasp. "Because it is not me you came to find, but the girl I used to be. I am no longer that girl. Young, naïve, compliant. I have learned what it means to be imprisoned. I have learned what it means to love and be loved.

Not what passes for love where we come from, but love, real love. To love another so much that you would be willing to sacrifice everything to be with them. And you care not but to bring me home."

"You don't belong here. Tell me that you won't be captured and tortured when others find out what you are. A cripple like that human could never protect you."

"Don't you dare speak of Flint that way. He was blinded saving me. That is a hero's honor. Were we in Shaidan he would be hailed round all the kingdom and set up high and watched after forever for his service. You know not of the scars of a warrior he carries. Not even you have so many."

Cutter's eyes narrowed and his lips clamped down into a thin line. Scars were a sacred honor amongst the fighters of her race.

"You do not know what we have been through these last fifty years. You gone. Father withdrawn. It has been up to me to run Shaidan. Without your grace, your powers, your delicate nature usurpers have come from all directions to try and take the throne. That guard out there." He pointed. "The one that stands between you and those dragons are the only thing keeping the infidels at bay back home. Countless battles we have fought. Thousands have died. I've had to lay with the virgins just to help repopulate our people. How I wish I could find love the way you have and be happy to sit and love and rejoice in it, but I can't. I am too busy producing a new generation and protecting our home. Only your return can end the wars. Only your marriage to a male of honor can bring to close what we've had to endure in your absence."

Zelle swallowed her shame. She was being selfish. A naïve child, like she had just professed she wasn't. To know what Cutter had been through tore at her soul. She wanted Flint.

To be with him, in his arms. But she had a duty. She couldn't just sit by and let her people, her brother, suffer.

All this time since remembering who she was she'd thought nothing of the plight of others. She thought only of herself and Flint. Never wondering if Cutter was all right. Not once thinking that her homeland may be in trouble. All those years of being a princess and she'd not once thought of her people. That wasn't how she'd been raised.

She nodded, her heart crumbling. "I'll go," she whispered.

He blew out a heavy breath. "Thank you."

She nodded.

"We just need to figure out how to get out of here."

"I have an idea, but it won't be pretty," said Zelle. "Let me use my power."

"It's too dangerous."

"It is dangerous and will require quite a bit of sacrifice from the guard. It'll weaken them. But if it works, it will get all of us home."

"How can I help?" he asked.

"I need to feed."

His eyes swirled with emotion. "The risk you take—"

"Is a risk for my people. If we are slaughtered here, it'll be worse for them, than if I do this."

Cutter stared at her hard for a moment and then gave her a curt nod. "I'll ready the men."

DAX STORMED INTO THE LIBRARY OF THE UNDERGROUND dwelling. He couldn't believe what was happening, and the fact that he was powerless to stop it made things even worse. He'd promised Flint he'd protect Zelle and now she was upstairs sucking life out of every male to increase her powers. He'd witnessed her explosion of power in the forest. Running after her as she bounded through the trees. The screams of pain and the indescribable high pitched whining sound they burst from her. The arc of white light that fanned out destroying everything in its path. He'd barely ducked behind a tree in time. The bark had peeled from the trunk of the tree along with the arms of his tunic. The experience was something he'd not soon forget.

He paced his half filled room. Empty bookcases and drawers stared at him. Someone had cleaned the place out in the months that he'd been off with Flint.

Dax slammed his fists down on a table splitting the wood. He roared in anger. Trapped between the dragons and the daemons, he was nothing but a bystander. He turned and punched a nearby bookshelf.

An object on the corner of the lowest shelf clattered to the floor. An ornate hand mirror. A memory surged. A vision of a beautiful woman with flowing silvery hair looking into the mirror and speaking.

Dax lifted the mirror with a shaky hand. It was set with a large red stone at the top. The slice of dread cut through his skin. He raced down the hallway, passing daemon after daemon that were lined up to meet with Zelle in Cutter's bedroom. He headed to Zelle's room and located her cloak on the floor. Rummaging through it, he found a broken red stone. The stone from her bracelet.

He held the stone to the red stone atop the mirror. Together the stones glowed brightly. His reflection dissolved and a small corridor of mirrors appeared. Dax stepped out into the hallway and peered around. There was no one in the hall. He slid into his own room and shut the door, locking it. He sat down heavily in the wooden chair making it creak.

Blowing out a deep breath he touched the mirror and his hand passed right through. He jerked away. The image shifted and changed until he was looking into a familiar room. Tall wooden walls lined with beautiful ornate paintings. A tapestry of a green dragon covered the floor. Pillows and covers of deep crimson silk dripped from the large wooden bed. A figure in the bed rolled over.

Klaus.

Dax growled deep in his throat.

He placed the mirror on the table as images of being in that room, on that bed with a silver haired woman laughing next to him, bombarded him. The last image was that of an army of dragons standing before him.

He took several deep breaths to calm himself. When he opened his eyes the mirror had gone dark. He pressed the stone again.

"Tanah Darah," he said, taking a chance.

The image shifted and zoomed forward darting here and there until finally he looked out into a room he'd not seen before. He wasn't sure how to do this. He'd been sucked through the mirror at the bottom of the pool but something told him that wasn't his first time.

"Sage!"

There was no answer.

"Sage!" Dax yelled again.

Still no answer. He'd said Tanah Darah but who knew where the corresponding mirror could be hidden. It could be hours or days until someone entered the room containing this particular one.

He just hoped that someone showed up before Zelle and the daemons of them got themselves killed.

"It's been two days Sage, I need to go check on Greeg," Sonya said.

"You can't," said Flint, following the group through the castle hallway. "What if they see you and kill you both? We'll not have anyone to communicate with."

"Nice to know you aren't concerned for me personally," Sonya replied.

Flint didn't care a whit about Sonya. He only cared about Zelle and Dax. Sonya and Greeg were a means to an end.

Over the last two nights Flint had eaten more and trained more than he had in months. He'd begun to feel like his old self, painful as it may be. He wasn't one hundred percent yet, but he was close. It amazed him that since losing his sight his other senses had become more acute. With Sage's tutelage he'd been able to tune into his other senses to use while fighting.

They'd arrived at a door. Someone pushed it open and Flint was hit with the scent of magick. Alchemy supplies came to mind. Dusts and potions, essences and other substances.

"You can't keep me here. I have a right to go check on him," Sonya said.

"Unfortunately, I can keep you here, as I am your king," said Sage. "But I won't."

"Sage if we lose them both–"

"Then I will have lost my best friends," said Sage. "You want to make sure Zelle is all right. Sonya wants to do the same for her mate."

Flint swallowed. There was nothing more to say.

"Sage?"

Dax's voice floated from somewhere in the corner. Sonya gasped.

"Dax?"

"He's in a mirror," said Sage. "Dax how did you—"

"It's a small hand mirror. I found it in the lair library. Look, there's no time to waste. You need to get down here. There are dozens of dragons and Zelle is planning something dangerous."

"What's happening?" Flint moved toward Dax's voice.

"We're trapped and have no food and little to drink. We need to get out of here. They're planning to fight the dragons."

"They'd be slaughtered," said Sonya.

"Zelle came up with a plan. She's going to use her powers on the dragons and then everyone is making a run for the rift."

"What about Zelle?" Flint asked. Panic pounded loud as thunder.

"She's going with them."

Flint covered his face with his hands. This couldn't be happening. He needed to go to her. If she faced the dragons, she died.

"We have to go," said Flint.

"The only way through is the pond. You'd have to swim blind," said Sage.

"We're talking about facing dragons, I think swimming blind is the least of my problems."

"Tie him at the waist to someone else, that way you can pull him up if need be," said Dax.

Voices floated out of the mirror.

"What, is a man not allowed to look in a mirror where you're from Liaos?" asked Dax.

There was silence.

"Dax? Dax!" called Sage.

"I have to go." Flint turned for the door and a cool hand dropped on his shoulder.

"We all have to go," said Sage. "Ready the guard, and tell your brothers, we leave immediately."

"We could send for Adrian's assistance," said Snow.

"No time," Sage replied. "We're on our own this round."

CHAPTER TWENTY SIX

R ed mist swirled around Zelle thicker than she'd ever experienced. The energy of her magick buzzed and snapped around her like a cocoon of fireflies. In the past hour she'd sucked essence from every one of her royal guard. Liaos stood before her, awaiting his turn. He stared at her, his face a mask. There was no hiding the red mist from him, Cutter, or anyone else.

"You lied," he said in a flat tone.

"No." Zelle shook her head. "Yesterday my mist ran purple. Today with all I have taken in, it has changed," she lied.

"Is there no going back?"

"I don't know."

"So there's a chance?" Hope lifted his features.

She didn't answer. She didn't want to lie to him, but as she would be returning home, the truth could make him unpredictable. And in the battle to come, they needed him. "Come, we have little time."

Liaos moved to her bed and sat beside her. She noticed how large his body was; larger than even Flint's. His short hair meant she couldn't run her fingers through it. His eyes bright as his hair, not dark like Flint's. He smelled of home, not of sweat and dirt and the road. A million tiny differences separated the two men. Things that she'd come to appreciate before, now left her raw and prickly. Everything about Liaos screamed to her that he was not the one. But she had to do this.

He lifted a rough hand and caressed her cheek with his knuckles and his lips met hers. They were warm and full against her mouth. He prodded her lips with his forked tongue and she withdrew from him.

"Not like that," she said.

With a heavy exhale, he dropped his hand.

"Lay down. That way if you become light headed you won't fall."

"Is that what you did with the others?"

What was the use of trying to hide it? He'd find out anyway. "Yes."

Liaos' aura swirled evergreen and black as he lay on the bed, never taking his eyes from her. One of his arms found its way around her waist and settled at the base of her spine. With all the contact and pheromones that she had been exposed to in the last hour, she had to take several deep breaths to keep from attacking him. He was different from Flint, but not unattractive. His alien type of beauty was something she had been raised to see as handsome. And his large, muscular body hadn't been unpleasant when they'd slept together before, though he'd never brought her pleasure the way Flint had.

"Do our lips need to touch?" he asked.

"No." She leaned in close, her hand sidling up his chest. She was inches from his face. Desire flooded his orange eyes. He exhaled once and she inhaled. She waited and breathed in again when he exhaled a second time.

Suddenly he pulled her on top of him and their lips met again. He kissed her harder this time. Everything about their contact was so recognizable. They'd been there many times before. His arms wrapped around her as she breathed him in. His taste was exotic and strong. Stronger essence she'd never had. His split tongue snaked into her mouth. She breathed him in again and he kissed her harder, lapping at the inside of her mouth, until a wave of nausea pulled her from him. She doubled over and dropped her head between her knees. The nausea grew along with her mist. With the food gone she'd not eaten in close to three days.

"I'm sorry." He pressed his hand into her spine. "I shouldn't have. I know that. But I've waited over half a century to feel you in my arms again. Hoping. Praying the gods would return you to me. I don't care that your mist runs red. You are not your mother. I know you. Have known you for so long. When we are wed, you will purify your mist in my love. Together we will break the curse."

She sucked in deep breaths in an effort to stave off the nausea that consumed her once more. Her stomach growled like a wounded animal. She was so hungry. They all were. They needed to get out of this place.

"I wish I could feed you," he said. "Bring you the carcass of a mandelor, cook it for you, and feed you with my hands."

To be fed by the hand of a warrior was a great honor, and showed tremendous humility and adoration. It was almost as sacred as making love.

"I should like to taste mandelor right now." The nausea

passed and she sat up. Liaos' eyes held nothing but concern and affection.

"Then let's get out of here and I shall catch one for you." He smiled revealing straight white teeth.

Cutter entered before she could answer. "Are you ready?"

She pulled away from Liaos and stood. "Yes."

Dax appeared in the hallway behind him. "Can I have a minute?"

"No. Yes." Liaos and Cutter said at the same time.

"Yes," Zelle said.

Liaos and Cutter left and Dax entered. "I got a message to Flint."

"What? How?"

"I found a mirror. They're coming, we just need to wait."

He was coming for her. Her smile fell. He'd be injured if he came, possibly killed. "No. Tell them not to. This isn't their fight."

"It's your fight, which makes it Flint's fight."

Zelle grabbed Dax by the arm. "You need to tell him to stay away."

"Do you really think he would stay away with you in danger?"

She scowled and turned from him. "You shouldn't have told him."

He turned her to face him again. "How could I not? I withheld information from him before and it almost ruined our friendship. I won't do that to him again. And I won't do it to you either. You are my friend and I'd risk my life to keep you safe. There is no stopping him from coming. And why would you want to?"

"Because he'll be hurt! He's in no shape to fight."

Dax chuckled. "Well, I suggest you don't tell him that when he gets here."

"No," said Zelle. "I won't. Because there's not going to be a need." She burst from the room.

"Zelle, wait!" Dax shouted.

She couldn't let Flint anywhere near Rasmuss, or Liaos, or any of them. Although she had to go back to Shaidan to save her brother, she didn't have to get the man she loved killed in the process. The mist expanded and contracted taking on a life force of its own as she raced for the exit. She couldn't hold it off much longer.

She knocked into the psychloc daemon from days before, but didn't slow.

"Zelle!" Cutter yelled.

She didn't care. She sprinted for the entrance and pushed the boulder wide. The cool air slapped her in the face. Behind her everyone followed. She stepped out onto the gravely ground, the rocks pressing into her bare feet. At first she heard nothing but the sound of leathery flapping wings.

A roar split through the night and she stepped out farther. A group of dragons clustered together toward the edge of the woods. She ran for them, with the guard right behind.

A dragon's head rose from the ground and swiveled her direction. Several climbed to their feet. They clicked and hissed in a language she did not recognize. From out of the middle of the cluster, a man in a blue robe appeared. *Rasmuss.*

"Welcome, Zelle." He smiled. "And welcome, Cutter."

"You kidnapped me," she said, still advancing on him.

"No, dearest, it wasn't me. But I did keep you safe this long while." He was younger, even more so than the last time she'd seen him. He appeared no more than forty.

"If not you then who?" Dax caught up and stood beside

her. Cutter and Liaos stood on her other side. The guard held back.

"Well, you do have quite the entourage. One befitting a princess of course."

"Wait for Flint," said Dax in a low voice.

The dragons hissed and clicked faster. Their eyes tracked Zelle and moved from her to Dax.

"You've been naughty." Rasmuss chuckled. "Your mist flows red. I'm sorry for that, truly I am. I tried to keep it from you. Was it the bear or the blind one?"

"Stop talking to me like you know me," Zelle spat.

"Oh, but sister, I do know you. I know you quite well."

"She isn't your sister," Cutter yelled.

Rasmuss laughed. "Well... not entirely. Zelle, I still want what's best for you. Come with me, and I'll let Cutter and the others go. Except the bear. I have someone who's been looking for you for a long while, Dax."

"You want her, you'll have to go through me," said Cutter.

"You'll have to go through all of us," Liaos yelled.

"I had hoped you'd say that," Rasmuss smiled. "I haven't had a real fight in ages." Rasmuss raised his hand. "Hunter! Attack!"

The dragons didn't move. Their eyes were all on Dax.

Rasmuss' smile faltered. "Hunter, attack!" he yelled again.

The dragons twitched and moved forward, but did not attack. Rasmuss spun on his heels and faced the dragons. He raised his arm and pressed the stone on a cuff he wore on his wrist. The stone shone green. A gem on the collar of each of the dragons lit up.

"Attack!" Rasmuss yelled again.

The dragons roared in agony and took to the air. They circled above as Cutter ordered his men into formation.

Dax pulled Zelle out of the way. "Don't do this," he yelled at the dragons.

One of the dragons looked down at Dax. It was nudged by another dragon and the two began to snap in midair at each other.

"You don't have to obey, you're free to choose," he yelled.

Zelle wasn't sure what Dax was getting at, but at least it was distracting the dragons from attacking.

"Kill them!" Rasmuss commanded.

A dragon broke from the pack and dove for Cutter and his men. Opening his giant mouth, fire flew from his throat as he passed overhead. Zelle screamed as Cutter and his men raised their shields to protect themselves.

The dragon continued past, reached out with a clawed foot and grabbed one of the guard. Pulling him into the air, it dropped him from high above.

Anger swelled inside Zelle. Her mist grew thicker and tighter like a binding rope. Cutter and his men regrouped and took cover closer to the entrance of Sage's hideout. Several of the dragons fought against each other. The roars above her were deafening.

Dax continued to stare into the sky. He spoke words in a language she didn't understand. Every once and a while a dragon would glance down at him. Rasmuss looked on, yelling for the dragons to attack. Every time he did, a couple more did his bidding. Five dragons dove at the guard. Cutter brandished his giant flamesword, attacking anything within reach. Several of his soldiers fired crossbows at the dragons as they passed but the attacks were useless against the armored winged beasts.

Zelle needed to do something. Her gaze trained on Rasmuss. She ran for him at top speed, knocking into him she shoved him to the ground. The air whooshed out of him and his eyes widened.

"Stop this," she demanded.

"Well, sister, I didn't know you had it in you." He laughed.

"Why do you call me that?"

"Because you and I are kin. We share the same mother."

"My mother is dead."

"Who do you think brought you here? She saved you from the same fate that she endured at the hands of your father."

Zelle blinked rapidly. It wasn't possible. He was lying to distract her. "Stop the dragons."

"I'm afraid I can't. My job is to bring you and Dax home. Come with me. Mother is waiting."

"Never!" Zelle dropped her face close to Rasmuss's and sucked in a deep breath. Her mist lapped at his face and arms. Rasmuss's eyes popped wide open as she sucked in his essence.

"Stop them."

"No," he choked.

Zelle breathed in again, deep and hard. Rasmuss's face paled. He pushed at her, but she'd grown strong in the past days. She was no longer a timid human. She sucked in again and then slender fingers gripped her shoulder and ripped her off Rasmuss, flinging her to the ground. Zelle looked up into vibrant red eyes. Rasmuss coughed and sputtered rolling on his stomach away from her.

"You have your father's gift as well as mine," Morgana said. "I'd hoped you would."

CHAPTER TWENTY SEVEN

Dax was at Zelle's side a moment later, lifting her to her feet.

It wasn't possible. She had seen her mother's body and wept on her mother's bosom until her father had ordered the body away.

"Hello, Lover." Morgana helped Rasmuss up as well. "Long time you've been hiding from me."

Zelle could do nothing but stare in disbelieve.

Morgana called to the sky and a giant dragon swooped down.

Dax rushed forward as Morgana and Rasmuss climbed onto the dragon. It hovered off the ground and roared.

He ground to a halt and turned toward Zelle. "Run!"

They headed for where Cutter and his men fended off the onslaught of dragons. Fire, ice, acid, all were shot in the guards direction. Only their daemon armor was able to keep out the worst of it. Cutter caught sight of Zelle and Dax and he and Liaos broke formation, running their direction.

"Get down!" Cutter yelled.

Without warning giant clawed feet pulled Zelle and Dax off the ground. Her stomach plummeted as she was propelled into the air. Her limbs flailed downward as if calling to the ground while her spine felt like it was being grasped by the heavens.

Cutter cursed and Liaos let forth a blast of fire from his hand in the direction of the dragon. The shot was high and it missed.

If Morgana got her to where they stayed, she'd be bound in the cuff again. She locked eyes with Dax as the night air slapped at her face.

"Do it," he said.

She remembered the last time she had released a blast. Dax had followed her and not been harmed.

"You could die being this close to me."

"Better dead than captive. Do it," he said again. "For both of us."

Zelle glanced down to see Flint, his brothers and the vampires rushing toward the fray. Her gut clenched at the though of him being hurt. She had to do this. No matter the cost. She took a deep breath, pulled her magick in tight.

"I love you all," she whispered, and then let her magick go.

FLINT SLOGGED THROUGH THE CHILLY NIGHT AIR IN HIS WET clothes. They'd run from the pond to the edge of the Wastelands. The sounds of battle drifted from up ahead. He held on to Gerall. Loca perched on his shoulder nipping and hooting alerts when something was in his way.

"Come on," said Erik. "Cutter and his men are pinned down."

"Where's Zelle?" he called.

"Look!" said Sage.

Everyone stopped abruptly.

"What is it?"

"It's a dragon," said Gerall. "Carrying two riders and holding Zelle and Dax in its claws."

"Shoot it down!" he yelled. "If they get her away we'll never find her."

Gerall moved his grip. Flint heard the creak of Gerall's bow as an arrow loosed.

"It glanced off. Their scales are too thick," he said.

"Gerall, you and I'll follow them."

"I don't think—"

A booming sound shook the ground. A pitiful roar split the night air. There was a flash of bright light that burned Flint's eyes forcing him to turn away.

"What the hell was that?"

"An explosion," said Sage.

"The dragon's falling!" cried Erik.

"Take me!"

Gerall grabbed Flint's hand and rushed forward. A blood curdling scream sounded behind him, but all other fighting stopped. The sounds of men in armor rushed by. Loca nipped Flint's ear and he stumbled over something. Gerall caught his arm and moved him forward.

Ahead the screeching of a wounded animal and the smell of burning flesh permeated the air. Gerall slowed and Flint heard cries.

"Where is she?" he asked.

"Cutter has her," Gerall replied.

REBEKAH R. GANIERE

"Take me." His throat was dry as the Ashlands that surrounded them. When they got close, Flint stuck out his hand and laid it on a sobbing armored shoulder.

"Flint." Her voice was gravelly and weak.

He knelt and felt her fingers on his face. The scent of blood slapped him and bound him so he couldn't move.

"Why did you do that? I came for you." His eyes welled with tears and he wished more than anything he could see her.

"I did it for you. I couldn't let you get hurt." She coughed and the wet gurgling sound stuck in his ears.

"That's not your job. I'm supposed to protect you. When will you learn that?" Salty tears burned rivulets into his cheeks.

She laughed lightly. "Silly human male." Her hand fell from his face.

"Zelle? Zelle?" He groped for her.

"You did this!" shouted Liaos. The sound of armor moving close made Flint tense. He was lifted to his feet by an unseen hand. "This is your fault. You took her, changed her. Ruined her. If it hadn't been for you, her mist would have been pure and we would have been wed and she would not lie in her brother's arms close to death."

Flint had no words. The rest of his group caught up. His brother's breathing hit his back.

"This is not Flint's doing," said Sage. "Princess Rapunzelle made a choice."

Suddenly Flint was struck with the truth of Sage's words. The truth for Snow, and the truth for Zelle as well.

The sound of flapping wings surrounded them. Air whooshed about like a vortex as dragons neared.

"Kill them," Cutter ordered.

"No," said Sage. "They don't want to fight. Look at them."

292

"Where's their master?" Anger fired through Flint at the thought of running Rasmuss through with his sword.

There was a murmur of confusion as the group moved to the injured dragon.

"They're gone!" someone yelled.

"We need to get Zelle home," said Cutter.

"No." Flint's gut clenched.

"Yes," said Cutter. Zelle moaned and Cutter moved close to Flint. Her scent mixed with blood. Flint stroked her silken hair and cheek. They were cold to the touch.

"I'm sorry," said Cutter. "She loves you. I know she does. But you are not equipped with the magick needed to heal her. I have to get her home to her people who can take care of her."

Flint's heart shuddered. If she went through, she wouldn't be able to come back. If she stayed, she died. Either way, he was going to have to live without her.

"We need to go, Cutter, before she goes into the Fade." Liaos' voice was hard.

"Can you promise me that she'll be taken care of and not cast out for what has happened to her here?" Flint asked.

"I promise on my life that no harm will befall my sister," Cutter intoned.

Flint brushed at his tears and nodded. He leaned in close and inhaled her scent one last time before kissing her cheek. "You are my love and my life forever," he whispered. Then he stepped back and listened as Cutter and the guard jogged away.

Pain deeper and stronger than any he'd known threatened to cripple him. "Dax. Where's Dax?" he asked.

"Over here," said Erik.

Gerall moved Flint forward. He knelt down and touched Dax's naked body in Erik's arms.

"Is he dead?"

"No, but he's out cold and it looks like he has a broken arm and leg at minimum. We need to get him somewhere warm."

"What the hell?" Hass said.

A large, hot presence loom over Flint's shoulder. The smell of charred cinders wafted off the creature. Fear rippled his abdominal muscles.

"What the going on?" asked Flint.

"I don't know," said Gerall. "The dragons, they're staring at Dax."

A mournful cry filled the air. Then another and another. The sound reverberated around them and shook Flint to his bones.

The sound of beating wings surrounded them as air pressed down. Then the heated presences were gone.

"What the hell was that?" asked Ian.

"Did you see their collars?" asked Erik. "They lit up suddenly, as if they were called."

"Come on," said Sage. "We need to get Dax home."

Flint climbed to his feet, trying to comprehend what had happened. His best friend was almost dead, and so was the love of his life. But even if Zelle did live, he would never feel her touch again.

A small hand slipped into his. "Come on, big brother." Snow laid her head on his shoulder. "Let's get you home, too."

Flint sighed and a tear leaked from his eye. His life was over. All he wanted to do now was pass into the Fade to be with the rest of his dead.

CHAPTER TWENTY EIGHT

Zelle gazed out her open window. From a distance the peony and tangerine clouded sky taunting her with their brilliance. The dark atmosphere of Shaidan loomed over her like her father's shadow. The lands that she called home were now alien to her. In the week that she'd been back she'd kept to her cream stone rooms, surrounded by her finery, and longing for the strong arms of Flint. A new prison. Polished and full of servant, but a prison nonetheless.

Her reunion with her father had been short lived when she realized the deterioration of his mental state. Cutter really had taken over the running of Shaidan. Advisors from around the lands had swarmed the castle at news of her return, but both Cutter and Liaos had forced them to give her space.

Even as she looked out across the black grounds of her homeland dotted with apple red trees, she could see preparations for her return celebration far below. Thousands upon thousands of people gathered from all over to catch a glimpse of her. Their hope for peace renewed. But Zelle didn't want to see them. For the first time since leaving her prison in Fairelle, she just wanted to be left alone in her high tower.

The door behind her opened, but she didn't turn.

"You haven't eaten again," said Liaos.

"The food upsets my stomach," she replied. Her eyes fixed on the swirling blue rift in the distance that separated her world from Flint's.

"You've been gone too long, I suppose. Is there anything I can get you?"

You can get me back to Fairelle. "No, thank you."

"Perhaps a broth would be easier for you."

"Mayhaps."

"Would you like to talk?"

"Not right now." She watched as the wind whipped the fallen leaves across the lake surrounding the tower.

"Then I shall see about your broth."

"Thank you."

Liaos tried, but every moment she was near him felt like a betrayal to Flint, and she agonized over what would happen with her mist. Their union had been announced by her father once more. They would wed within the month. But she'd come to a decision in the last week- one that neither Cutter nor Liaos would like very much. One thing was for sure however, she would not end up like her mother.

She still couldn't understand how her mother was alive. When she'd told Cutter and Father they'd not believed her. No one seemed to have seen Morgana but she herself, and Dax. Her heart squeezed. She didn't even know if he was alive or dead. Or Flint, or Snow, or any of Flint's brothers. She covered her face with her hands and refused to cry again, trying to calm the agony that tore at her soul like a caged animal.

She turned from the large open window. Her stone walls and floor were so different from the gray stone of Fairelle. Her cream bed was adorned with blue pillows and silks of different shades. She'd made the servants change to those colors as soon as she'd awakened from her injuries, so she could feel closer to the colors of Fairelle. Even the thin dress she wore was the color of Fairelle's cerulean skies. Her gaze traveled to the tray of food and her stomach growled. She wrapped her arms around herself in an effort to stave off the hunger pains.

She'd barely eaten since her return. The wildness of the game churned her insides to the point of nausea. There were no berries, no fruits, no breads in Shaidan. Only game and roots and drink.

Luckily for her the temple priestesses had performed the rite of healing on her to a degree that had saved her life. Though she couldn't find it in her heart to thank them. She'd much rather have died than live the rest of her life away from Flint.

"Princess?"

She turned to the door. "Enter."

A female dressed in the fawn colored robes of a virgin appeared with several young in tow.

"Hello, Highness. I am Arena. I thought that perhaps you might want to meet some of the new royal offspring."

Zelle's gut clenched as she was reminded of Cutter's duties. There were half a dozen children. Two girls and four boys in ages ranging from small child to early adult.

"Hello," Zelle said.

They each murmured a reply. There were two boys and a girl with Cutter's coloring, the others she assumed, look like their mothers. She had never thought about the offspring before.

"Where are you raised?"

"They are raised in the temple, with us," Arena said. "Until they come of age. Then the boys are trained as royal guards, and the girls are prepared for a life as a virgin."

"Is that what they would choose?"

Arena smiled. "I'm sorry?"

"The children. Is that what they want for their lives?"

"I... I don't really know, Highness. That is how it has always been."

How had that plight escaped her notice before? "And the girls who become temple virgins, they are sent away to other lands to be prepared for other royal males?"

"Yes, Highness."

"Away from their families, from those they love and have been raised by?"

"Yes, Highness."

"And what of you, Arena? Is that what happened to you?"

Arena looked at the floor and swallowed. When she made eye contact again her shoulders were straight. "To be a temple virgin is a great responsibility. We honor the gods and our king by being in their service. To bear a child of royalty is our birthright and privilege."

Zelle didn't think that all such virgins appreciated the way things were run in Shaidan. She knew all too well what it was like to be stolen from those you loved. The fear of being bound to open yourself up to a male you did not know or want. The burden of duty. Being back in Shaidan, it had all been made fresh again. She wished she could see Arena's aura to tell if she was lying, but the atmosphere was so different in Shaidan that she could no longer see them.

"Thank you for coming to meet me," she said. "I'm sure we shall see each other again soon."

"Of course." Arena lifted her eyes once more. "All praise the gods that you have returned safe to us."

The children repeated the mantra and the group left.

This was not the life she wanted for herself. This was not a society she wanted to live in. One where children were produced out of duty and then ripped from their mother's arms to service the gods and their king.

Zelle loved Cutter, and felt responsible for the burdens he carried, but one thing was clear as glass. She could not stay here. She needed to find a way back to Fairelle.

CHAPTER TWENTY NINE

WESTFALL, FAIRELLE WINTER, 1211 A.D. (AFTER DAEMONS)

4 MONTHS LATER

F lint smoothed down the flank of his steed Ripper with a stiff brush, his fingers rigid from the cold. What had started out as small adjustments and tasks to do had become his daily routine. After the heartbreaking first weeks, waiting in Tanah Darah for any word about Zelle's condition, his brothers had brought him and Dax home. Dax had broken his leg, arm, wrist, and several ribs in the fall, but his body had been miraculously uninjured by the blast that had killed the dragon as well as possibly Rasmuss.

While in Tanah Darah, Flint had gotten his hands on the book Zelle had used to call Cutter, but no one could decipher the spell. Written in Daemonic the only one who would've been able to read it was Rasmuss. After Flint had argued for days with his brothers about riding down to the mages and demanding they find him, sanity had won out.

"If Rasmuss is still alive, which I highly doubt," Gerall,

had said, "we cannot go looking for him. Or let him know we are looking to bring Zelle back." Of course Gerall had been right.

Upon arriving home Flint had been torn by his joy for Jamen and Scarlet, as well as his pain at his own loss. His old room had been just the way he'd left it. Even the tunic and breeches he'd tossed on the floor still awaited his return. The scent of tobacco and alcohol had permeated the room and it had taken months of airing it out and washing everything he owned for the smell to lessen. It'd taken just about as much time for him to finally get past the shakes and dry out after a three week binge. It had been Scarlet who had put her foot down and thrown out all his bottles of alcohol before throwing him into a tub and scrubbing him with his clothes on. Ever since, she and Jamen had taken to caring for him personally. It had been Scarlet who had set him up with things to do around the house and in the stables. For the first month after getting sober she'd kept him so busy he'd done little more than eat, sleep and work.

Loca hooted from the rafters of the barn and Flint stopped brushing. Someone with a slight limp crunched across the snow cover drive.

"Dax. What brings you out to the barn this morning?" He began brushing again, moving around to the other side of Domingo.

"Just wanted to speak to you for a moment."

"Something wrong?"

"No..."

Flint stopped. He'd known this talk was coming for months. He'd tried to stave it off as long as possible. But the majority of Dax's bones had healed.

"I'm leaving for Cinder's in the morning."

Dax had been struggling since the fight with the dragons. They'd talked about what had happened and Flint had known it was only a matter of time before he moved on. He deserved to know the truth and to find his people, but Dax had become like a brother to him over the last year.

"Do you need company?"

"No. Thank you, but no. You have a life here you don't need to go chasing after mine."

Flint stopped and turned his gaze toward Dax. "I'd go. You know I would."

"And I would appreciate it. You're the closest thing I have to family. But I don't know how dangerous, long, or where this journey is going to take me and it's best that I do it alone."

Flint had the urge to argue, but he couldn't because in all honesty, he had no desire to travel anymore.

He nodded. "You always have a room here, and if you ever need us, you know we'll be there."

"Thank you."

"Make sure you take the hand mirror so you can keep in contact."

"I will."

"How about I finish up and we have one more sparring session before you go? I still owe you a black eye from the last time."

Dax chuckled. "You're welcome to try and repay that debt."

"I'll be in soon."

Flint listened to the sound of Dax walking across the snow dusted ground to the house. His thoughts turned to Zelle once more. Her smile, her soft hands, the peace she brought with her. He'd tried to make a life for himself at the manor house.

Overseeing things like disputes among the renters, the horses, and Snow's aviary. Small things, meaningless really, but they kept him busy and gave him lots of time alone, which was what he wanted.

He placed the brush on the stall railing, grabbed an apple and gave it to the horse to munch on before he walked out of the barn. He rubbed his hands together and yearned for a warm cup of cider. Loca landed on his shoulder as he headed toward the house. Long shadows cooled his skin as evening approached.

It was exactly fifty-six steps from the barn to the solar door. When he opened it, the sounds of the crackling fire filled his ears as the scents of cinnamon and spice warmed him. Loca hooted and flew from his shoulder.

His skin prickled.

Someone was in the room with him, though he couldn't see them. The shadows that had consumed his vision months ago had all but gone dark now except for the corners.

"Who's there?"

Loca made a small hooting noise somewhere in front of him. Flint breathed in deep, trying to steady his nerves. "I know you're in here and I asked who you are. If you are in my home, you know who I am and I'm not one to be trifled with."

"Not be trifled with huh?" said a soft voice.

Flint's throat went dry and he reached out to steady himself on the table. Her scent wafted over to him and he had to blink back tears that threatened to spill. It wasn't possible.

"Zelle?" he whispered.

"Hello, Flint."

"You're... Are you really here?"

"I am."

"I… how? How did you get here? Did someone call you? Bring you?"

"No. No one summoned me. I came on my own."

His body ached to rush to her and feel her for himself. "But… but I thought that wasn't possible. Daemons can't come through to this side."

"Not usually."

Flint shook his head, unable to comprehend what was happening.

"Why don't you sit down?" She took him by the arm and sat him in a large chair by the fire.

He wanted to hold her. To kiss her. She took a step away and he grabbed for her hand. She squeezed tightly and then moved away. He could hear a chair being hauled closer.

He leapt to his feet. "Let me get that for you."

"It's all right, I have it." Her breathing was hard and she puffed with exertion.

A chill ran through him. "What's wrong? Were you hurt in the fall?"

"No." She sat in the chair with a creak and reached for his hand again. "No, I wasn't hurt. I'm fine, quite tired from the trek, but I am well. Sit."

"Wait." Flint tried to wrap his mind around her words. "You walked here, all the way from the rift? By yourself? Zelle, do you know how dangerous that was? Plus it's freezing outside."

"It wasn't too bad. A man with a wagon gave me a ride from the edge of the Grasslands to here."

"But still, the walk from the rift to the Grasslands is half a day at minimum." He touched her face and she pressed her cheek into his palm. "You shouldn't have done that. You need to rest." Flint dragged her to her feet.

"Flint, wait—"

He pulled her close, but froze when their bodies connected. She was different. Flint ran his hands over her face to her shoulders. They'd rounded and filled out slightly. He traced down her arms to her belly. It was large and protruding. He ran his fingers over the top of her bump and felt a small kick from under her skin. His mind went into overdrive and he fell into his chair.

"You're with child."

"Twins, actually."

Flint took several deep breaths. *Twins.* "Liaos?"

"No. I was never with Liaos after... Anyway, this wasn't how I wanted to tell you but they're ours. Yours and mine."

Twins. He was having twins.

"I understand if you don't want me, but I thought you had a right to know."

"Wait, what?" Flint lifted his head.

"I am ruined, according to my people. Liaos would no longer have me once he found out. Which I was grateful for. My father wanted me executed, but Cutter intervened. I was to be locked away in my shame. Instead I fled."

Flint jumped from his chair and took her in his arms. "I want you. How could you think I would not want you?" He pulled her face to his and kissed her softly. "I want you. I love you. I want all three of you. I'm yours." He knelt in front of her and pressed his lips to her stomach before wrapping his arms around her waist. She was so big that he could barely get his fingers to touch. His eyebrows knit together. "Wait, you shouldn't be this big so soon."

"My people grow quicker than humans. We are only pregnant for about five months. But I have a feeling it will go longer than that for me, since the babies are half human."

"So you could have the babies any day?"

She chuckled. "Yes. But I'm sure it will be another month or more."

Flint jumped to his feet. A month. He only had a month to get things ready for his children to be born. His children. He could barely contain his joy. "But I don't understand. How did you get here?"

"I walked through the portal. Or should I say, Cutter smuggled me to the rift and then I walked through."

"But the rift was sealed so daemons couldn't cross into Fairelle."

"It is, but it doesn't keep humans from coming through. And our young are half human. So the rift had to let us through. I waited until they were big enough though, to be on the safe side."

"What if it had killed you?"

"Living there without you was as good as death to me. And for our children it would have been worse."

Flint pulled her in tight once more. The press of her form against his sent tendrils of happiness weaving through his muscles, filling his entire being. "I love you," he said.

"I love you too."

Flint kissed her lips and his body awakened with desire.

"Well are you just gonna stand there kissing the princess or are you gonna make an honest woman out of her?" asked Ian.

There were several snickers to Flint's left. Zelle broke the kiss and laughed. Flint wrapped her in a tight embrace.

"I don't know," said Hass. "If I were her, I might want to go for someone better looking, like me, perhaps."

"No way in hell," replied Flint.

"I have something you might want." Erik pressed something into Flint's hand. A ring.

"Oh!" Zelle said with a slight jump. "I have something for you too." She pushed away from him and rummaged through a bag. She returned and settled him into his chair. "Close your eyes."

"I already can't see."

"Just do it."

Flint chuckled but obeyed. She slid something up his nose and over his ears. It was lightweight and he could barely feel it.

"Open your eyes slowly."

This was silly. He opening his eyelids a fraction. A red haze came into view. He blinked several times and the blur cleared. He gasped. A red tinted Zelle stood in front of him. To his left Erik looked on, arms crossed, and smiling. Hass, Ian, Jamen, Dax, and Gerall moved forward, all smiling.

He could see.

It was red, and a bit blurry around the edges, but he could see. His gaze traveled to Zelle. Her slender form heavier with pregnancy. In the red haze her purple eyes had taken on a vibrant magenta appearance. He reached up and took off the glasses. His vision faded. He placed them back on.

"How did you get these?"

"Cutter helped me make them. I used a portion of the broken stone that Rasmuss used on me, to bind my essence to the glass. They heal your eyes, but only while you wear them."

"Did it hurt you?"

"No. I gave up a portion of my vision to create them though. My vision is no longer as sharp as it used to be and the evenings will be darker. Not by much, but I fear I will never be good at needlepoint and sewing again."

"I'll hire someone to do it for you."

He looked around at his brothers. Joy oozing from every

pore. He had the woman he loved, his brothers, and children on the way. He had peace.

He got down on one knee and slipped his mother's ring onto Zelle's finger. "Rapunzelle, will you be my wife, my life and my joy, for as long as I live?"

She smiled widely. "For as long as I live."

EPILOGUE

Zelle awoke to Flint's muscular arm draped over her bare chest. She smiled and snuggled close to him. His body had changed so much since the first time she'd seen him. His once thin and gaunt he was now filled out and muscular again. Strong and healthy he was worthy to be one of her royal guard. Even his use of weaponry had increased to a level she didn't think possible, due to his blindness. But somehow losing his sight had enhanced everything else, so he preferred to not wear the glasses when he fought. But for all of his tough exterior, his heart was as soft as the downy pillow she lay her head on.

She traced a new scar on his chest. The outline of it still red and puckered. After they'd been married by Erik, Flint had taken her up to his bed and before they made love- insuring her mist would never flow red, she'd performed the ritual of soul-binding. Taking a piece of herself and tethering it to him, she'd not only bound them together, but for as long as she lived as well. Unless some fatal accident befell one of them, Flint would live for another several hundred years by her side.

For all of her happiness with Flint over the past three months, she couldn't shake the nagging patch of dread that clouded even her sunniest of days. Rasmuss was still out there. And even if he was not, Morgana most certainly was.

Flint snored loud enough to wake himself. She chuckled and he awoke further, smashing her into his chest. She ran her fingers lightly over his scars as he bent his head and kissed her.

"Good morning, my beauty." His dark eyes stared at her blankly.

"Good morning, my warrior. Did you sleep well?"

"With you in my bed, I always sleep well." A smile played across his lips and he kissed her again. "And I awake well, too." He kissed her, pressing his arousal into her belly. His tongue mingled with hers and sparks lit up her spine. Every day with him it was like this, and this was how she wanted it always to be.

"Did you sleep well?" He trailed light kissed down her neck.

"Of course."

He stopped. "Bad dreams?" He smoothed her hair.

"No worse than usual." Her voice quavered only slightly.

He kissed her and sucked her bottom lip into his mouth. "I will find them and kill them. That is my vow. I will feel his blood as it runs down my sword. Rasmuss will pay."

She stroked his cheek. "I know, my warrior." The gnawing dread caused her throat to clench tight.

"They'll never take you again. You're safe here." He kissed her again and their tongues blended sending shockwaves of desire traversing her body. He rolled on top of her, his bare skin on hers. She let out a moan of pleasure as he kissed his way down her throat to her stomach. Wiping all bad thoughts from her mind.

"Flint." She tangled her fingers in the soft chocolaty curls on his head.

"Yes, my love?" He licked her naval.

A distant cry stopped her, mid-thought. They ceased moving. Each holding their breath.

Two closer cries followed the first.

Flint sighed. "Maybe we should get a home of our own. Baby Kellan wakes the twins too soon every morning."

Zelle snickered. "You would never move away from Jamen just because his son is an early riser. And besides, the twins wake him up in the afternoon so we're even."

"You're right, as usual."

"Did you doubt?"

Soon the twins demanded attention.

Flint kissed her once more. "I'll get them." He hopped from the bed and pulled on his breeches and tunic as she threw on her nightdress.

"You don't have what they want."

"Yes I do," he replied. "I have you."

Flint reached into the first honeywood cradle that he'd crafted by hand and pulled Lucia from her rosy colored blankets. Lifting her to his shoulder he spoke softly into her silvery hair. The baby quieted as he brought her over and placed her in Zelle's arms. Then he walked to the second cradle and pulled dark haired Marcus from his matching cradle.

"My boy." Swaddled in robin's egg blue blankets, Flint rocked the baby in his arms.

Zelle smiled as Flint kissed Marcus' head and stuck his pinky in the baby's mouth to suckle on. The twins beautiful white auras were almost blinding in the morning light.

Flint lounged next to her and smiled. His aura swirled in a cloud of peaceful rosy pink. Though he still had the glasses she'd made, they gave him headaches so he only wore them when they had company or he had to go out.

Sitting on the bed, feeding her daughter, happiness swathed her. With Flint by her side, and her children loved and protected, what more could she ever need? Purple mist drifted off her skin and surrounded her daughter. This was the life they were meant for.

CINDER THE FAE

FAIRELLE BOOK FIVE

By Rebekah R. Ganiere

CHAPTER ONE

VILLE DEFEE, FAIRELLE - LATE SUMMER, 1212 A.D. (AFTER DAEMONS)

T he coins slid across the counter one by one, scraping the glass and making Cinder's nerves shred.

A pompous, buttercup yellow hat that she could only assume was the latest fashion in fae society, adorned the local fisherman's red hair. His bright fern colored tunic, embroidered in golden thread, cost more than her shop earned in a week. But for all his finery, he couldn't hide the excess of drink in his cheek and excess food from his waistline.

She scooped the coins into the register and slammed the drawer, trying not to let her irritation show. She plastered on a smile, handed Silas his bag and thanked him for coming. Taking the man's money was easy. Having to stand his smell and manners was something else altogether.

His pale blue eyes scrutinized her.

"Was there anything else, Silas?" If she were to be leered at, it wouldn't be by a fisherman who smelled like a scuttle fish dipped in love potion perfume. She rubbed her nose at the nauseating mixture.

She tried to brighten her smile, but the flicker in his eyes told her he wasn't buying it.

He gave a crooked grin, revealing teeth so white and straight only magick could have done them. "That's Baron Silas to you, Cinder. You forget your place since your father's death."

Her eyes narrowed, and heat licked her cheeks up to the tips of her ears, deepening her anger. "My place stays where my father put it. His death did nothing to dilute my blood."

"How naïve you are, girl." Silas pulled himself up to his full six-foot height and scratched his jutted, cleft chin. "I might be able to secure you a place, however."

Cinder's skin crawled like spiders covered her, and she struggled to swallow the bile that scorched her throat. She might be considered a lowly shop girl by some, but she'd be damned if she'd let someone like Silas look down on her.

"I'm just fine where I am, thank you."

Silas leaned in and stroked Cinder's cheek with his long pudgy finger. "How long will you deny me? Do you think you can do better?"

Her thoughts traveled to Rome and her gut clenched. Though she'd loved him for years, he was the one fae she could never have. That didn't mean she'd stoop so low as to accept Silas though.

Suddenly Silas grabbed Cinder's face. "You are nothing more than a *Tingafae*. I'm a Baron. What makes you think you can deny me anything?"

Anger roared through her breast, and she shoved out her hand. An icy blast of cerulean magick burst from her fingertips and hit him square in the chest. He flew a foot from the counter and hit a display table, knocking over a tower of tea canisters, and sending them spilling in every direction.

Silas flipped to his feet, hat askew, and advanced on her. "You little–" He stopped short as diamond white magick arced between Cinder's fingers.

"Get out," she warned. "My father may not have left me much, but he sure left me his temper. And the next time you lay a hand on me, Silas, you'll wish that jolt was all I'd done to you."

He stood, chest puffed out, cheeks as red as cinnamon candy. For a moment, she questioned whether she'd gone too far, but Silas would be too embarrassed to report what had happened.

The bell over the entrance rang, and someone stepped into the shop, but Cinder couldn't see around Silas' bulky form. Silas glanced sideways, toward the door, and relaxed his stance.

"Problem?" asked the newcomer.

"No." Cinder smiled at Rome and shoved her hand below the counter, flinging off the magick. "Silas stumbled."

Cinder waved her other hand, and the tea canisters righted themselves. She sucked in a breath, trying to stave off the fatigue that seeped into her muscles from the use of magick.

Rome strode toward the counter, his highly polished boots clunking on the wooden floor. His boyish smile and sparkling, azure eyes cheered her instantly; just as they had for the past sixty years.

He ran his fingers through his messy, chestnut hair and chuckled as Silas struggled to retrieve his purchases. The small vials had rolled in every direction.

"Tinctures for your foot fungus again, Silas?" Rome picked a piece of horehound candy from a dish and popped it into his mouth.

Silas gave up on the last vial which had rolled deep under a cabinet and stood. "It's from standing in sea water so much."

It was a lie. Silas had several human fishermen down south that brought him their catch every week. Though it was forbidden to have dealings with humans, no one saw the harm. Not the gate guards that looked the other way for a few coins, not the fae who loaded in the fish, and not the fae who paid for the fish.

Silas' eye caught Cinder's for a moment and then he looked at Rome. "Well, I must be going."

Rome waved toward the door. "Don't let us keep you."

Silas bristled and gave a tight smile as he bowed. "Your highness." He turned to leave.

"And to Lady Cinder?" Rome asked.

Silas' back straightened and his shoulders bunched. He turned around slowly. His gaze fell heavily upon Cinder, but then he smiled genuinely.

A shiver crawled up Cinder's spine.

"Lady Cinder, I hope you have a pleasant day." He inclined his head and then strode from the shop.

As the door slammed shut, Rome let out a bark of laughter. "What an ass."

"He certainly is." Cinder's eyes stayed glued on the door as she stilled her anger.

Rome looked at her, and his smile fell. "What happened?"

Cinder swallowed and met his gaze before looking away again. "Nothing."

She picked up the lid to the jar of horehound candy and replaced it, then grabbed a cloth and scrubbed at a spot on the glass counter.

Rome continued to look over her. He had ever been her loyal protector. Standing up for her with anyone who dared to put her down or treat her as a lesser. But she didn't need him getting in the middle of her battles. Not this time. She could handle herself.

He reached out and touched her face gently, placing his fingers just where Silas had before. Cinder swatted his hand away and rubbed her cheek. Rome's eyes narrowed.

"*Afa Kalinda Mae.* He touched you."

"No, he didn't." Cinder ground the cloth on the invisible spot. Out of the corner of her eye, she saw Rome bite his bottom lip and scan the shop floor. She knew that look. He was replaying what he'd seen.

"Rome—"

"I'm going to kill him." He rushed to the door, but Cinder was right behind him.

"*Dota.* Don't, Rome, please." She grabbed him by the arm.

His handsome face twisted into a mask of anger.

"He had no right to lay a hand on you. He should be punished."

"Please. If he reports me then I'll have to go to a hearing for using magick on him. You know what could happen to me. And if I lose my father's shop what will I have?" The begging coated her mouth like soapy water, making her stomach roil. But she knew this side of him. The royal side, the just side. His father's side. She took his hand and squeezed it like she had when they were kids and scared.

After a minute, his face softened, and he squeezed her hand in return. "You always have a place to go, Cinder. I'd never let anything happen to you."

His sincerity struck her hard in the heart.

She sat her fists on her hips and blew the hair from her eyes. "I know, but I can't rely on you to get me out of trouble. What kind of reputation would I have then?"

He laughed. "Since when do you care what other people think?"

"I don't, but it would be nice to marry someday, and who would want a woman with a tarnished reputation?"

"We've been friends forever. People know that."

"Yes, but what kind of female friend gets the Prince to help her out of trouble with the law?" She wiggled her eyebrows at him.

Rome's expression grew serious again. "You've never spoken of marriage before."

She shrugged though her insides squirmed. She'd not thought about marriage much, except to Rome. But Silas had been right. Due to her father's not claiming her as his heir before he died, she had little to no standing in the fae community at all. Men with higher bloodlines wouldn't want a woman like her.

"Well I can't spend forever waiting around for you to ask me, can I? Not that I'd say yes," she joked.

A sly smile grew across Rome's face. He brushed a hair behind her ear then ran his finger along the outside to the apex. "As if you would ever curb your independent side enough to be bound by the rules of being a princess."

The tone of his voice struck her as serious, and something else replaced the playful glint in his eye. Like he was prodding her, testing her. She swallowed hard at his nearness and the desire to kiss him burned deep inside like it had ever since he'd kissed her in the field of sungolds ages ago.

"I might." She leaned into him, taking in his wonderful, lemon balm scented cologne. "If the right prince came along."

His face held mock offense. "Oh?" He grabbed her around the waist and brought her hips into contact with his. His deep blue gaze sucked her in. "Am I not the right prince?"

319

His words held the same teasing tone he always used, but his eyes were fixed on her like nothing else existed at that moment. What was he playing at?

In the past months, something had changed with him. Ever since the night Flint Gwyn had come asking for help and Rome had carried her home, something had been different. Nothing she could put her finger on but his words seemed a bit more earnest at times and his actions more meaningful. All she could assume is that it had to do with his father's desire for Rome to finally settle down.

The most eligible male in the kingdom, Rome was prone to flirting, but she knew what his life held. Parties, dignitaries, delegations, festivals, royal everything. Always on his best behavior. Always smiling and judicious and… a royal wife. One with grace and poise; one that didn't break the law or combine her magick with a mage to help a human. And most importantly, that had pure blood. Blood was the most important. Always had been.

Which was why, no matter who her father had been, how close he'd been– or how close her step-uncle now was to the king, she would never be a princess.

So why did it feel like he was asking her if she was really interested in the job?

Her heart ached for him. Yes, Rome was judicious and a stickler for the law as the prince. But with her he was someone else altogether. He was funny and kind hearted. He always listened to her problems with her stepmother and offered logical advice. Something she herself wasn't prone to giving. He never saw her as a commoner, and he treated her with respect. They'd shared every hope, every dream, every new beginning with each other. He knew her inside and out. Her good, her bad and her ugly, and he was still there.

She stared at his lush, full lips and wondered if they would taste the same as they had the time he'd kissed her, when they had played seek and find as children. She'd pushed him away then, afraid that he was only toying with her like she'd heard he had with other girls. And as he'd never tried again, she could only assume he had been testing the limits of their friendship.

"What's going on here?" Came an angry voice from behind them.

Cinder stumbled as Rome let her go. Her stepmother came through the back curtain and walked to the counter. She took one look at Rome, and her anger melted away instantly.

"Why Prince Rome, I'm so sorry, I didn't recognize you. How are you this fine morning?" Cinder's stepmother glided toward them, a toothy smile, wide as the moon, planted on her face.

Cinder stepped aside, bumping into a table of herbs, as her stepmother shoved a burgundy silk cloak into her arms. Cinder bowed and moved to hang it up.

"Tell me, your highness, what can I get you today?"

Cinder peeked over her shoulder to see her stepmother link a slender arm in Rome's and pull him into the middle of the room. His eyes never left Cinder's, and her cheeks flushed with warmth as she walked to the back room. She bit back her shame of being treated so low in front of Rome and hung the cloak on a hook near the rear door. She listened to her stepmother chat at Rome as she lit a fire in the small stove and put on a kettle for tea.

Cinder knew the drill. Stay out of sight, pretend she didn't exist, unless someone needed something magickal made.

Cinder pulled up a stool and tended the fire, flicking sparks off her fingertips while listening to the light tinkle of laughter from her stepmother out front. Her heart sank, thinking of Rome and his offer to help her.

Her father had been an advisor to the king. But since her father's unexpected death, five years before, Cinder had been forced to be the breadwinner for her stepmother and half sister. Her father came from a respectable bloodline, and he'd taught her everything he knew about magick, as well as herbs. He'd left her stepmother the apothecary, but the woman knew nothing about running it. Fancy parties and charming men she could do, but providing for herself and her daughter was beneath her.

The curtain was thrown aside, and Cinder's head whipped up. Her stepmother's eyes narrowed on her, and Cinder's gaze traveled toward the shop floor. Had a customer arrived? She hadn't heard the bell ring.

"Prince Rome would like to speak to you about his grandmother."

"All right." Cinder swallowed hard and kept her eyes on the floor. She crossed to the curtain, biting her tongue to keep from saying what she really wanted to. Her stepmother grabbed her by the arm, digging long nails through her thin dress and into her skin. Cinder's gaze caught her stepmother's and for a second she could swear the woman's eyes flashed red.

"Remember your place, girl. You are nothing more than the product of a fling with a seductress. Only I and my daughter Olivia carry the name of Rondell."

Cinder dropped eyes again, and her ribcage squeezed her like one of her stepmother's magick corsets. How could she forget her place when she had so many people willing to remind of her of it? The slashes to her pride burned white hot.

"Yes, Stepmother."

The woman gave a guttural, wheezy hiss. "How many times do I have to tell you not to call me that? Are you dense?"

"No, Lady Sabine."

Sabine thrust a parchment with a list into Cinder's hand then brushed past her, grabbed her cloak and headed for the back door. "Bring those potions by the house when you break for lunch. I have some clients coming in that need them. And it's a complete mess back here. You are to straighten up before tomorrow."

"Yes, Lady Sabine."

Sabine's gaze raked over Cinder. "Tomorrow, see that you wear something nicer as well. I don't want anyone thinking that I can't afford to keep you well enough. And please, for the sake of the gods, put some shoes on those hideously enormous feet of yours."

Cinder crossed her bare feet and swallowed but said nothing as Sabine swung her cloak around her and stepped out the back door. She tried to keep her anger contained, but the blue tendrils of magick had already begun to swell within her, like a floating lantern.

It was Cinder and her magick that kept both the shop and her stepmother in style. Without her magick, Sabine would be forced to do the work herself. If anyone looked as if they couldn't afford nice clothing, it was Cinder herself.

For the first time, the desire to run away crossed Cinder's thoughts. It would be hard out in the world of Fairelle, and she would miss Rome all of her days, but perhaps the Gwyn brothers would help her. They'd ever been kind to her and more like family than her own. Her ribcage squeezed, Ville DeFee was her home. So why did she never feel like she belonged there?

Rome peeked through the curtain into the back room and glanced around. "Is it safe? Did she go?"

Cinder sighed. "She's gone." She walked to her flat shoes and picked them up, looking at them. "Do you think my feet are hideously enormous?"

Rome chuckled. "What?"

"Nothing." She slid them on.

Rome shook his head and stepped in. He folded his arms and leaned against the back wall.

"I don't know how you do it, Cinder, I really don't. I couldn't put up with a woman like that."

Anger pierced her, and the need to stand up for her step-mother crossed her thoughts. But she couldn't pretend. Not with Rome. He knew her too well. "She and Livy are all I have. Even if she doesn't want me," she finally said.

The bell rang, and several sets of footsteps entered.

"I need to go."

"Me too," he said. "But I'm going to bring my grand-mother in tomorrow. She's got a cough that worries me. And I wanted to speak to you about something. Something important."

"You can tell me now."

He shook his head. "No. I want to do it when we have a bit of time."

She planted a forced smile on her face. "I'll be here."

Rome wrapped her in a hug and kissed the top of her head. "It'll get better. I promise."

Her cheek brushed against his chest, and the scent of him made her eyes close as she inhaled.

If only she knew who her mother had been. If only her father hadn't died before claiming her as his heir and giving her his name. If only she'd tried harder to win his affections. If only, if only, if only...

"Helloooooo?" Came a call from the front of the shop.

Cinder backed away. If only I were someone else.

He shot her his winning smile and pointed at her. "I'll see you tomorrow."

She nodded and ambled to the curtain.

"And Cinder?"

She glanced back.

"Your feet aren't hideously enormous. Only moderately enormous."

She flicked her fingers and a hand towel flew off the work-bench in his direction. He ducked out the rear door, and the towel hit the glass window instead of his face.

He laughed as she glared at him. A smile snuck across her face, and she shook her head before going to the front of the store.

If only she'd let him kiss her again and again when they were young.

ROME WALKED INTO THE KITCHEN, ON THE FIRST FLOOR OF THE castle and plucked at his tunic from the long walk from Cinder's apothecary. From the apothecary he'd gone to tend to the duties his father had asked of him.

Rome scanned the plethora of food on the counter.

"Prince Rome. Is there something I can get you?" asked Bess the cook.

"A piece of pie if you have it, Bess. Thank you." His stomach growled loudly.

In the past months, his father had added more and more

responsibilities to Rome's plate. Not that he minded, it was his duty, but Rome was no fool. He knew the real reason. His father wanted him to settle down. His thoughts went to Cinder and their encounter from that morning.

Rome sat at the round wooden table in the corner and undid the top buttons of his jerkin. Ever since Flint Gwyn had shown up, something had changed. Seeing her break the law, by combining her magick with Stil, and almost getting herself killed, made feelings he'd pushed aside for decades roar to the surface. A protectiveness that had him wanting more than just friendship. Just knowing that Silas had insulted and touched Cinder made Rome want to banish the fishmonger's entire family from Ville DeFee.

But in the past months there had been more than just the feelings, there had been the thoughts as well. Thoughts of life with her. And life without her. Of what he'd have done if she'd died that night. She was so willing to risk her life helping someone else. It was one of the things about her that he loved and hated most. She always followed her heart, no matter the cost to herself. Whereas he was bound by the law. Bound by his duty. Bound to his kingdom.

The fleeting moments he spent with her were the happiest times of his life. Going to see her in her shop. Having her up to the castle for a walk. Eating with Stil and the three of them playing games. Things they'd done for decades. Things that were becoming harder to find the time to do with all the new responsibilities. And not seeing her on a daily basis had him even on edge about wanting her to be with him constantly.

Despite his father's fear that he'd never marry, Rome had thought about it quite frequently of late. The problem was... he had no idea how he was going to convince his father to let him court Cinder. And honestly, Rome wasn't sure he could court her. He didn't want to ruin their friendship and he was under no delusion that she would change who she was and conform to the life of a princess.

Bess set down a large piece of goldenberry pie. "Anything else I can get you, highness?"

Rome picked up his fork and his mouth watered. "No, thank you."

Bess nodded and headed back to the long table piled high with food. Rome glanced around to find the head cook making a list and going over it with several other servants. For the first time he noticed how many servants were about. Where only Bess and two others were usually in the kitchen, there were currently close to half a dozen people.

Outside the kitchen maids ran here and there, and the butlers barked out orders to the footmen. So much commotion for a weekday. He tried to remember if there was a special occasion he'd forgotten about, but nothing came to mind.

"Why is everyone so excitable today?" he called to Bess.

"For the feast of course."

"A feast?" He shoveled a bite of the crisp tart fruit into his mouth. There hadn't been a feast in the castle since his mother's death. "What's the celebration?"

Bess's eyebrows knit together. "You are."

"Me?" Rome wracked his brain again. What day was it? "It's not my birthday."

He shoveled several large forkfuls of pie into his mouth, and then poured himself a cup of ansleberb wine.

Bess wiped her hands on her apron and licked her lips. "You may want to speak with your father, your highness. I could be mistaken."

The nervousness that shrouded her left a gnawing feeling in Rome's stomach. Bess looked like a cornered cat as she

327

waited to see if he would ask her anything else. All appetite gone, Rome set down his fork. If Bess was correct, and there were festivities planned in his honor, there could only be one person behind it– his father.

Pushing out his chair Rome stepped around the table. He gave her a reassuring smile and squeezed her arm.

"Thanks, Bess."

She nodded but wouldn't meet his eye.

He remembered his father's rushed appearance as he'd strode down the hall with Phinneaus that morning, asking Rome to go out and see to the guard. Had it been a ploy to get him out of the castle?

His mind went wild with ideas as he walked along the stone passage leading to the upper courtyard. The sunlight struck him with warmth as he crossed into the open space. A beautiful white stone fountain stood in the middle. Several swans swam as pink water sprayed in time to the sounds of a solo violin playing nearby. Maids bustled to and fro carrying fabric and decorations from one side of the castle to the other. Above, several of the court dressers used their magick to hang a crystal candelabra ten feet in the air.

Damn. Not good. He crossed to the entrance.

A maid with a large carpet bowed low, knocking into him and forcing him back out the door. "Excuse me, your highness."

He gave her a tense smile and waited for her to pass before continuing into the front hall. Everywhere he looked, servants prepared for the celebration. Vases were being polished. Paintings dusted. Flowers revitalized to the perfect state of bloom. Rome hadn't seen the castle that bustling in a long time. But for all the beautification, anxiety wound tight inside him, like a string ready to snap.

He walked past the ballroom and dining hall to the grand staircase and jogged up to the third floor. The noise died down, but there were still maids making beds, footmen stocking fireplaces and polishing every surface. There was definitely going to be a party. The guest rooms hadn't been that cleaned in close to a year, which meant his father was expecting company. Noble company.

He rounded the corner and continued up to the fourth floor, then to the fifth, where his father's rooms were. All the curtains had been opened, and the smaller, quieter area had a light, airy feeling to it. Something glittered in the large window to the left and he walked to it to see what it was. Down below in the courtyard glass tables were being set up in two long rows. Swathed in tablecloths, he watched as placemats were set out down the line. The castle was as abuzz with action as the city far below it.

He looked out over Ville DeFee. The brightly colored buildings, in hues of pinks, purples, and blues, were a stark contrast to the heavy golden gates and lush farmlands that surrounded the city. Beyond the farmlands were the dull brown woods that offered, even more, protection from the rest of Fairelle.

His gaze traveled to the part of the city where Cinder's shop stood and then beyond, to where her smaller home was smooshed between a hundred other tall, thin houses locked together on the sides. He had intended on going to see her that morning, but his father's need for him to help out had taken prescience. The door to his father's study stood ajar and voices floated out.

"This isn't right Alfred," said Rome's grandmother.

"And what would you have me do mother? He's no longer a child. It's time he stopped acting like one."

Rome's ears prickled and he stepped from the window and headed for the open door.

"Your Royal Highness, I too feel this is best. Not just for Prince Rome but also for all of Ville DeFee." Phinneaus, his father's advisor, spoke in his normal jovial manner.

His grandmother tsk'd. "This isn't the way. He needs to decide this on his own."

"I didn't get to decide, and things worked out quite well for me."

"That was different. You'd already known her."

"Your Royal Highness, with all due respect, he's been given ample time, and he hasn't even shown the slightest interest in a girl," Phinneaus said.

"Shut up you sycophant. Ever since you became my son's advisor you've had nothing but one bad idea after the next."

"Mother—"

"I apologize, Queen Mother," said Phinneaus. "I meant no disrespect."

Rome raised a shaky hand and knocked on the door.

"Enter," called his father.

Rome straightened his shoulders and pushed his hair out of his eye.

"Ah, Rome!" His father clapped his hands and smiled. "I'm glad you've returned. I have some wonderful news."

"Do you?" Rome's gaze strayed to his grandmother. Her small, slender form leaned heavily on a brass cane. Her eyes held sadness, and she smiled at him weakly before coughing twice.

"We're having a feast." His father advanced. "And after the feast, a contest."

"Contest?" Rome's mouth went dry.

"To find you a bride." Phinneaus had been appointed after

Cinder's father had died, even though he wasn't much older than Rome.

"Excuse me?" Rome looked from Phinneaus' friendly face to his father's gleeful eyes.

"It's time you grew up and married my boy. I'm not a spring fae anymore, and your grandmother has only fifty years or so left. We want to see you happy and wed with young ones of your own," said his father.

"Oh no." Rome's grandmother raised her hand. "You keep me out of this. I've already told you I'm against this whole thing. Besides, fifty years is still a long time for him to fall in love, marry and have faelens."

Rome caught his father's scowl.

"Enough is enough." The King donned his most royal voice and gripped Rome's shoulder. "You need to take responsibility. Stop gallivanting around with Stil and hanging out at Cinder's shop."

"What's wrong with Lady Cinder?" Rome crossed his arms.

Rome's grandmother's eyes glittered with interest.

"There is nothing wrong with Cinder. You know how fond of her I am. Her father was like a brother to me. And Phinneaus is her step-uncle. But it's time to put childish friendships behind you and look to your future."

"You need a wife of good breeding and with clean bloodlines," said Phinneaus. "And as fond as I am of Cinder, you know that with the death of her father, and him never claiming her, Cinder has no more pedigree than–"

"I wouldn't finish that sentence if I were you." Rome's fists clenched so tight his knuckles ached. He would be damned if he'd let anyone, especially the self-important Phinneaus speak against Cinder. Though she might not have the pedigree she carried more dignity and respect than the sniveling Phinneaus had in his left pinky finger.

Phinneaus held up his hands. "I mean Cinder no offense. Cinder is like family to me. I simply mean that she has no bloodlines to claim her."

Phinneaus' handsome face, with his long hair, so blond it was almost white, pulled back into many braids, looked strikingly like his sister Lady Sabine. Only more feminine.

"I love Cinder," said his father. "But a princess needs to be of proper breeding. And as you refuse to pick a bride for yourself, we will hold a competition to find one for you."

How long had they been planning this? How had he not seen the signs? His father had hinted at the fact that he'd wanted Rome to marry, but this was so… obvious.

"Why can't you just let me pick in my own time? I'm sure if you will just-"

His father held up his hand. "It's too late. Announcements have already started to go out to the noble families."

Rome's gut squeezed. Married. His father wanted him to win a bride like a carnival prize. How could he think that would go well?

"A test, in three parts." Phinneaus shook his hands from his overly flamboyant, turquoise robes. "Three different houses of magick. To make sure the bloodline is pure and strong."

Rome's heart beat so wildly, he was sure it would give out. He didn't want any old female, especially not one that would entertain the idea of a contest, to get a husband.

"Three tests. So there could be three winners? Then what?" he asked.

"Well," his father shrugged. "We'll just have to figure it out if it comes down to that, but I doubt it will."

"I wouldn't be so sure," his grandmother muttered.

"And who's eligible to enter this contest?" asked Rome.

"All maidens who can trace pure bloodlines back at least four generations." His father beamed, as proud as a rooster crowing.

Rome paced, staring at the creamy walls. How in the world had his life fallen into such a mess?

A contest to find him a wife. The person he was to sit with, to talk with, to sleep with and make love to. To have his children, raise them, and spend the rest of his life with. The idea was ludicrous. His grandmother was almost three hundred years old, and she had been married to his grandfather for over two hundred and sixty of them. That was a long time to be with someone you met at a contest.

"Rome, surely you must see that this is the best way," said Phinneaus. "I know this may feel a bit rash, but you'll get to choose from the best and most beautiful our kingdom has to offer."

"I don't want the best and most beautiful, I want to choose for myself."

As if he hadn't been exposed to enough preening, overeager supposedly noble females already. He didn't need a contest to have fae women throw themselves at him. Strong willed, stubborn, rule breaking, beautiful, gentle, kind. Those were the kind he liked. Or at least, one in particular.

Rome stopped. What if he could beat his father at his own game? He smiled despite himself. What if Cinder could produce four generations of pedigree- then she could enter. Or, he could get her a fake set. Even if she didn't want to, he could convince her to do it as a favor. Surely she'd want to help save him from marrying someone else. Hell, she'd broken the rules to help a human get a girl out of tower. Entering his father's contest should be nothing to her. And there was no one like Cinder when it came to magick. She'd surely win. If she did he could prove to his father that pure bloodlines weren't everything, and that Cinder was good enough to become his wife. That she was indeed princess material.

But what if she said no? What if Cinder didn't want to help him? Or be a princess. The thought stuck him like a lightning rod to the chest. Worse yet... what if she didn't want to be his wife?

He had never told her how he felt about her. Though now that he looked back on it, his reasons seemed foolish. He'd been with women before, but none he'd fancied for more than a romp or two in bed. Funny how Cinder, who wasn't considered noble enough to become his bride, had more pride in herself to fall into a man's bed. Even his.

Memories of the one and only time he'd dared kiss her darted into his mind. They'd been young at the time. Playing seek and hide while on a picnic. He'd found her, but she'd run from him, and he chased her to the ground. They'd rolled in a patch of sungolds, and her laugh had infected him so that he'd wanted nothing more than to kiss her. So he had. But within a minute, she'd bucked him off and smacked him in the chest.

"You may be the prince but you have no right to me or my lips, Roman Geoffrey. The next time you feel so inclined to use me for kissing practice, you better ask permission first."

He'd been crushed that she'd think he'd been using her, but admired her even more for standing up for herself. Few girls then, or women now, would stand up to a prince and tell him no. But Cinder had never treated him like he was better than she was.

They'd been friends for decades. And he'd cared for her that entire time. But what if she'd never cared for him as

ZELLE AND THE TOWER

anything more than a friend? His chest squeezed. Even so a friend would help him with the contest, wouldn't she?

He spent more time with Cinder and Stil than anyone else. But what about when he wasn't with her? Was she spending time with someone else? Certainly she would have mentioned suitors.

She had to care for him the way he did for her. She had to. Because if she didn't... His mind was made up. There was no more time for lollygagging. His father was putting on a contest to win him a wife and he needed to know if Cinder had feelings for him or not.

Rome strode from the room.

"Rome? Rome!" his father called.

"Let him go, your majesty," said Phinneaus.

Rome didn't stop. It was rash and unprecedented but he needed to know. Had to know. Right then, whether or not Cinder cared enough for him to enter the contest. Not the silly flirtations they had been bantering with, but if she truly cared.

He raced out the front door and down the winding steps to the village below. Though he'd already made the trek that morning, it didn't matter. He'd waited too long already – and now they were out of time.

ROME REACHED CINDER'S SHOP OUT OF BREATH. HE SLOWED at the side of the building practicing what he would say to her. He ran his fingers through his hair and buttoned his jerkin. He needed to look presentable or she wouldn't believe him when he asked her true feelings.

He waited for his heartbeat to stop thundering and though he'd caught his breath, his heart refused to calm. Finally he wiped his sweaty palms on his pants and sucked in a breath. It was now or never.

Rome rounded the building to the front door and tried the knob. It didn't turn. Stepping back he looked through the front window. A sign floated into view.

I've gone to see a sick customer on the far side of town. The shop will open again in the morning. My apologies for the inconvenience.

Rome sighed and looked around. He could go to her house and wait, but he had no inclination to be stuck with Lady Sabine all afternoon. He blew out a heavy breath. There was only one thing he could do- go home and wait until the morning when he brought his grandmother back to be looked at. All in all... it was going to be a very long day.

To read more go to your nearest retailer!

Dear Reader,

Thank you for taking the time to read *Zelle and the Tower*. This series is due to my love of fairytales and the fantasy genre. I have loved writing all of these characters in new adventures and new relationships. I hope that you will enjoy the rest of the series of our strong women and honorable men.

If you enjoyed the book, please take a moment to leave a review on your favorite retailer. Your reviews make all the difference to an author and the success of books.
If you'd like, email me and let me know what you liked about the book or who your favorite character is. I love hearing from readers. It makes writing so much more fun when I hear from my readers.
VampWereZombie@Gmail.com

To find out more about me and my Upcoming Releases, Join my Street Team for Swag and Freebies.

I also love connecting with readers! Stalk me everywhere!
I look forward to hearing from you!
Rebekah R. Ganiere - BOOKS WITH A BITE

NEWSLETTER

To claim your Two FREE Books and find out more about
Rebekah R. Ganiere and her other Upcoming Releases
You can Go Here:
www.RebekahGaniere.com/Newsletter

Made in the USA
Columbia, SC
16 March 2024

32919298R00209